DOGMA DAYS OF SUMMER

DOGMA DAYS OF SUMMER

THE ELVEN PROPHECY™ BOOK FIVE

THEOPHILUS MONROE

MICHAEL ANDERLE

LMBPN

DISRUPTIVE IMAGINATION

LMBPN Publishing
PMB 196, 2540 South Maryland Pkwy
Las Vegas, NV 89109

Version 1.00, September 2021
ebook ISBN: 978-1-68500-454-5
Print ISBN: 978-1-68500-455-2

CHAPTER ONE

Missouri summers suck donkey balls. Not that I'd know what sucking donkey balls is like. I imagine it would be an unpleasant experience for all but the strangest of humans. It was so hot I was pretty certain even Satan would get heat exhaustion if he ever dared leave the comparatively temperate climate of Hell.

It wasn't just that we'd endured seven straight days of hundred-degree heat. It was the eighty-five percent humidity on top that made it unbearable. Living "off the grid" at the junkyard ranch, we were dependent on portable generators and portable air conditioning units. Even the old farmhouse where Layla and I stayed—along with Agnus—didn't have central air.

All three of us huddled around the unit, hoping to catch a gust of cool air. It was the opposite of how we'd gathered around campfires when I was in the Boy Scouts. Not just because we were seeking coolness rather than heat, but because in the Scouts, we used to sing songs, do skits, and have a jolly good time. All *we* were doing was bitching.

"My God," I prayed (because I'd never take the Lord's name in vain), "it's so fucking hot!"

"No shit, Reverend Sherlock," Agnus, my talking cat, retorted.

1

That's what Agnus does. He's an expert retorter. I'd call him retorted, but, you know, that wouldn't be politically correct. Cordially challenged. I'll go with that.

"It's just Sherlock. Without the reverend. I was defrocked, remember."

"You bloody heretic," Agnus shot back. "This heat is God's way of burning you for your damnable doctrines."

"If that's the case, he's punishing you, too," I pointed out.

Agnus snorted. "I know I'm a heretic. I'm a cat. We worship ourselves. At least if your pretender god burns me to death, I'll have eight lives to spare."

"Would you two just shut up?" Layla asked, pushing herself between us in an attempt to catch some cool air for herself.

"*Reeeorrrrow. Hissss!*" Agnus responded in his native feline tongue, clawing at the air in Layla's direction.

I chuckled. "You do a great imitation of her."

Layla rolled her eyes. "We're all on edge. It never got this hot on New Albion. I'm not used to this."

"We need a distraction," I said. "If we're not thinking about how miserable it is, maybe it won't feel as hot."

Layla peeled off her shirt. "This enough of a distraction for you?"

I stared at Layla wide-eyed, trying but failing to lift my eyes to hers. "We're trying to get cold. You're just making me hotter."

Layla smirked. "Well, that shirt is soaked. It's not going back on."

I shook my head. "I didn't say you should put it back on. Sometimes, the heat is worth it."

Agnus gagged. "Go to your room, you two."

"And leave all the air conditioning to you?" Layla asked. "Nice try. We're going to do it right here."

"All right. So long as I can watch."

"Not happening, buddy," I said, scooping Agnus up with one

arm. He flailed in my arms, meowing in protest as I tossed him into the bedroom and closed the door.

"Now, shall we proceed with our…distractions?" Layla asked, wrapping her arms around my shoulders as I grabbed her by the waist and pulled her in close.

POP!

I sighed. "Dammit. Agnus clawed a hole in the air mattress again."

"That's what you get!" Agnus shouted from behind my closed bedroom door.

"Ignore him," Layla said, pressing her soft lips to mine.

I kissed her back, ignoring the sound of claws on wood that indicated Agnus was doing his best to break through the door. He'd opened doors before, back at our apartment, but the doors in the old farmhouse didn't quite fit right. Even if he managed to turn the knob, he didn't have the strength to push it open.

"Get on your knees," Layla said, pulling away from our kiss.

"On my knees?" I asked.

"Just do it," Layla whispered seductively into my ear.

I knelt. Yeah, we men like to pretend that we're in charge. The truth is we're only in charge when we're allowed to be. Layla lifted her high-heeled shoe to my chest and pushed me down onto my back before she climbed on top of me, straddling my mid-section as she dug her nails into my chest, ripped off my sweat-soaked shirt, and locked me into another kiss.

Knock. Knock. Knock.

Layla broke our kiss. I sighed. "Seriously?"

Layla pressed her finger to my lips. "Just ignore it. Whoever it is will go away."

My incredibly alluring and irresistible elven wife reached down and unfastened my belt.

Knock. Knock. Knock. Knock. Knock.

"Stop screwing and answer the door!" Jag shouted from the other side.

"He isn't going to go away," I said. "You'd think he smelled our pheromones or something."

Layla scratched her head and stood up, leaving me lying on my back on the hardwood floor. "What is it, three times in a row he's interrupted us?"

I rolled over and got to my feet. "I swear, he'd better not be bothering us for another grocery run."

"Probably," Layla said. "You have access to all of Aerin's accounts. I told you to turn it all over to Rina. She's the head of the drow now that Aerin is gone."

"She is not gone," I said, opening up the bedroom door. Agnus bounded out. I looked at Aerin's sword, propped in the corner of the bedroom. "She is still with us, and she told me to manage her assets."

KNOCK. KNOCK. KNOCK.

"Just a second, Jag! We aren't decent!" I shouted.

"But you're the only one who can talk to her when you touch that sword," Layla said. "You really expect Rina and the drow to just take your word for it? From their perspective, all of Aerin's money belongs to the drow."

I put on a dry shirt. "Technically speaking, but I was her husband."

"Yeah," Layla said. "But the drow don't allow men to have money of their own."

I snorted. "All I know is that Aerin said I might need it. There's no telling if the drow will fully accept Rina's authority since, once again, the only evidence that Aerin wanted her to take charge is based on my word."

"She thinks the drow might defect?" Layla asked.

I shrugged. "I don't know. I could ask her. I think she just wants to be sure we have everything we need for the war and that we aren't hindered by drow politics."

"And if they think you're holding them ransom by controlling all their money—"

"Aerin's money," I snapped, walking to the front door and opening it.

"Hey, Casp," Jag said.

I folded my arms. "What do you want, Jag?"

"I'm sorry to bother you again, but the giants are getting restless. They still won't talk to the drow. Gronk just said if you won't lead them against the elves, he will. They've started making armor."

"Making armor?" I asked.

"From all the junkyard scrap," Jag said. "They want to take the fight to the elves."

"Where's Brag'mok?" I asked.

Jag shrugged. "He's the one who said I should come and get you."

I sighed internally. "Why didn't he come himself?"

"Probably because he's smarter than I am. Didn't mean to interrupt your fun."

"What fun?" I asked, shrugging.

"Oh, come on, Casp. You mean to tell me you weren't hitting that?"

"That?" Layla asked. "I'm a *that*, now?"

"No disrespect intended, Princess," Jag said.

"Well, if you must know," Layla said, putting her arm around me and running her hand down my stomach. "I was getting ready to hit *that*."

Jag looked at us wide-eyed and speechless for a good three seconds.

"What can I say," I said, shrugging. "She likes to be in charge."

Jag shook his head. "Right. So, yeah. Like I was saying…"

I laughed. "All right, we'll be right out. The last thing I want is a disgruntled army of giants on my hands."

CHAPTER TWO

I stepped back inside and moved briskly into my bedroom. Stepping over my recently popped duct tape-covered air mattress, I glanced at Aerin's blade as I grabbed my tennis shoes.

I sighed. It occurred to me that she'd know what to do. Our relationship was awkward, to say the least. But I needed her. So, I grabbed her sword and, loosening my belt a little, I stuck it through. Not the best way to carry a sheathed sword, I suppose. But I was a former preacher, not a samurai.

Not that I was going to use the blade. But Aerin's soul was bound to the blade and if I touched it, I could speak to her. More importantly, as long as I had the blade on me, she'd be able to hear what the giants had to say. If anyone had an answer for how to make peace between them, the drow, a legion of fairies, and my cat… Well, it would be her.

It's not that I wasn't a good leader. However, leading a congregation is very different than leading an army. As the pastor of a small church, leadership was more about inspiration than method. Sure, a lot of ministers out there pore over their church growth and mission *strategies*, but the way I saw it, that level of intervention just complicated things. Sharing our faith with others, I always felt, should be natural. Not pushy. Something that happens while we go about our lives expressing compassion and forgiveness and loving people. When people got curious and wanted to know why I have hope, I was happy to share. Otherwise, in my mind, I didn't have any business telling someone what to believe. I lived a life tied to my beliefs, and if people wanted that for themselves, then I was there to guide them.

Great virtues when it came to the Kingdom of God. Not so much when it came to leading an army. It was becoming a big problem. I was always something of a pacifist. I abhorred violence. Always did. Still do.

All you need is love? Used to believe that.

But violence was all the giants knew. It was how they'd fought King Brightborn on New Albion, and it's how we were going to have to stop him before he took over the world.

I stepped outside, and a buzzing sounded over my left shoulder.

"Hey, Trixie," I said. Trixie was the newly-crowned fairy queen—blessed by the Furies to rule the Seelie court and help us defend the Earth.

After they'd defeated the Unseelie court, the fairies led by King Develin, we'd gained a significant advantage over Brightborn and the elves. With the fairies at our side, we could create portals through the ether that allowed us to travel to anywhere I could visualize. When Brightborn had lost his Unseelie fairies, he'd also lost that ability. I figured we'd find him sooner than later. Especially since fairies can sense magic when it's cast anywhere in the world.

However, it had been two months since then, and we had no leads. The only thing I knew was that some of the elves, mostly civilians, had been brought to the Earth by King Brightborn and were settled in the arctic, close to the North Pole.

I know what you're thinking. There are elves at the North Pole! Wore those jokes out weeks ago.

"How goes it, Caspar?" Trixie asked in her usual perky tone of voice.

I shook my head. "The giants are getting restless. We need to find Brightborn."

"He's not using magic," Trixie said. "If he was, I'd know it. How much harm could he be doing?"

"Magic isn't what makes him a threat," I told her. "All things being equal, I'm probably more powerful than he is. It's his political savvy and his ability to con world leaders and work behind the scenes that frightens me the most."

"He'll have to use magic eventually," Trixie said. "That's the only reason he has the attention of the world's leaders, right?"

I nodded. "Eventually, yes. I'm just afraid by the time he does, it will be too late."

"We'll keep looking," Trixie said. "At least he can't find you now that we have this whole ranch cloaked!"

"Hiding us from the government is probably the bigger issue," I said.

Trixie nodded and buzzed off, presumably to gather the rest of her court and go on another elf-finding expedition. They'd been searching the globe since the confrontation with King Devlin. They could move inconspicuously, and they could go virtually anywhere on Earth in an instant. They were our best chance at finding Brightborn. Until we knew where he was and exactly what he was up to, we had little choice but to stay in hiding. Especially since Brightborn had the US government in his back pocket. The Furies had told us that he had the governments of the world feeding on the bullshit he'd extended them with his open hand.

Gronk—not the NFL tight end, the leader of the giants—had the rest of his warriors gathered around him and was fitting them with breastplates and pauldrons made from the parts of junked cars. Targigoth, the giant's high priest, was sitting alone on a pile of trash. Was he meditating? Who knew. But he wasn't partaking in Gronk's battle preparations. That was something, at least.

Brag'mok stood beside Gronk, already wearing a full set of rusty armor.

Layla, meanwhile, was checking in on the drow. While Layla wasn't a drow, she was an elf. More importantly, she was female. The drow were more likely to talk honestly with her than me.

"Looks like you're ready for a fight," I said, approaching Gronk.

"We can't just sit here," Gronk said.

"But how are you going to fight if you don't know where to go?" I asked.

"We don't know where the elf king is," Gronk said. "But we know where the elves are. If we attack, he'll have to respond. It's the only way we can draw him out."

I shook my head. "But we don't know that those elves are inclined to fight. Layla says that they're just citizens. They're probably distraught over the loss of their homes."

"They are elves," Gronk said. "So is your wife. As well-intentioned as she might be, I understand why she wouldn't want to fight."

"It's not that," I said. "Those elves are victims of Brightborn's schemes the same as anyone else."

"Our purpose is clear," Gronk said. "The giants were charged from the beginning to serve the Earth. To guard and protect it. Would you spare the elves at the cost of your world?"

"He is right, Caspar," Brag'mok said. "We don't have to kill the elves. But if we capture them or even just threaten them, Brightborn will have to respond. As it is, we're allowing him to gain allies, to consolidate more power by the day. We can't wait any longer."

I rolled my eyes. "The fairies won't take you there. How do you expect to march on the North Pole from Missouri?"

"Exactly like that," Gronk said. "We'll march there."

I snorted. "You can't walk to the North Pole. It's not possible."

"We'll take an arctic cruise," Brag'mok said.

I rolled my eyes. "A cruise? Seriously? How in the world are you going to get an army, with weapons, onto a cruise ship?"

"We'll commandeer the ship," Gronk said.

I shook my head. "That's a horrible idea."

Gronk shrugged. "Waiting for Brightborn to show himself when he's ready is a better idea, you think?"

"No," I said. "We're looking for him. Trixie is taking the fairies on another expedition today."

"They won't find him," Gronk said. "I've been fighting the elven king my entire life. Trust me. If he doesn't want to be found, he won't be."

I nodded. "But we can't attack a bunch of unarmed elves, Gronk. That's not the answer. If we do that, we're no better than Brightborn."

"We have to do *something*," Gronk said. "If there was another way to get his attention, we'd do it."

"Maybe there is. What if I could draw him out? Brightborn still wants to put forward Layla as the chosen one of the elven prophecy. If he had a chance to capture her…"

"You're going to use your wife as bait?" Brag'mok asked, incredulity in his voice.

I shrugged. "I don't know. It's just an idea. But she's the one thing we have that he wants. All I'm saying is give me a chance to come up with something to draw him out. If it doesn't work, then we'll go with your plan."

Gronk grunted, then removed his makeshift breastplate and set it on the ground. "Very well. We accept that you are, in fact, the chosen one. We'll give you one week to figure something out. After that, we're leaving—with or without you."

CHAPTER THREE

"Most of those elves at the North Pole don't even know what Brightborn is doing!" Layla vented in frustration, gripping the porch railing on the front of the farmhouse.

"I tried to tell them that," I said, "but they're convinced that they have to do something to get your father out of hiding. We have a week to figure out something else."

Layla sighed. "If we come out of hiding, my father will know where to find me. He'll make a move."

"That's what I suggested," I said.

"Wait," Layla said. "You proposed using me as bait?"

Dammit. "You just had the exact same idea!"

"Yeah, but that's different than you suggesting it for me." Layla grunted, folding her arms.

"It wasn't like I was committing you to it," I said. "Besides, bait isn't the right word. Gronk called you bait too."

"See, that's because it's so obvious."

"What is?" I asked.

Layla snickered. "You're a master baiter."

I snorted. "Am not. Not recently, anyway."

Layla chuckled. "And to do it for my father…"

I stared at Layla blankly. "Doing it with *you*, for your father."

"Nasty, nasty, Reverend Cruciger." Layla smirked.

"What are you talking about?" I laid the innocence on thick. "I was discussing bringing you out in public to lure your father out of hiding."

Layla grinned. "Sure you were."

I sighed. As fun as it was to laugh about it, we were under pressure. "Seriously, though, Layla. We need to talk about this."

"What's there to talk about?" Layla asked. "You and I both know that even if my dad caught me, he couldn't keep me. Not with the angelic magic I have."

Layla raised her hand, showing off the two rings that together gave her access to celestial power. So far, we'd barely scratched the surface as to what she could do. She could teleport like I could now with fairy power. The biggest difference was that she didn't need to clearly visualize her destination. Her power had come in handy when we'd taken on the nightcrawlers in New Albion. "So does he."

"Then we have to convince him that you're willing to go with him," I said. "That you won't run. Otherwise, he'll see right through it."

Layla shrugged. "He'll probably see through it anyway. Just because I *say* I want to go with him doesn't mean I will. My father rarely keeps promises he makes to his enemies, and he's not foolish enough to trust that we will."

I scratched the back of my head. "We have to try. We only have a week. How'd your conversation go with Rina and the drow?"

Layla shrugged. "They're restless, too. They're eager to avenge Aerin. But they won't go into battle without her blade."

"So they won't fight if I don't."

Layla nodded. "Since you're the only one who can wield the sword and connect to her, they're shit out of luck."

"What about Elrand?" I asked.

Layla shook her head. "He's still mourning. As a male and one long since exiled from the drow, his wellbeing isn't exactly at the top of Rina's list of concerns."

"I wish he could talk to Aerin like I can. I mean, he just got his daughter back, then this happened. I can't imagine what he's going through."

"You should talk to him," Layla said. "You have experience counseling the bereaved. Maybe if you brought the blade, let him speak to Aerin."

"I tried that. Several times. He doesn't want any part in that."

Layla cocked her head. "Well, why not? If he's distraught about losing his daughter… I think most parents who've lost children would do anything to be able to speak to them. He could speak to her any time you're available."

I nodded. "Everyone mourns differently. They say there are certain stages of grief that people go through. I suppose there are. But in my experience, no one goes through any one of those stages the same way."

Layla frowned. "So you're just going to let him sit on the junk piles alone all day, every day, feeling sorry for himself?"

I nodded. "I can't tell someone that the way they're grieving is wrong, Layla. When he is ready to come down and wants to talk to Aerin, he knows where to find me."

"You realize he's the only one of us who has any experience wielding magic on Earth? The drow haven't done much more than enchantments for centuries, and I've only had experience wielding magic on New Albion. I know he's mourning, but we could use his help."

"I realize that," I said. "But if he isn't ready, he isn't ready."

"Have you asked him?"

I bit my lip. "Well, no. But maybe you have a point. The drow don't give him the time of day. The giants couldn't care less. Maybe he just needs to feel needed."

"What's the worst that will happen if you try asking him for his advice?" Layla said.

I laughed. "He might kick me off his mound of junk and shout, 'This is Sparta!'"

"Sparta?" Layla echoed. "Why would he call it that?"

I waved a hand. "Never mind. I guess you haven't seen that movie."

I glanced across the junkyard. From the front porch of the farmhouse, we couldn't see the giant or drow camps. They were on different parts of the twenty-acre plot of land behind the farmhouse. Piles of old kitchen appliances, atop old abandoned cars, and random junk I couldn't even identify lined either side of the gravel road that led from the closest paved road to the junk-yard ranch.

It was on one of those junk piles, separated from the rest of the drow, that Elrand perched. Elrand had lived as a hermit for a decade. He'd spent that time in his stone circle working with magic, evoking the Furies, and God knows what else. When I'd invited him to stay with us, I figured I was doing him a courtesy. Aerin, communicating through her sword, said she thought it was a good idea.

I kissed Layla on the cheek and made my way down the porch steps. One of the boards was loose and lifted every time I stepped on it. I'd have to nail it down again at some point. One of those to-do items that wouldn't take all that much time but for some reason never gets done. Eventually, someone would trip on the thing, and I'd have to do it.

I walked over to the junk heap Elrand had chosen for a throne. How the hell had he even gotten up there? Surely he got down to eat, pee, whatever. I felt bad that I hadn't taken time to think about it before now.

I was so occupied with maintaining a semblance of peace on the junkyard, which had become a melting pot of different races from cultures totally alien to one another. Layla represented

New Albion's elves, who had been at war with the giants for centuries. The drow, elves of another sort, had been in hiding on Earth for centuries. Jag was the only other fellow human who stayed with us at the junkyard ranch. Since he was a bodybuilder —an interesting subculture in its own right—and I was a former minister, even he and I were from very different worlds. Then, of course, there were the fairies. The Seelie court consisted of a contingency of fairykind that had endured intense persecution at the hands of the elves on New Albion. They'd only recently returned to Earth and were still feeling out their new role as the protectors of Earth's magic.

But Elrand was different than all of the above. Yes, he was a drow. However, he rejected the drow ways, and despite being exiled by his daughter, persisted in his belief that magic was something to embrace even if it put him at odds with the fairies who had previously guarded the Earth.

He and I had a lot in common, in an odd sort of way. He'd been exiled. I'd been excommunicated. He'd resisted the matriarchy in his culture. I'd resisted the patriarchal powers that be in my former denomination, and now I was pitted against my own country's government. Unlike me, Elrand didn't have a new calling or a new purpose to embrace. If it hadn't been for Layla, the elven prophecy, and the pressure to save the world (no biggie, right?), I don't know if I'd be handling the loss of my ministry career any better than he was handling the loss of his daughter. I had AA, which kept me grounded—even though, technically, I could fly. Elrand had…a pile of trash. The only thing to keep him company up there was a swarm of flies.

Elrand was a thin man. His sunken cheeks gave the impression that he might be suffering from malnutrition. He was rather vigorous, though, so it probably wasn't that. He was, like all of the drow, dark in complexion with pointed elf ears. He had a long, white beard that nearly reached his waist. It was glorious. I'd always envied men with long, thick beards. I don't know if I could grow one. I never had the patience to get much beyond a stubble. Too damn itchy.

I grunted. I wasn't about to climb the trash heap. Instead, I drew on the elements of air and aether and floated to the top, lowering myself beside Elrand.

"Show off," Elrand said, snorting.

I chuckled. "Not what I was trying to do. I'm just too damned lazy to try to climb this mountain of garbage."

Elrand shrugged. "It's peaceful up here. Apart from the flies."

I swatted at one when the dang thing landed on my forearm. I missed it, of course. It landed there a second time, about a second later. I swatted and missed, again. "Little buggers. Between those things and the heat radiating off all this junk, I don't know how you survive up here."

"What do you want, Naayak?" Elrand asked.

I scratched my left arm. "Just figured I'd come and visit with you. I noticed you and me, we don't fit in around here."

"You're the chosen one. Of course, you fit in."

I sighed. "People look to me for hope. They want me to lead. But honestly? I don't even know where to begin. Everyone is from different worlds. They all want to save Earth from Brightborn for different reasons, and they want to do it in different ways. Meanwhile, I'm supposed to unite them and lead them and I'm as clueless about what to do next as anyone else."

"Never been much of a leader, myself," Elrand said. "I'm more of a loner. A hermit. An outcast."

"Aerin was a leader," I said.

Elrand snorted. "She was. Why don't you ask her for advice seeing as though you're the only one who can talk to her anymore?"

I sighed. "I do. But it's different to take advice, to consider what to do next, and to actually lead people."

Elrand snorted. "I'm not much of a follower either, in case you couldn't tell. Not sure I'll be of much help."

I lifted the bottom edge of my t-shirt and used it to wipe the sweat from my brow. "Except that's the thing, Elrand. Maybe you don't need to lead or follow. But I do know that you have more experience working with the elements, with the Earth's magic, than anyone here."

"I'm not as powerful as you are, Naayak," Elrand said.

I nodded. Naayak Nightshade was the name they'd given me. It meant "hero." The first part did, anyway. The surname was Aerin's. Since drow custom mandates that husbands take their wives' names, and I'd married both Aerin and Layla by drow rite, in their minds, I belonged to my wives. "You might not be as powerful as I am, but you know more about magic than I do. You're efficient with what you do. If it wasn't for you, we couldn't have evoked the Furies, we wouldn't have the Seelie court at our side, and Brightborn would still have the Unseelie helping him monitor the use of magic and teleport around the globe. If it wasn't for you, Elrand, we wouldn't have a chance at all."

Elrand picked at a hangnail on his left thumb. "I'm glad it helped. It came at a cost, though."

"Aerin."

Elrand nodded. "I just can't get my mind around it. She fell on her own sword."

"The prophecy said—"

"I know what the prophecy said, Naayak," Elrand interjected. "I know *why* she did it. That doesn't mean I can accept it or understand it. Sometimes I wish there was no prophecy."

I took a deep breath. "You and me both. It's a blessing and a burden."

"I get that." Elrand swiped a fly off his nose. "I know that's how Aerin felt."

"She didn't believe she had a choice," I said.

Elrand huffed, his breath fluttering the stray whiskers of his mustache that fell over his upper lip. "What if the prophet was full of it? Taliesin, I mean. What if it was all a bunch of nonsense meant to give people hope as they fled their persecutors on Earth?"

"I'm sure that was a part of it," I said. "The Book of Revelation served that purpose. People today read it like a newspaper, trying to imagine what might happen in the future. In fact, virtually every symbol or metaphor in that book referred to the Roman empire in cryptic terms and to things going on in the world at that time. The message about the future wasn't about tribulations or marks of the beast but about a future victory over oppressors. It was meant to give people hope that there would come a time when persecution would end. When suffering and even death would end."

"Still waiting on that one, aren't you?" Elrand asked.

I nodded. "The point is that the book wasn't meant to scare people about the future. It was meant to console people who were enduring hell on earth with hope. With the elven prophecy, the scrolls being revealed over time, and the last scroll being different for each race that possesses the prophecy, this is something else."

Elrand nodded. "We still don't know what the last scroll that the New Albion elves possess says. Maybe Brightborn already knows, and that's why he's hiding."

I sighed. "I wish I knew the answer to that question. Honestly, Elrand, I'm flying by the seat of my pants. It's hard to know how to lead people if you don't know where you're going. I've always told myself that I should just do the next right thing. But how can I even know what that is? The next step forward for a blind man on the edge of a cliff will probably be his last."

Elrand shrugged. "Sometimes it's easier to see what you shouldn't do next than what you should."

I nodded. "Like march an army of giants on defenseless North Pole elves?"

"The giants have seen most of their race wiped out by elves. They believe they are here to fight to protect Earth. I can't help but think that vengeance has something to do with their desire. Could you blame them if it does?"

"You're probably right. They've lost so much. All of us have."

"Loss is a funny thing," Elrand said, staring at the clouds. "Some feel like they have to act. They have to move forward. Others, we feel like we're paralyzed. Like if we move at all, we'll have to put who we lost even farther in the rearview mirror. It's hard to admit when something that you'd held out so much hope for in the future is now only a part of the past."

"It doesn't have to be in the past," I said, gesturing toward the farmhouse where I had Aerin's blade. "She's willing to talk to you, Elrand. I know that it's not the same, having to hear her words as I relay them, but I promise you that she can hear you."

"Last time, it was so painful," Elrand said. "I wish there was a way to bring her back. If my girl had died the normal way, if she'd moved on, I'd have hope that she was at peace. Or perhaps preparing to be reborn, reincarnated. It's hard to imagine her soul bound to something so mundane, like a blade."

I nodded. "I get that. You know, when we were in the forest and she read the words of the prophecy, she didn't hesitate. She knew what to do and did it. I can't imagine having that kind of resolve, especially if it involved a blade to the gut."

Elrand smiled sadly. "My Aerin was a special girl."

"Aerin *is* a special girl, Elrand. What would it mean if we just sat on our asses and didn't move forward after all she sacrificed? She did what she did for a purpose. We have to honor that."

Elrand nodded. "You're right. But what do you suggest?"

"Somehow, we have to convince the giants that they don't need to attack the elves at the pole. That we can get to Bright-born and stop him without resorting to terrorizing civilians. We were thinking of putting Layla out there as bait. I'm not sure it would work, though."

Elrand shook his head. "Using your wife as a dangling carrot isn't going to move the jackass forward."

I chuckled. "Right. I think no matter what we do, he'll see through it. We've resisted him and his plans too many times for him to believe that we're serious. Not to mention, it isn't like we're in a position of total desperation here. We scored the last victory, and he's playing coy."

"What you need to do isn't make a desperate offer," Elrand said. "You need to act from a position of power, do something aggressive that will threaten him but reflects a form of confidence owing to your last victory."

I nodded. "I agree. Any ideas?"

"Like you said, no one anywhere has more experience working with earthen elemental magic than I do," Elrand said. "What if we showed the governments that we could offer them more than Brightborn?"

I bit my lip. "That might work. The only reason he has their ear is because he claims he can offer something they can't get elsewhere."

"But if we have something better, bigger, even more powerful, and we're willing to offer it without making them beholden to a one-world government with you at the head…"

I saw where he was going. "But can we really? It isn't like we can just give them magic. Most humans don't have the capacity for it."

"You can unite the world without ruling it, Naayak. What Brightborn promises is unity, too. *A unity contingent on his dominion.* What you offer is the potential for both unity and independence. To heal the world while preserving freedom."

I nodded. "Do you think I can show them enough to get them to buy into it? And can we do it in a week?"

Elrand tugged at his beard and smiled. "Definitely. But you'd better be ready for a fight once we do. Brightborn won't hesitate to try to eliminate you."

"He'll hesitate if only because mine and Layla's souls are still bound," I said. "If I die, she does, too. He's still convinced he can present her as the chosen one."

"There are ways one can be eliminated without being killed," Elrand said. "While I haven't engaged the elven king as you have and certainly don't have the insight on his behaviors that Layla does, you can be certain he has a plan. Are you willing to fight?"

I shook my head. "I've learned a few evasive moves from Brag'mok. I'm still not much of a fighter. Never have been. Don't believe in it. The only power I have against him is my magic."

"And my daughter's blade," Elrand said. "How'd you like to learn how to use it properly?"

"All the drow can wield their blades better than I can," I said, shaking my head. "They've been training all their lives. How can I gain their skill in just a week?"

Elrand grinned, flashing his yellowed teeth. "You suppose the magic that connects you and Aerin when you wield the blade merely offers you the chance to talk to one another?"

I shrugged. "I suppose I pushed it aside when Aerin warned me of the dangers. I haven't considered anything more, and Aerin hasn't mentioned any extra benefits to our union."

"She may not have realized the possibility. But there are none among the drow more accomplished with a blade than Aerin. If you know how to access her knowledge, then her skill and yours can be united when you wield her sword."

"Can you show me how to do that?" I asked.

Elrand shrugged. "Maybe. But we'll never know unless we try."

"Are you're sure you're ready to do that? So far, you haven't even wanted to talk to Aerin through me."

"You've given me much to consider, Naayak. What you've said about the prophecy rings true. Aerin did not relegate herself to the past when she fell on her blade. She's placed herself—and you —in a position to do what must be done now."

CHAPTER FOUR

I had two things to learn from Elrand. First, I had to do whatever magic would get the governments' attention. Jag would help with setting up the demonstration. We'd probably use St. Ensley's— the church building that the former Elf Gate cult used to use for meetings.

Jag owned the building. We hadn't gone there in a while, figuring both the President and Brightborn probably had agents watching the place. Of course, the suitability of St. Ensley's depended in large part on what exactly Elrand had in mind.

I had a few ideas. Brightborn's whole schtick was that he could use magic to heal the planet from the effects of pollution and reverse climate change. I wasn't sure how he intended to do that. I suppose I could fly all around the globe and use the power of air to extract carbon from the atmosphere.

Somehow.

I wasn't entirely sure how it would work. It wasn't like I could just chase the carbon away with a newspaper and broom handle. I wasn't even convinced that Brightborn could do what he was promising. Not that it mattered. All he had to do was convince the rest of the world that he could. Given the inability of scientists to come up with viable solutions to the problem, most of the world's authorities would be ready to deal, even if that meant ceding authority to the global empire he intended to establish.

Layla stayed at the junkyard ranch. She was getting along with the drow surprisingly well. The drow warriors were experts with the blade. Layla was skilled with the bow. She was also well-versed in elven battle strategies.

So was Brag'mok, but from the opposite perspective, having fought against Brightborn's forces. However, since Brag'mok had sided with his fellow giants over me on the idea of assaulting the North Pole, he wasn't being much use to the drow who needed to learn how to fight effectively against Brightborn's elven legion.

Elrand and I fairy-portaled to his old cabin in the woods, where his temple—the circle of stones we'd used to summon the Furies—stood. It wasn't too far from the ranch. Taking fairy portals to the middle of nowhere came with fewer risks than using them to travel to highly populated areas. I could only visualize my destination based on my recollection of it. In the city, there was always a risk that someone had moved things around, or worse, might be standing exactly where the portal opened on the other end.

So far, I hadn't killed anyone by portaling into them, but I had gotten stuck in inanimate objects. All it took in those instances was another portal to free myself from whatever I got stuck in. I'm not sure the same solution would work if I teleported into a person or an animal. I wasn't especially eager to find out, either.

We appeared right in the middle of the stone circle. Elrand had forged it some time ago as a way to practice magic without being detected. For some reason, the stones contained the magic inside, and the fairies who became the Unseelie court couldn't sense it.

For a decade or so, Elrand had lived alone in these woods and used this stone circle to shield himself while he devoted almost all of his time to experimenting with any magic he could figure out how to wield.

"When I first came here, exiled by my daughter, there were trees. But maybe half as many," Elrand said.

I looked around. "All of these trees look a lot older than ten years old."

Elrand grabbed a wooden staff that he'd left leaning against one of the stones that formed his circle. "This staff fell from one of the first trees I grew."

"One of these, here?"

Elrand nodded. He stepped between two of the stones and put his hand on the largest tree around. The trunk was as wide as a car. It extended around a hundred feet into the skies, and its branches formed a canopy over the rest of the forest. "This tree is only about nine years old. Just celebrated her birthday."

"Her?" I asked.

Elrand shrugged. "Some trees have preferred pronouns."

"Hmm," I said, raising my eyebrows. "You think growing trees like this will be enough to threaten Brightborn's plans?"

"Trees remove carbon from the atmosphere," Elrand said. "They enrich ecosystems and establish new ones where they thrive. Many people cry that we should save the trees. In truth, we need the trees to save us."

I shook my head. "I don't know. I'm not saying I don't believe you. I'm just not sure I'll be able to sell it. Can we do something like this in a week?"

"You can harness earthen magic with probably a hundred times the potency that I'm capable of. Imagine turning a desert into a flourishing forest in a matter of minutes. Barren lands into a thriving jungle. I don't know what Brightborn has shown them, but I can't imagine it's more impressive than that. Tell me, what does Aerin think of this idea?"

I grabbed the hilt of the blade that I had sheathed and tied it to a belt loop on my shorts. Yeah, a t-shirt and shorts with a sword at one's side were a little silly-looking. But it was too hot to wear pants, and I wasn't concerned with style. Not to mention, I doubt that swords were an accessory any of the summer catalogs identified as a recent trend. If you think tight-rolled jeans and fanny packs are out of style, well, I'm old enough to remember when those things were cool.

Swords, though? I missed that fashion trend by a few centuries.

"Aerin, can you hear me?" I asked. I didn't feel much when I touched the blade—a light warmth.

Of course, Caspar.

"You've been listening, right?"

I have. I don't think you should do this as part of a show. Start planting forests. Plant them everywhere. Start solving the problem. It'll take the wind out from under Brightborn's sails.

"But will it stop the giants from attacking the elves?" I asked.

Tell Brag'mok your plan. Perhaps he can stall them.

"What does my daughter think?" Elrand asked.

"She thinks we should start planting forests. As many as we can, everywhere we can. If we can undermine Brightborn's efforts, we may be able to avoid war altogether."

"She thinks the war can be averted?" Elrand asked.

"Well, that was me thinking out loud," I said. "Wishful thinking. I don't think Brightborn's plans for world domination will be so easily put to rest."

"It will take time for people to buy into what you're doing," Elrand said.

There's no telling how much power and influence he's already attained, Aerin said. *I imagine he's offered people more than a way to slow down global warming. He probably promised to give them access to magic as a military power.*

I nodded. "Aerin believes that Brightborn has likely sold the government on the idea that magic can be used for military purposes."

"I agree," Elrand said, pinching the tip of his beard. "But he's using fixing climate change as a ruse to allow politicians to hide their real agenda behind something that appears noble. Remove that, and they'll have a harder time answering questions about why they're so willing to cede authority to a one-world elven empire."

"So this probably won't stop Brightborn at all," I said.

"Probably not," Elrand said. "But it'll give him reason to come after you, which is what you want, isn't it?"

"It is," I said, chuckling to myself. I couldn't believe that I wanted him to come and try to kill me, or abduct me, or whatever he would try to do to get rid of me. But we had to get him out from hiding, somehow, if we were ever going to stand against him. If the giants attacked the elves, everything we planned could backfire.

I was certain, Brightborn had presented the elves to the governments of the world as refugees escaping a harsh and failing world, attacked by what they called "orcs." Never mind that the giants, aka orcs, were trying to protect Earth. Take one look at an elf—regal, perfect skin, beautiful. A giant, on the other hand? Barbaric by appearance. Green, leathery skin. Their bottom incisors, and the resulting underbite, gave a distinct impression that they very well might want to eat you. In this world, the elves checked every box on the standards of beauty lists. The giants looked like monsters. There wasn't any question in my mind how the world would see it if the giants launched an assault on defenseless North Pole elves. More than that, the world would probably come to their defense.

"Funny," I said. "The protestant reformer, Martin Luther, once said that if he knew the world would end tomorrow, he'd plant a tree."

"Wise," Elrand said. "Though one tree probably isn't enough. Scientists estimate that if we planted a trillion trees, which would require land roughly twice the size of the United States, it could remove roughly two-thirds of the carbon in the atmosphere."

"Okay," I said. "So if the world might end tomorrow, I need to plant a trillion trees."

Elrand smiled. "Not necessarily. To meet the one trillion mark, we'd need a hundred and twenty-five trees planted for every person on Earth. Probably a few more. The logistics of that would be staggering. But you could do it quickly by using your power to create larger, healthier trees and assisting them with propagation."

"We could certainly use the shade back at the junkyard ranch," I said. "It's so much cooler out here in the woods without the summer heat beating down on us constantly."

Elrand smiled. "Want to practice?"

"Sprouting trees?"

Elrand nodded vigorously. "Use the stone circle to focus your energy. I suspect you won't need it for long. Think of the stones like training wheels. You'll need to channel the element of earth through the stones, speak to the trees all around and ask them to lend their seeds to you. Then, you'll have to touch upon the life in the seeds using the element of aether."

"Trees have spirits?" I asked.

"All life has spirit, Naayak. After that, call upon the elements of water and earth to nourish the young seedlings. These three elements are what you require to sprout a forest. Then, once established, the element of air can engage the trees—to flutter through the leaves, to carry their seeds further that the process might continue, and of course, to produce life-giving oxygen and remove carbon from the air."

"So the only element we won't use is fire, I presume," I said.

Elrand cocked his head. "Not necessarily. Fire may be sent ahead to lands where new forests will grow. It removes the underbrush, cleans the forest floor of debris, and nourishes the soil. All the elements will be required in order to do as I promise.

First, find land in need of trees. Use fire to clear the area and water to ensure that it remains contained. Then, speak to the trees, carry their seeds through the air, and invest them with aether, water, and the nutrients of the earth. With the right balance, you'll see mighty trees emerge in mere minutes."

I nodded. "I guess my original idea of broadcasting from St. Ensley's is off the table."

"Probably," Elrand said. "You'll need a larger area to demonstrate this."

"All right. Well, let's practice. If we still need to work on my sword-fighting skills, or at least on how to draw on Aerin's skills, I may need a break between these things. Using the amount of magic as you're talking about to plant a forest like this will be exhausting."

"Not with a stone circle to focus and amplify your magic," Elrand said. "Once you get accustomed to working with stones and harnessing so much power beyond the stone circles, you'll be more adept at working even without them if necessary. Of course, even once you reach your potential, there may be times when using stone circles might still be of benefit. As you'll see, now you should be able to establish a dozen or more trees with very little demand on your power."

"But you're talking a trillion trees," I said.

"Eventually," Elrand said. "Even *you* can't plant that many overnight. You should at least give yourself the weekend."

I smirked. "Surely it'll take longer than that."

Elrand chuckled. "More trees, invigorated by magic, will produce more trees. Each one you plant will require less magic than the one before it. Once you get rolling, it will come as easily as breathing. At least, I suspect it will work that way for you since your power is so much more potent than mine."

"Cool," I said. "So, how do we start?"

"How do you feel about killing two birds with one stone?" Elrand said.

I shrugged. "Not really a fan of the senseless killing. But I appreciate the metaphor."

Elrand smiled. "There's a field not far from here that's mostly overgrown with weeds and bramble. Since Aerin's blade is enchanted with both her spirit and fire, perhaps we should clear it that way rather than using fire magic directly."

"You want me to clear a field with a flaming sword?"

"Why not?" Elrand shrugged. "If you're worried about conserving your energy, why not work on your sword skills at the same time?"

CHAPTER FIVE

I gripped the hilt of Aerin's blade as Elrand and I stood at the edge of the clearing. There were no trees. A lot of thistle and bramble. Weeds of every variety, including poison ivy.

"Looks like a great habitat for snakes," I said.

"They'll leave," Elrand said. "They can live just as well under the cover of trees as they would in a field like this. You won't be unsettling their homes."

I raised my left eyebrow. "I'm sure they'll find new homes. But for now, there are still snakes!"

"You're afraid of snakes?" Elrand asked. "Why?"

"Well, duh," I said. "Because they are *snakes*!"

"That Genesis story in your Bible gives them a bad rap," Elrand said. "They aren't so bad."

"Aren't so bad?" I asked. "My belief in the Bible has nothing to do with my dislike of snakes. At least, not consciously. I suppose I have a subconscious revulsion to snakes, given the fact that I grew up believing it was a snake who came and screwed up the paradise that Adam and Even were given. Ultimately, though, it's the whole biting thing that turns me off."

"Most of them are probably harmless garter snakes," Elrand said.

I shook my head. "Probably, but I don't take time to evaluate what a snake *might* be. If I see a slither, I run hither and thither!"

Aerin was giggling in my mind as I held her blade. *Probably just a few copperheads.*

"Just a few copperheads?" I echoed. "Are you serious right now?"

Elrand cocked his head.

"Your daughter is giving me shit," I said.

A smile spread across Elrand's face. "That sounds like my Aerin. Look, Naayak. You'll be fine. Just allow Aerin's instincts to take over."

I've only been bitten by snakes four or five times. You'll be fine.

"Four or five times!" I shouted.

Aerin giggled.

"She's messing with you again, isn't she?"

I snorted. "Yeah. She is."

I've never been bitten by a snake, Caspar. You'll be fine. Trust me.

"All right," I said, scratching my head with my free hand before raising Aerin's crescent-shaped single-edged blade in front of me. "What am I supposed to do?"

"Allow Aerin to guide you. Let her direct your steps, your swings, your every move."

"Fitting," I said. "Let the drow woman tell the man what to do."

Oh, shut up, Caspar. You know it's not like that.

I giggled. Aerin had gotten rambunctious in death. In a strange way, she was freer. Less burdened by the pressure of the prophecy, leading her people, and navigating our polygamist marriage as a third wheel. I think I liked this Aerin better. If nothing else, she was more fun than before.

"Those drow women can be real bears," Elrand said, smirking. "If only you knew Aerin's mother."

He's right. My mom was way stricter with her men than me. I think she used to spank dad regularly.

I snorted. "Your wife used to spank you when you misbehaved?"

"Tell Aerin to stop telling tales," Elrand said. "That never happened. Not exactly, anyway."

Aerin giggled in my mind.

"All right, so how do I do this exactly?" I asked. "A spell? Do I need an element?"

Elrand shook his head. "Everything you need is already there, in the connection forged between you and my daughter. The rite that bound your souls, when you took your rings, united your souls forever. You may only be married to Layla now in this life, but your soul will forever be linked to Aerin's. What you require is not a spell or magic of any sort. It's less a matter of drawing her power, her abilities, out of you and more about getting yourself out of the way and letting her take a seat in your conscious mind."

I'm already in your subconscious mind. When you hold the blade, our binding is complete, like a closed circuit connecting my soul in the blade to your soul and your body.

"Wait, Aerin," I said. "So you can read my subconscious mind, not just the thoughts I'm having at the moment?"

Yeah. You know, for a guy with so many fantasies, you sure hold back a lot. I wish I'd known you were so freaky before!

"I am not!" I said. "We're not talking about this in front of your dad. It's weird."

Elrand cocked his head.

It's okay, Caspar. Everyone has a freaky side. Most people are too buttoned up by society to gain the confidence to ever express it.

"She's reading my mind," I said, "and giving me more shit about stuff that I'd generally prefer people not know about."

"That's the connection I'm talking about," Elrand said. "Don't resist her access, don't try to block her out. Let her connection to your mind flow through your body."

"This is something you've done before?" I asked.

"Not exactly," Elrand said. "The connection you and Aerin have is unique."

"Then how do you know this will work?" I asked.

"It's all theory, really," Elrand said. "The drow have written tomes on magical theory but practice very little. It's a disparity I've striven to correct. This is one of many ideas established in drow scholarship that I've not yet been able to test. I'm eager to see if the theory bears out in practice. I will step aside. Speak to Aerin, allow her to guide you until her thoughts become your own and your action become as one."

I nodded as Elrand took a step back to observe from afar. "All right, Aerin. You ready for this?"

Let's give it a go!

I held the blade in front of me with both hands. "Like this?"

Not so stiff! Relax your shoulders, widen your stance.

I grabbed the blade in both hands, spread my feet apart, and tried to loosen up. Relaxing is hard. I learned that doing yoga with Layla. Every time I relax one part of my body, I become aware of the tension I'm holding somewhere else.

It's not a baseball bat. You aren't trying to pummel something with the blade. Everything you do, when you swing it, should be smooth. Forceful, with intention, but also fluid. Can you sense the fire enchanted in the blade?

I nodded. "I think so. But when I wielded the blade before, when we were in Pruitt-Igoe, it wasn't fire. It was something else that came from the blade. It severed the Unseelie from the elves."

That's right. We have to be careful not to use that aspect of the blade's magic. It's on account of our binding that the blade has that ability in your hands. But the blade has always been enchanted with fire, too. Allow me to worry about the magic that the blade is channel-

ing. You focus on letting my influence help you use the sword properly and effectively.

"All right, well, here goes nothing." Still in a batter's stance, I took the blade in my left hand and swung it at the weeds that grew five feet tall on the edge of the clearing.

The blade burst into flames and seared the weeds as the blade cut through them effortlessly.

Keep going. I could feel that.

I swung again, taking out another swatch of leaves from the overgrown field. Another swipe and then another. The next thing I knew, I was spinning around, taking out large sections of the field at once. The weeds I cut burst into flames, but the fires didn't spread. Once the flames did what I intended, they died out.

I tossed the blade from one hand to the other and spun counter-clockwise. Every swipe felt more natural, instinctive.

We're doing it! It's like we share the same body!

I laughed out loud. She was right. It was exhilarating. I felt like a samurai warrior, cutting my way through the brambles with ease as I flipped, spun, and turned one-handed cartwheels. All Aerin. I couldn't do so much as a somersault on a padded floor on my own.

It didn't feel like she was possessing me. Aerin and I were partners, working in sync, our minds united and bodies—hers, the blade, mine, flesh and blood—melded into one.

I found myself doing a backflip, an arc of flames coursing from the blade over me as I landed on my feet. I looked around. Had I already cleared the whole field?

Elrand was smiling and clapping. "That's my girl!" he shouted.

Aerin giggled with glee in my mind.

"It sure was!" I said. "There's no way I could have done any of that without her! I didn't even notice any snakes!"

Elrand chuckled as he made his way toward me through the charred clearing. "I saw a couple slither back into the woods. I'm sure there were others."

I shrugged. "Well, I didn't notice. I was so lost in the thrill of it."

Elrand squeezed my shoulder. "Let's return to the stone circle and see if we can repopulate this field with some mighty oaks, maples, and pines."

CHAPTER SIX

I sat in the middle of Elrand's stone circle. There had only been a few times I'd used all five elements for a given task. Usually, I'd use water if I needed a quick drink or provide a cooling off for the folks at the junkyard ranch. The only advantage of living in such a humid part of the country was that I could always draw water from the air. I'd used fire for, well, starting fires. The drow had items enchanted with fire magic already, so they didn't need it so much. But I'd started a few bonfires for the giants since they arrived from New Albion. Air and aether I used to fly. Fairy magic didn't use the elements. It was a separate type of magic that Trixie had left within me when she'd bonded with my consciousness.

However, there weren't many tasks that required all the elements to work together in concert. What Elrand was proposing would take a lot of focus. Still, I was excited to try it. I was also interested to see how casting within the stone circle would help me conserve energy. I'd used magic there before, separating each element to summon the Furies. I'd evoked air and aether from within to fly out of there and stop an earthquake at a nearby fault line. But I hadn't used the combined elements to work extensive magic. Certainly nothing like this.

Elrand gave me basic instructions, reminding me of the combination of elements in the order that was needed to establish a flourishing forest. Evoking the power of air, the wind would carry the seeds from nearby trees into the clearing. Water and earth would be evoked to nourish the seeds; aether would help them germinate and grow at an above-average pace. I had no more use for fire. That part was done.

Aerin's blade was back in its sheath. I sat cross-legged in the middle of the stone circle. First, air. Elrand was right. It didn't take much effort to harness the wind from within the stone circle. With a whirlwind rising around the circle, the trees around the stones released their seeds into the air I channeled. Acorns, seeds, pine cones, the wind shook it all loose, moving at such speed that none of it fell to the ground.

I asked the wind to carry the precious load to the clearing I'd burned out before. Then, I dropped the water I gathered from the humid air over the clearing. I saw it all happen in my mind's eye. After all, it wasn't just the elements I wielded. Elemental spirits belonging to each element were contained within me ever since I conquered them all in the trials. It was as if the elementals went ahead of me and broadcast their vision back into my mind.

With water soaking the ground, I asked the earth to nourish the seeds, and I asked aether to spur them to life. I saw saplings sprout from the ground. They grew fast, reminding me of watching a tree grow on time-lapse imagery.

But this was in real-time.

From the vantage point of aether and earth, I was *inside* the trees, one and all of them at the same time. I was swimming in sap. My roots spread through the earth. I moved my point of view to the perspective of air, and from the skies, I saw the saplings grow into giant trees that towered over the rest of the forest.

I felt a hand on my shoulder. I barely noticed. So many sensations and visions were coursing through my mind. It took all my concentration to extract myself and return to my human eyesight.

"You've done it, Naayak." It was Elrand's voice. I lifted my hand and rested it on his.

"That was amazing," I said as he helped me to my feet. "I've never experienced anything like that. So much happening at once."

"You've given the elements their charge," Elrand said. "Now nature will sustain what you've planted."

I nodded. "I feel amazing, not tired at all. All the magic I cast, or how much I felt I was casting… Those stones took everything up a notch."

Elrand patted me on the shoulder. "Just imagine how much you could do with a larger circle, channeling more magic?"

I shook my head. "I just have to figure out how I can recreate this on a large enough scale that it will get Brightborn's attention. Something that huge will be intriguing to the governments and undermine his position with them."

"There are other fields around here. I'm sure you could repeat what you just did," Elrand said.

I bit my lip. "Maybe. That might not be enough. It's one thing to see something on video. Even on a live stream, people will always question it. Especially if I do it out in the middle of nowhere. Maybe we could produce a teaser video out here? We'd have to invite the media, the government, anybody and everybody who wants to see us do it live. It wouldn't need to be a forest of this size. But it would need to be somewhere that people would see it. Then they couldn't deny it was real."

"You have a location in mind?" Elrand asked.

I smirked. "Busch Stadium is probably out of the question. That would just tick people off. You don't want to mess with people's sports. Maybe I could do it at St. Louis Arch? There are open fields there, a park, plenty of space that anyone could come to. The visual impact of growing trees next to a recognizable structure so people can get an idea of the size of the trees I can grow, and how quickly I can do it, would be hard to ignore."

"I think that's brilliant," Elrand said. "First things first, I need to talk to Jag. We need to produce the invitation fast and get it out there. Something that will show what's possible, explain the significance of it in terms of climate change, and we'll have to disseminate the footage as far and wide as possible."

CHAPTER SEVEN

Jag wasn't an expert videographer. He'd run the webcam streams from St. Ensley's back when I was undergoing the elemental trials. Still, we didn't need a Hollywood production. The simpler and less edited it appeared, the better.

Elrand and I took a fairy portal back to the junkyard ranch. I almost forgot it was Saturday. Dwight came every weekend with his eighteen-wheeler so we could make a supply run. He had mostly local and regional trucking routes and was usually available. Since I had access to Aerin's money—I suppose she'd been something of my sugar elf—I'd have to go along.

Layla was already there, along with Jag, ready to roll.

"How'd it go?" she asked.

"Fantastic," I said. "I think I have a plan. but we're going to need a lot to pull it off."

"You've got me most of the day," Dwight said. "Anything you need, we can get it."

Dwight was a nice guy. He'd joined the Elf Gate cult shortly after Brag'mok had kidnapped him to commandeer his rig. In the process of all that, Layla and I saved him, and he'd seen enough that he couldn't go back to life as it was. Dwight was a Marine veteran. With war on the horizon, he was ever eager to help. He understood what was at stake, and as he put it, he hadn't risked his life fighting for his country only to have politicians cede their power to an otherworldly dictator.

I ran through the plan with Layla, Jag, and Dwight. First, we needed to create a video intriguing enough to get the public's attention on me when I grew trees at the Arch. Elrand and I had already decided I'd duplicate what I'd already done. Call the first time a rehearsal. It was simple and impressive.

"What we need is a drone," Jag said.

"I agree!" Layla added. "Think how impressive it would be to see a whole forest spring up out of nowhere from above?"

"I like that idea," I said. "I wish we had a scientist or someone who could explain the science of how trees absorb carbon from the atmosphere, all of that."

"I think you should do it," Dwight said. "You might not be a scientist, but you're educated. When you talk, you sound like you know what you're saying."

"Still, it would be helpful if we had a scientist or an environmentalist," Layla said. "Someone with credentials in that field. No offense, Caspar, but when someone hears your degrees are in theology and religion, some people will tune you out straight away."

I nodded. "I'm aware of that. But I don't know if we'll find anyone we could interview soon enough, and I refuse to involve someone without full disclosure of what might be at stake."

Layla nodded. "Good point. I wouldn't put it past my father to target anyone involved. We'd have to protect anyone who was willing to participate."

"The data is out there," Elrand said, approaching us from behind. "I may not be a scientist, but I have read the research. The credentials are with the universities and institutions that conducted the studies. All people need to know is that with a trillion more trees on Earth, climate change can be reversed."

"When they see that Caspar can produce trees that quickly," Layla added. "I'm not sure we need much more than that. All we need is to present a viable alternative to allying with my father. Then, when Caspar demonstrates it live, I can't imagine that my father won't respond."

"I hope you're right," I said, hopping into the passenger side of Dwight's truck. Jag climbed up beside me—not my person of choice to sit next to on a supply run. He smelled like the gym even though he had been working out on the ranch for the last several weeks. Maybe it was the gym that smelled like Jag.

"The usual stops?" Dwight asked.

I nodded. "We have the same list. The usual supplies."

"But we need to stop somewhere to buy a drone," Jag added.

When we'd first moved in, we'd made our supply runs closer by, hitting up the local Home Depot, Wal-Mart, and truck stop so we could fill all our gasoline cans. The whole junkyard ranch was powered by small generators. The giants lived mostly in makeshift huts built from scrap. The drow had tents. Still, we kept a semblance of air conditioning going in the farmhouse, we needed a station to keep our phones charged, and had several deep freezers and refrigerators for all the food we stored for everyone who lived on the ranch. When you're feeding giants, that's a *lot* of food.

Lately, we'd been running into the city and shopping at Costco, where we could get most of what we needed in bulk. It made things easier than loading up a dozen shopping carts at Wal-Mart.

Luckily, Costco had drones with video recording abilities. Jag said it would be sufficient. He'd be putting the whole video together on his phone, anyway. Since the drone streamed to his phone, from there, he could splice the footage into the makeshift documentary/promotional piece we were planning. It was convenient.

Giant bags of rice, bulk packs of toilet paper, lots of canned foods, frozen meats and vegetables, and a shit-ton of milk. I half-wondered if we'd be better off just buying the cow. It would certainly mean a lot less that we'd have to, um, *mooooove* into the ranch every week.

Stop groaning. I know you're laughing on the inside.

We'd probably need more than one cow, anyway. Then you'd have to agree that my jokes were the best you'd ever *herd*.

See what I did there?

I know. I know. I'm just practicing. Some day, after all, I'd like to become a dad.

CHAPTER EIGHT

With everyone at the ranch fed and all the supplies restocked for another week, I wanted to talk to Brag'mok before we headed to Elrand's stone circle to produce our pseudo-documentary. There were advantages to this whole plan, one being that it would distract the giants from their plan to attack the North Pole elves. Any effort that would undermine Brightborn's plan was a win in my book—unless it resulted in innocents becoming collateral damage. If we could score a victory on a diplomatic level without any bloodshed, that was far preferable.

Brag'mok had been, aside from Layla, my closest friend in this whole prophecy affair. He'd taught me how to fight. He'd helped me get an advantage over the elves more than once. There's no telling how much worse things would be if it wasn't for him. Still, I understood. He'd gone from believing his entire race was wiped out to discovering that there was a small clan of giants left on New Albion. We'd brought them here to fulfill their ancient purpose, to defend the world against any threat. The elves, and Brightborn specifically, were a threat.

Sure, Brag'mok and I were friends. But he'd fought against Brightborn's legions since he was just a teenage giant, and he knew that he was here with the rest of his race to fulfill a sacred duty. When push came to shove, I suppose I couldn't blame him if he sided with the other giants. Still, I had to talk to him. The giants would be stronger if we were all united rather than trying to launch an assault against the elves alone. And we'd be a more formidable force with the giants as well.

"I understand the giants' impatience," I said. "We have to be careful."

Brag'mok snorted. "It's not the time it's taking. Gronk lacks confidence that you have what it takes to wage a war."

"But the prophecy…" I sighed.

"Targigoth agrees that you are the chosen one," Brag'mok said. "You will unite the peoples in the end. But that doesn't mean you are the one who is meant to lead us in the war that will likely happen first."

I bit my lip. Brag'mok was right, of course. None of the prophecies said anything about war. We'd been presuming that war was likely, but I'd held out hope that it was avoidable. If the prophet had any idea who he was choosing, or whoever did the choosing that made me the chosen one, I wasn't the man to lead armies. I was a preacher. In my experience, a sermon was just as likely to put people to sleep as it was to fire them up. My experience wasn't the kind that would rally troops against an enemy, and I knew almost nothing about battle strategies.

"We still need to stay together," I said.

"Gronk does not wish to be your enemy, Caspar," Brag'mok said. "We are on your side. But you must realize that when you're in a war with Brightborn, you don't get many opportunities to seize an advantage."

"We *have* the advantage," I said. "We have fairies. He doesn't."

"Yes," Brag'mok said. "But how long do you think it will be before he has the world at his side ready to hail him as emperor, or whatever term they want to give him to make themselves feel better about the fact that he's the new king of kings, the president of presidents."

"I have no idea," I said. "But we have an idea. A way to convince the world that they don't have to give Brightborn authority in order to heal the planet."

Brag'mok lifted an eyebrow. "You really think most of the world's governments care about climate change and the health of this world?"

"I think some do," I said.

"As much as they care about power and might?"

I bit my lip. "Probably not."

"You may be a pacifist, Caspar. But Brightborn's plan has never been about starting a war. He sent Hector here years ago to start planting seeds in the minds of powerful people. It was Brightborn's plotting that led to the Elf Gate cult. His strategy from the beginning was to convince Earth's authorities to give him power, not to wrest it from them by force. By refusing to fight or by avoiding it until all else fails, you're allowing Brightborn to pursue the strategy he's intended from the start."

I shook my head. "If there's a war, people will die."

"How many people will die, humans especially, once Brightborn exacts his tyranny over your world?" Brag'mok asked. "He's already destroyed one planet. Do you believe he'll save this one? The ways he'll use Earth's magic for his own gain will have consequences, Caspar. He must be stopped before it gets to that, and that's what we, the giants, along with the Furies and the elementals, were first created to prevent."

I nodded. "But that's not me. I'm not a fighter."

"But the elementals dwell within you," Brag'mok said. "They are aligned with your spirit. You are a part of this battle as much as the giants or the Furies."

"I understand that," I said, "but wouldn't it make sense that the three protector species were created to defend the world in different ways? War might be the strength of the giants. But the elementals belong to the planet. They are most powerful in peace and harmony rather than in conflict and war."

"If Brightborn should succeed and take control, do you think the Furies will sit back and allow him to manipulate the Earth's power? They almost destroyed a whole city because they were evoked and angered by an injustice."

I snorted. "I was there."

"How many do you suppose will die if the Furies unleash the powers of the Earth after Brightborn starts manipulating this planet to suit his purposes?"

I sighed. "I don't know. Look, Brag'mok, I get it. We might have to go to war. How is assaulting unarmed elves just? How can it be the answer?"

"It's what's on the table," Brag'mok said. "If we don't move soon, we may never get another chance."

I shook my head. "Brag'mok, if you allow innocent people, even elves, to be slaughtered because you think that the ends justify the means, how does that make you any different than Brightborn?"

"Sometimes it isn't about justifying a means by its end, Caspar. It's about having no justifiable means toward a better end and having to choose the lesser of various evils."

"Is that really what this is about, Brag'mok?" I asked. "Or, after Brightborn wiped out millions of innocent giants—men, women, and children—is this a demented attempt to even the score?"

"Tell me, Caspar," Brag'mok said, scratching the back of his head. "If you discovered a nest of venomous serpents in the crawlspace of your home, under the nursery where your newborn child was sleeping, would you not eliminate the snakes before they had a chance to make their way into your home and harm your child?"

"I would," I said. "But we're talking about elves, not poisonous snakes. Just because they've had vile leaders, oppressive rulers who've done great evils, they are not by nature an evil race."

"You are blinded by love."

I shook my head. "Layla isn't evil despite being raised by a tyrant. It isn't my love that makes me see her as good. It's because she's good that I love her. You're better than this, Brag'mok. You know what I'm saying is true. Those elves at the North Pole aren't legionaries. They're people displaced from their homes, anxious about their place in this world. If they follow Brightborn, it's because they don't know better. He is their king, and he promised them a new home. They aren't wrong to want that even if Brightborn's plan to accomplish that is."

"Even if you convinced me, Caspar, Gronk is our chief. He is not amenable to persuasion."

"Well, who died and made him chief, anyway?" I snapped.

Brag'mok narrowed his eyes. I regretted my words the moment they came out of my mouth. Seriously, Caspar? After a whole race was subjected to genocide to throw out a line like that?

"I'm sorry, that's not what I meant."

"I know what you meant," Brag'mok said. "Good luck with your plan. But if it does not succeed, Gronk will order the assault."

CHAPTER NINE

I walked into the farmhouse where Layla and Jag were working on scripts for the video. Agnus was lounging on my duct tape-patched bed, scrolling on my iPad with his paw.

"Any progress?" I asked, taking my iPad back from the cat.

"You rampallian!" Agnus shouted.

I cocked my head. "What did you call me?"

"A rampallian, you mountain of mad flesh!"

I glanced at my iPad. "You're reading Shakespeare? Seriously?"

"The bard has the greatest insults!" Agnus piped up.

"I told him we needed good wording for the script, and Agnus was convinced that he needed to craft a literary masterpiece," Layla said.

"So he's studying the greatest playwright in the history of the English language? Agnus, we don't need anything that refined."

Agnus stared at me. "Not so much brain as ear wax, ye have between the ears."

"It's best if he thinks he's helping," Layla whispered in my ear.

I shrugged. "All right."

"You long-tongu'd babbling gossips! Tell me what you speak behind my back," Agnus demanded.

"Technically, above your back," I said. "Since you're a cat and on the ground."

Agnus narrowed his eyes and glared at me. "You elvish-mark'd abortive rooting hog!"

Layla tilted her head. "Elvish-mark'd?"

"Thou that was sealed in thy nativity," Agnus continued. "The slave of nature and the son of hell!"

"What does that even mean?" I asked.

"Cursed from birth," Jag said. "Elvish-mark'd was a phrase at the time meant to describe those who were marked out at birth by evil fairies in spite."

I snorted. "You know Shakespeare?"

"I majored in Western Lit in college," Jag said.

"You went to college?"

Jag winked at me. "I'm not all brawn, Caspar. I'm also brains."

"Too bad he can't hear Agnus," Layla said. "They'd work well together."

I bit my lip. "We don't need a masterpiece here. We just need something quick but persuasive. Short but powerful."

"Come on, Jag, you bolting-hutch of beastliness!" Agnus shouted.

"He can't hear you, Agnus," I said.

"What did he say?" Jag asked.

"He said you're a beast," Layla said. "Albeit with a bit more flourish."

"A bolting-hutch of beastliness?" Jag asked. Layla nodded. "That's one of my favorites. I'm impressed. Especially for one highly fed and lowly taught."

Agnus looked at Jag and hissed. "I do desire we may be better strangers."

"I don't think he appreciated that," I said.

"Let's just keep it simple," Layla said as Agnus returned to the iPad and continued scrolling through Shakespeare's Macbeth.

"What a lump of foul deformity," Agnus muttered under his breath.

The front door creaked open.

I turned as Elrand entered the room. "Elrand, I'm glad you joined us. We're struggling with this script."

Elrand nodded. "Be that as it may, do you know what happened to the giants?"

I stared back at Elrand blankly. "What are you talking about?"

"They're gone. One minute they were gathered around their junk heaps, fitting themselves in armor. I turned around, and they were gone."

"How could they do that?" Layla asked. "The fairies haven't returned."

Elrand shrugged. "Perhaps one of them has been melded to a fairy before and can create his own fairy portals."

I snorted. "They told me they were going to commandeer a cruise ship."

Elrand raised his eyebrows. "And you believed that?"

I shook my head. "I didn't know what to believe. But if they can create portals, then they need a visual to go there. I'm pretty sure that none of them have ever been to the North Pole."

"Not even Brag'mok?" Elrand asked.

"They can travel the ley lines," Layla said. "We learned that the giants could do that when B'iff did it."

"That makes sense," Elrand said. "The ley lines on Earth are all connected. They intersect at the poles."

I slammed my fist on the wall. "I can travel the ley lines, but only because I can control the magic that flows through them. The giants seem to have a natural ability to do it. If they make it into the ley lines, I won't be able to bring everyone with me."

"Not necessarily true," Elrand said. "You can create fairy portals."

"Yeah, but…"

"Hold on," Layla said, raising her hand. "I think I see where

Elrand is going with this. You could take the ley lines to the poles alone, then take a fairy portal back here and cast another one to take all of us to the pole with you."

"Exactly what I was thinking!" Elrand said. "If you would allow me to finish my thoughts!"

Layla giggled. "Sorry. I got excited."

"Well, so much for saving the trees and saving the world," I said.

"Not necessarily," Elrand said. "We have a grander purpose than stopping the giants. Our plan would still undermine Brightborn."

"I agree," Layla said. "We still need to do that."

"All right," I said. "Elrand, you and Jag work on the video plans…"

"Excuse me, you fustilarian!" Agnus interjected.

I held up a hand. "Sorry, Elrand, Jag, and Agnus work on the video."

"I can hear the cat," Elrand said.

"Must be a pointy-ear thing," Jag said, grinning.

Elrand and Agnus both stared at him blankly.

"Sorry, was that offensive?"

I shook my head. "Layla, grab your bow. I'll take Aerin's sword. We need to stop the giants before they enter the ley lines."

CHAPTER TEN

I hoped I wouldn't have to use my sword and Layla wouldn't have to use her bow. The last thing I wanted was to have to fight against my allies. But given the giants' penchant for solving problems with violence, we couldn't take anything for granted.

I formed a fairy portal, visualizing the place at the confluence of the Mississippi and Meramec rivers where the ley lines intersected. I grabbed Layla's hand, and we jumped through together.

The giants were there, standing at the shore. Gronk and Brag'mok were arguing with each other in their own language. I couldn't make out a word, but I approached them no less.

"What the hell are you up to?" I asked. "You agreed to give me a week!"

Gronk huffed. "It's Targigoth."

"The high priest?" Layla asked. "What did he do?"

"While you were inside, Trixie returned," Brag'mok said. "She went straight to Targigoth, and he left through a portal with her."

"Where did they go?" I asked.

Gronk snorted. "He's been telling us all along that we need to learn what the seventh elven scroll reveals concerning the elves before we act. The fairy must've found Brightborn, and he left with her to retrieve it."

"The last prophecy can't be opened without the elven high priest," I said. "And he's back on New Albion. I took him there myself."

"With Trixie," Brag'mok said. "Targigoth could go there himself to find him."

"But he's going into Brightborn's court," I said. "That can't be good."

"Which is why I insist we assault the elves immediately," Gronk said. "We need to do something to get Brightborn's attention so Targigoth stands a chance."

"But why would Targigoth go there alone, without any backup?" Layla asked.

Brag'mok sighed. "Like Caspar, Targigoth prefers diplomacy to war."

"But he's a young priest and naive," Gronk said. "I believe he intends to offer Brightborn a deal. To retrieve the elven priest and return him in exchange for knowledge of whatever the final elven prophecy reveals."

I bit my lip. "That's actually not a bad plan. But we promised Echor the chance to live out his days uninterrupted back on New Albion. He could have stayed with us. I offered it, but he insisted."

Layla grabbed my arm. "Caspar, there's something I should tell you."

"What's that?" I asked.

"Alone," Layla said, glancing at Gronk and Brag'mok. "I haven't told anyone yet for good reason."

Gronk and Brag'mok nodded as Layla and I took a few steps away, far enough that they couldn't overhear what she had to tell me.

"When you were still passed out in the forest after you stopped the earthquake, Echor passed the authority of the elven priesthood to me."

I stared back at Layla blankly. "That's exactly what your father wanted!"

Layla nodded. "He figured we would need to open the prophecy later. But it wasn't Echor's idea. It was Targigoth's."

"So Targigoth isn't going to offer Brightborn Echor…"

Layla shook her head. "He's going to offer him me."

I grunted. "Why the hell didn't you mention this to me before now?"

Layla shook her head. "Because Echor told me that no one should know. Not even you."

"Why the hell shouldn't I know about this?" I said. "If I'd known…"

"What would you have done, Caspar?" Layla asked.

"I don't know!" I said. "I'd have done something!"

"You would have gone after the prophecy yourself."

I shrugged. "Yeah. Maybe."

"You didn't know where Brightborn was," Layla said. "Meanwhile, what about the giants and the drow, who needed you to unite them?"

"Well, I've certainly failed at that," I said. "Maybe everyone would have been better off if someone else was in charge."

"You kept the peace," Layla said. "The giants and drow don't agree on much. The only reason they've stayed at the ranch this long is because of you."

"All this stuff is over my head," I said. "How can I even *begin* to lead them when I don't know a thing about war, or even diplomacy for that matter? I'm a freaking preacher, for Pete's sake! At least, I was."

Layla put her hand on my shoulder. "Leaders don't have to be experts at everything they're in charge of, Caspar. What makes a leader is the ability to identify the talents in others and to unify them in a common purpose."

I sighed. "There's that unity word again. You know, what I'm supposed to be about as the chosen one."

"Exactly," Layla said. "Has it occurred to you that if you brought Gronk and Rina together, if you allowed them to give their input rather than just hoping that they'd do what you say, when you say it, that maybe we'd be more unified about what needs to be done next?"

I scratched the back of my head. "They're too different. They hardly speak at all. How am I supposed to get them to agree on anything?"

Layla knocked on my forehead with her fist. "Hello, McFly! That's exactly why *you* need to bring them together. The one thing they have in common is that they believe you are the chosen one!"

I rubbed my forehead. "Why'd I ever show you that damn movie?"

Layla smirked. "Because you wouldn't stop giggling about B'iff's name, and you had to show it to me so I understood what you found so funny."

I chuckled. "That's right. Damn, I miss that dude. I wish he was here. Brag'mok is great, don't get me wrong. But that giant, he understood sacrifice."

"If I remember right, you thought he was your enemy until the very end. You barely knew him," Layla said.

I bit my lip. "I guess you're right. Someone gives their life for you, and you start to convince yourself that you had more of a relationship with them than you did. But he was the one who I thought was fighting you in the alley. He's the one who stalked us in his pickup truck."

"And he came to believe in you, giving his life because he believed so much in what you were meant to do," Layla reminded me.

I sighed. "I remember."

"You have what it takes to unite the giants, the drow, the fairies, everyone," Layla said. "They *will* follow you, Caspar. But you have to believe in yourself first. A leader has to be confident if nothing else. No one wants to follow someone who's wandering aimlessly as if he were blind."

I nodded. "All right. Lets talk to Gronk and Brag'mok."

"Don't tell them about the prophecy," Layla said. "Or about me being the high priest."

I nodded. "I won't. But I don't see why they shouldn't know about it."

Layla shook her head. "The giants are not as unified as they seem. Otherwise, Targigoth wouldn't have gone off on his own. Brag'mok and Gronk wouldn't be at odds about whether to attack the elves or try to rescue their priest. Until we know for sure that they all stand with us, we should keep this information to ourselves. We can't risk word getting to my father somehow."

"All right." I walked back to Gronk and Brag'mok. "Here's the situation as I see it. We don't know where Targigoth went. But I am confident that he and Trixie wouldn't go off alone without telling us anything without good reason. There may be reason to believe that they went to the North Pole, but again, we don't know that for sure. Here's the thing. I'm not an expert in battle or war. I don't know much about politics or diplomacy. But I *am* the chosen one, and it's my job to unify the peoples. So that's what we're going to do. We're not going to stand here at the confluence of the ley lines and fight over it. We're going back to the junkyard ranch. We're bringing the drow into the conversation. This impacts them, too."

"I still believe that we need to attack," Gronk said.

I nodded. "That might be. If that's what we all decide together, I'll back you up. But we have to make our next moves *together*. That's the only way we win this war."

CHAPTER ELEVEN

"So, here are the options we have on the table," I said. We were sitting around a table we'd made from an old door and milk crates gathered from the junkyard. "Gronk and the giants want to march on the North Pole. At least, they did until Targigoth took it upon himself to go on a mission with Trixie to try to recover the last scroll of the elven prophecy. We were planning on creating a video to undermine Brightborn's relationship with the governments and draw him out of hiding. What is the position of the drow?"

Rina stood up from her folding chair and rested her hands on the table. She and Jag exchanged nods. They were an odd couple, but admittedly, a cute one. "Aerin believed it was our sacred duty to protect the prophecy and support the chosen one. But we cannot remain here waiting for something to happen. We agree, should Targigoth fail, we must make an effort to take the prophecy from the elves."

"Then we are in agreement," Gronk said. "We must march on the North Pole. If it does not lead Brightborn to us, it will, at the very least, offer a distraction so that Targigoth can succeed."

"But we mustn't attack," Rina said.

"What the point of marching there if not to fight?" Gronk asked.

"To win over the elves," Layla said. "With my celestial magic, with everything I know, I can convince them to follow me rather than my father."

"Or they'll brand you a traitor and try to kill you," Gronk said.

"In that case," I interjected, "you'll have your war."

"And we'll fight beside you," Rina said.

"But we're still making the video," I said. "We have to stick to the plan."

"Why?" Layla asked.

"We have to trust that Targigoth knows what he is doing. Trixie wouldn't lead him into a trap. Whatever he's up to, there has to be a reason why he didn't tell us in advance."

Gronk snorted. "It's because he knew it went against what I intended. His concern is the prophecy. My concern is ensuring that the elves don't have a chance to do to this world what they did to ours."

I nodded. "This is your world, Gronk. Always has been. It's why the giants were created in the beginning."

"So if we must fight, you will fight with us?" Gronk asked.

I nodded. "If it comes to that, if there's no other choice, I will."

"What about the video thing?" Jag asked. "We're still on with that. How soon do we have to get it ready?"

"Targigoth has already left," I said. "We can't waste time on scripts. We need to shoot it now, get it out there, and invite those who will come to see what I can do first thing tomorrow."

"By tomorrow?" Jag asked. "It would take me all night just to edit this video, much less get it sent out on all the right channels."

"No edits, Jag," I said. "We don't have time for that. It will be crude, but all that's important is that they hear our explanation of what we think is possible and see it happen. Keep it simple. Record me in the stone circle. Switch the drone feed and get a good shot of the forest springing up from the ground. Come back to me, and I'll tell them when and where to be if they want to see me do the same thing in person."

"I still think we should move ahead to the pole," Gronk said.

"We'll go together," I said. "I can travel the ley lines just as you can. I'll take you with me so we can choose a strategic spot to bring everyone else to, and then I'll portal us back here, and we'll take everyone with us back to the North Pole."

"Why not do that before you make this video?" Gronk asked.

"Because," I said, shaking my head, "we don't know how the government or Brightborn will react to the video. When I show up at the arch to perform my public demonstration, I need backup in case someone attacks. I'm saying I need you, Gronk. I need all of you."

"We need each other," Rina added.

Gronk nodded. "Very well. This is a better plan."

Layla put her hand on my shoulder and squeezed. It was either her way of saying, "I'm proud of you, Casp," or saying, "I told you so." Either way, I'd take it.

Preparing the video also gave the giants and drow time to coordinate their efforts. The drow didn't require heavy armor. That wasn't the way they fought. Their style depended on speed and agility rather than brute force. Float like a butterfly, sting like a bee. The giants had more of an Incredible Hulk *smash* style. They were more agile than you'd think, given their size, but they weren't going to avoid a lot of blows with their size. They had to focus on protecting themselves, absorbing blows, so they could counter-strike with a devastating attack.

Still, the drow could use a little armor. Breastplates to protect their vital organs. Helmets. Forearm protection. The giants were great at reforging scrap, so this gave them a chance to work together on something.

Layla, Jag, Elrand, and I gathered the supplies Jag said we'd need for the video. It wasn't much. Jag planned to use his phone to record my introduction and the drone to record the trees rising from the ground. Other than that, we just needed a few lights since where I'd be standing in the stone circle was heavily shaded and an external microphone.

I was about to form my fairy portal when I felt a large hand on my shoulder.

I turned. "Brag'mok?"

"I want to come with you. I want to help with the video."

I shrugged. "Not sure there's a lot to help with. This is going to be a pretty simple production."

Brag'mok nodded. "I want to say a few things."

I raised my eyebrow. "Like?"

"People need to know what's at stake. They need to hear how Brightborn destroyed New Albion. They must know that his promises are hollow, that he'll do the same to this world if they trust him."

I bit my lip. "A lot of the people watching won't even know who Brightborn is."

"But the governments will," Layla said. "I think it's a good idea. If Brightborn perceives this video as a direct threat to his plan, and there's no way he won't see that this plan diminishes whatever he's offering the world's governments, he's more likely to react."

We didn't have a Shakespearean script. I'd have to shoot from the hip. Agnus would be disappointed. Elrand gave me the statistics about how a trillion mature trees would effectively reverse climate change. I knew the basic argument and, due to the many Sundays back in the day that I showed up at church ill-prepared to preach after drinking all week, I'd developed keen improvisational skills. Now I'd be able to use those talents without the challenge of speaking through cottonmouth and the sensation of a jackhammer pounding at the inside of my skull.

Layla held the smartphone to record my introductory speech and my spell casting in the stone circle. Jag operated the drone. After we got all that recorded, Layla would record Brag'mok's speech. I wasn't sure how people would react to seeing a giant. They weren't just large humans. They looked like orcs of Tolkien or World of Warcraft lore. The elves even referred to the giants as orcs disparagingly.

The live streams we sent out before had already shown the world elves—my success in the trials, my marriage to Aerin, my whirlwind tour of the children's hospitals. But this would be the first time most people ever saw a giant. It would be shocking to some people. At the very least, it would probably encourage more views which could only work to our benefit.

Elrand might have been a better candidate to address the science of trees, photosynthesis, and climate change. However, I was already a fairly well-known public figure due to the live streams we'd sent out before. The world needed to hear it from me.

Elrand showed me another treeless field filled with brambles and poison ivy that I could clear with fire and use as the site to plant our new grove.

I knew what to do.

Layla started recording.

"My name is Caspar Cruciger. Some of you know me as the Reverend Cruciger due to the miracles we performed at hospitals across St. Louis and the demonstrations of elemental magic we've broadcasted in the past. Today, I come to you with an important message. I have a way that we can reverse climate change and still maintain our way of life. Scientists have long recognized that if Earth had a trillion more mature trees that they would remove most of the carbon from the atmosphere. It would take more than a hundred trees to offset each person's carbon footprint. You probably haven't heard about this because until now, it hasn't been a viable solution. The land required, not to mention the time it would take to grow so many trees to maturity, has led most to discount such a project. Today, however, I intend to show you that I have the ability to make this a reality. If you're impressed by this demonstration, but imagine that what I'm showing you is the result of a Hollywood-style production, I'm inviting any who are interested to join my friends and me at noon tomorrow, at St. Louis Arch. I will demonstrate this again in person so you can see it with your own eyes."

I sat down cross-legged in the stone circle. I was better able to focus in a seated position than standing. Jag already had the drone in the air.

I called for the element of fire, and the heat coursed through my body as I sent a torrent of flames across the field that Elrand had shown me before. This was my second time doing this, so I was more efficient.

Once the flames subsided, I watered the ground. My body cooled off in turn. With wind, I carried the seeds of many trees throughout the forest into the clearing and added aether, life. The seeds started to grow. The saplings grew into trees that towered over the rest of the forest.

"We've got it," Jag said. "You ready to record your portion, Brag'mok?"

The giant nodded. Layla fixed the camera on us as we stood side-by-side.

I looked into the camera. "There is a visitor from another world, an elven king by the name of Brightborn who has convinced our world's governments that he alone can save our world. But at what cost? This man beside me belongs to an ancient race of giants. They were once charged to protect the planet from any threat, but they were cast out in the middle ages, along with the elves, when fleeing persecution. He has a warning for the world that our leaders must heed."

"Thank you, Caspar," Brag'mok said, his voice shaking with nerves. "The elven king has destroyed our former planet. A place we called New Albion. He wasted all of the planet's magic to wage wars against my people. Millions of giants like me died at his hand as we fought to prevent him from coming to your world. But now he is here. He makes grand promises that he cannot keep. Does he have a solution that could solve problems like global warming? Maybe. But it will come at the price of your freedom. My friend Caspar offers another solution. He attaches no strings to what he promises. If you would like to see more, then join us tomorrow at St. Louis Arch. The future of your world, and your freedom, depends on it."

CHAPTER TWELVE

It took Jag about an hour to splice the videos together and get them uploaded. He shared it through the same channels we'd used to disseminate our broadcasts before. Last time, we'd managed to get the attention of national media. Surely, we'd have at least as much success now. The world needed to see this. Not just the video we'd just recorded, but the demonstration we'd planned. If all went as planned, we wouldn't need to record anything the next day. The media outlets would take care of that.

"We have a problem," Jag said, scrolling through his phone.

"What sort of problem?" I asked.

"The social media outlets are closing down my accounts. Saying that I violated misinformation policies."

"Misinformation?" I asked. "You have to be kidding. Who the hell decides what's real and fake information anyway?"

Layla snorted. "Probably your government."

"Well, that's just great," I said. "So much for freedom of speech."

"Just the start," Brag'mok said. "Once Brightborn has full compliance from the world's governments, there won't be anything that gets out there that he doesn't want to be seen or heard."

"It's not all a loss," Jag said. "Some of the news networks picked it up. We can only hope at this point that they'll let it… Wait… What the hell?"

"What is it?" I asked.

"My freaking phone isn't connecting to the internet now!" Jag exclaimed.

Layla and I exchanged glances. "Probably not a coincidence," Layla said.

"You can probably send me the video over Bluetooth," I said. "I don't think the government knows about my burner phone."

"So much for all the President's talk about freedom and liberty," Jag snorted. "I thought you said when you met with him, he was steadfast about not allowing Brightborn to gain influence."

"Yeah," I said. "That was before Brightborn wiped out an army when he came to Earth and before all the shenanigans with my legal situation a few months back."

"We knew they were looking for us," Layla said. "That's why the fairies shrouded the ranch."

"They'll be able to trace my phone to the closest tower," Jag said. "They might not see us, but they'll know we're somewhere close to here."

"This is my fault," Elrand said, shaking his head in the corner. "The video was my idea."

"It's not your fault," I said. "It was a good idea. We didn't expect they'd go to these measures to silence us."

"Then what do we do?" Layla asked.

"We stick to the plan. Tomorrow, we go to the arch. I'll grow a whole forest. Not just one tree. Let them try to explain *that* away. At the very least, the video is in the hands of some media outlets. Even if the government doesn't let them broadcast it, hopefully, someone will find a way to get the word out to the public."

"What are we going to tell the giants?" Layla asked.

"The truth," I said.

"Are you sure?" she asked.

I nodded. "Yes. Brightborn works through deceit and subterfuge. We have to be honest with each other. They have to know what's going on."

"They'll want to fight," Layla said.

I nodded. "When we go to St. Louis tomorrow, we might need them to."

———

We couldn't wait until the next day. They'd be expecting us. They'd be waiting for us. We had to go immediately. The few media outlets who had gotten our video before the powers that be shut it down wouldn't be there. If they got the message at all, they'd be expecting us to come the next day at noon.

Still, if I birthed a whole forest of sky-scraping trees around the arch, there wouldn't be anything the government could do to keep that a secret. Too many people would see it. Cars, driving by on the nearby interstate, people living in the tower apartments with a view of the arch would notice. The government wouldn't have any way to get rid of the trees without making a scene.

The giants didn't have all the drow fitted in armor, but many of them were—including Rina. I had Aerin's sword in hand. Chances were, we wouldn't be coming back to the junkyard ranch. If the authorities were tracing Jag's phone, it wouldn't be long before they'd come looking for us. If they couldn't find us on account of the fairy veil, who knew, they might just carpet bomb the place to Hell. There weren't many people in the area. Hardly anyone else would notice. The collateral damage would be minimal.

A ley line ran through the Mississippi. It was convenient that the river ran along the state line next to the arch.

I formed a fairy portal and connected it to my memory of

the foot of the steps leading up to St. Louis Arch. I'd put my trees under the arch itself, but I figured our appearance would be less obvious at the bottom of the steps. Also, we'd be closer to the river if the shit the fan and we had to bail into the ley lines.

The drow and everyone else couldn't do that. I'd have to portal them somewhere downstream. But the giants and I could ride the ley lines to the North Pole, get a visual, then come back to get everyone else.

According to Elrand, who was an encyclopedia of knowledge on all things trees, the tallest tree in the world is Hyperion. It stands at three hundred eighty feet in Redwood National Park. St. Louis Arch is about six hundred thirty feet—one of those facts you come to learn living in the city. I didn't have any Redwood seeds, and even if I did, growing trees that high would have been a tall order.

See what I did there?

The point is, if you can stop laughing at my awesome jokes long enough to listen, I probably wouldn't be able to create a tree as tall as the Arch. But even if I got some, enhanced by aether, to approximately half its height, the world would have to take notice.

I stepped through the portal to make sure we weren't going to materialize inside some poor tourist when we came through. All was clear. No sign of any government agents. They weren't expecting us until the next day. They'd probably be there, then. I went back through.

"Coast is clear!"

Gronk and Rina issued their marching orders to their respective troops. The giants went through first. The drow were right behind them. Then came Layla, with Agnus in her arms, followed by Elrand and Jag not far behind. I pulled up the rear.

It felt like leaving home for the last time. I almost shed a tear thinking about the junkyard ranch. Would we be able to go back?

I hoped so. It wasn't fancy. It was a junkyard, after all. But after being there a few months, the place had started to feel like home.

Jag had the drone. He couldn't broadcast the feed from his phone, but we planned to try to send it from mine to the networks. We didn't know if it would go through. I'd have to send it to a few rogue news sources, not just the major news networks. They were more likely to be free of government intervention in their reporting. I also added a repeated introduction to the broadcast, just like the one I'd given in the stone circle.

It was important that the message got out. People needed to know why I was doing this, what it meant, and how the governments of the world were being manipulated by the elven king.

Without the aid of the stone circle, this was going to take more out of me than it had before. Brag'mok, Elrand, Rina, and Layla stood beside me as we climbed the staircase leading to the grass beneath the Arch. Several tourists were on the grounds already. Many of them were taking pictures of the Arch from the ground, others were entering the underground passage to where they could take a wonky elevator ride to the top of the monument.

It was called the Gateway to the West. It was a monument to America's westward expansion. There was a small museum inside dedicated to the theme. I'd been there many times. The arch tour was an underwhelming experience. The elevators were small space pods that people crammed into like sardines for the ride up. When you got to the top of the Arch, you could feel it sway in the wind.

Little did the tourists realize what they were about to witness.

"Here goes nothing," I said, sitting cross-legged on the grass. "Any words of encouragement?"

"Maintain your focus," Elrand said. "You have more than enough strength to succeed."

"I believe in you, Caspar," Layla added, kneeling to kiss me on the cheek.

"Peace, ye fat guts!" Agnus added.

I cocked my head. "More Shakespeare?"

"From Henry IV," Agnus said. "Good luck."

"We are united at your side," Brag'mok said.

I focused my mind, calling on the power of air and sending it through the surrounding park to gather the acorns and seeds from the trees and carry them to the ground beneath the arch.

I called on the element of water, gathering a large, dripping bulb from the Mississippi and guiding it over the clearing before dropping it to moisten the soil. Then, I drew on aether and poured life into the seeds.

Trees burst from the ground, crackling as they grew from saplings into full-size trees. The species of trees around the arch weren't large. Not like the oaks I'd grown before. But I could grow them larger than they would normally get. Sweat gathered on my brow, both on account of the summer heat and due to the exertion of channeling so much magic.

They didn't grow as tall as I'd hoped, but they were still impressive specimens. Twenty trees, all growing beneath the Arch, reached almost a third of the height of the monument, several times larger than the same trees would ever grow naturally.

I heard Jag's drone buzzing overhead. He was capturing this. The sound was hypnotizing. My head felt light as if I'd been suspended upside-down.

I released my magic and got to my feet, stumbling as the world spun around me. Brag'mok caught me and steadied me with his strong, giant hands.

BANG!

"I've been shot!" Brag'mok shouted.

"What the…"

"A sniper!" Layla shouted, readying her bow.

BANG!

A sharp pain struck me in the leg. I screamed.

I focused my magic. I healed Brag'mok, visualizing the wound in his shoulder closing. He picked me up and took off running down the stairs with me in his arms.

"Quick," Layla said, putting her hand on my leg and focusing her magic on my wound. The pain turned to a tingle, then subsided. "To the river!"

I didn't have much energy left. Would I be able to traverse the ley lines like this? There wasn't time to wonder.

"Gronk," Brag'mok said, "we need to hit the ley lines. Caspar, you should get the rest somewhere safe. You can rendezvous with us at the North Pole."

I nodded. "We can do that."

I focused my fairy magic and opened a portal. I needed to keep us near the ley lines, in a place I could visualize. I connected the portal to the confluence of rivers, several miles south of the arch where the gateway to New Albion had formed before.

We weren't going there. But we needed to get someplace safe.

Who the hell had shot me? Was it someone from the military? One of Brightborn's legionaries? It was impossible to know. But we were out of the sniper's line of fire at the bottom of the stairs. At least temporarily.

Rina ordered the drow through the portal.

Brag'mok set me on the ground. Jag caught me as my legs wobbled.

"Help him through!" Layla shouted.

"Got him," Jag said, sweeping me up in his arms into a fireman's lift before running through the portal.

We emerged on the muddy shore where the Mississippi and Meramec rivers met.

Once everyone was through, I closed the portal.

"We don't have long," Layla said. "They don't know where we are, but they will be coming after us."

Jag set me on the ground and retrieved his phone from his pocket. "I got the video. Still no signal."

"Send it to me," I said.

Jag nodded and started scrolling on his phone.

"I don't know if I have enough energy to make the trip," I said. "Traveling the ley lines takes magic."

"They don't know we're here," Layla said. "Take your time."

"I need to get this video out," I said. "I can feel my strength returning. But it'll take me a while.

"Drow!" Rina said, barking orders at her warriors. "Surround Naayak. Keep him safe while he recovers."

The drow formed a circle around me. They had their blades drawn. I wasn't sure what good their swords would do if another sniper came upon our location or, worse, some kind of military helicopter or bomber. However, it was comforting to have them around me, protecting me.

"They were waiting for us," Layla said.

I nodded as I pulled my phone out. Jag had sent the video to me. "Just imagine how much worse it would have been if we'd waited until tomorrow."

"But we did it, Caspar," Layla said. "The trees are there. They can't deny what happened."

"Once this video is out, people will know why," I said. "I just pray that people know what to do with it. That it doesn't get wiped from the internet."

"Send it to everyone you can think of," Jag said. "The more people who have it, the more likely people will see it."

I bit my lip. "Good idea. I'll make sure all the former members, the people who came to support me at St. Ensley's, get it."

I scrolled through my contacts. It was a short, relatively small video file. It didn't have Brag'mok's warning at the end like the first video we'd made, but it had my introduction. Hopefully, that would be enough.

I sent it to my friends. Philip, my former bishop. Cecil, the man whose daughter I'd healed, who had always supported me and had connections to a lot of people in the city. He'd brought hundreds of people to hear me preach. If he got this to them, I hoped, they'd get it out to as many other people as possible.

I texted to say that the video needed to be seen by as many people as they could get it to. I'd have to trust they'd pull it off. I also shot it off in an e-mail to several news networks and smaller internet news publications. Right-wing presses. Left-wing presses. It didn't matter. The threat to our liberties, the threat that Brightborn posed, was bigger than the divide that represented Americans' political affiliations.

Hopefully, the word would get out. People would know why I grew those trees, what they represented. I'd planted literal seeds in the ground, but I hoped I'd also planted seeds of resistance. I had to believe that people would realize the threat and come together to protest what was happening.

I *had* to believe they would.

I finished sending the video off and pocketed my phone. "This thing won't make it once I go underwater, into the ley lines."

"Might as well leave your phone here," Jag said. "Just in case, we can maybe dig it up later."

"Good idea," I said, finding a rock and lifting it. Thankfully, there weren't any snakes curled up underneath it. I set my phone face-down in the mud and set the rock back on top of it.

I returned to my feet. "I'm feeling pretty good. I think I can do this."

"Are you sure?" Layla asked.

I nodded. "This can't wait. Besides, the giants are alone at the North Pole. I don't want them to get any ideas of attacking prematurely."

"You're going to the North Pole, Caspar," Layla said. "You aren't dressed for that."

I nodded. "I'm just going to get a visual. I'll come back to bring the rest of you with me. Hard to find winter coats this time of year, but whatever you can gather to prepare, I'd get it."

"Well, we could call Dwight," Jag said.

I lifted the rock back off my phone and retrieved it before handing it to Jag. "Just put it back there when you're done, so we know where to find it.

"I'll do you better," Jag said. "If I can get Dwight to take us on a supply run, I'll get some ziplock baggies."

I nodded. "Not a bad idea. But we're going to the North Pole. What are the chances we'll have service there? Even so, this phone has a basic pre-paid plan. It would be nice to know if the video is reaching people, so we know what to expect when we come back."

"You're a man of faith," Layla said. "We'll just have to trust that the message will get out. That the people will respond."

I nodded. "All right. Well, I'll see you soon. If I don't get turned into a block of ice on my trip."

CHAPTER THIRTEEN

Diving into the Mississippi isn't like riding the Lazy River at Six Flags. It was muddy. I couldn't see two feet in front of my face. I'd also seen an article not long ago about how two bull sharks had somehow made their way up the river and were found near St. Louis. Hard to believe, right? Totally true. And they'd only found two. Surely there were more lurking in the current, just waiting for some yummy preacher meat to chew on.

Thankfully, I didn't encounter any sharks. The only thing I'm more terrified of than snakes is sharks. There was a better than average chance that there were a few cottonmouths nearby. That would be all I'd need—to get shot and bitten by a snake in one day.

The farthest I'd ever traversed a ley line before was between the confluence of the Mississippi and Meramec rivers and Meramec springs. Just a little longer than two hundred miles. Needless to say, traveling a ley line all the way to the North Pole would take a lot longer, and a lot of it wouldn't be beneath a river bed.

Entering the ley lines directly isn't a skill I can easily describe or explain. The giants could do it because their bodies were so resilient. The force in the ley lines would tear most people apart. A regular elf or a common human wouldn't be able to survive more than a few minutes. I could only survive because of my ability to harness magic. I could absorb the magic that would dissolve anybody else and use it to propel me forward like one of those canisters in the bank shooting through the tube to the teller.

It was exhausting, like casting large amounts of magic usually was, but because I had a constant source of magic and wasn't drawing from the elementals within me, I could hurl myself forward as long as I could stand it. Since I was traversing through magic, not through normal space, I moved *fast*.

It was hard to say how fast I was going. The magic that flowed into me was invigorating even as the same magic flowing out of me, propelling me forward, was tiring. It was a little like chugging energy drinks while pulling an all-nighter. My body was getting more exhausted even as the energy pouring into me kept me alert, if a little shaky.

My heart rate was through the roof. It may have been because I was inhaling magic rather than oxygen. Even so, the magic healed any damage that oxygen deprivation caused.

How was I supposed to know where I was? I learned quickly that traveling ley lines via magic doesn't come with GPS. If I popped up and I wasn't in a riverbed, would I be able to get back into the ley line? I wasn't sure. I hadn't ever encountered a ley line other than those that ran under rivers. Holy crap. Why didn't I think about these problems before I dove headlong into the Mississippi and hitched a ride on the ley lines northward?

If all the ley lines intersected at the poles, I could only assume that there'd be some change in sensation when I hit the pole or another confluence of ley lines.

My mind remained alert, but the fatigue settled into my body. Once I left the ley lines, and the magic wasn't coursing through me, I'd probably pass out. I still had Aerin's sword on me. The last time I passed out, when I unleashed a ton of magic trying to stop an earthquake, she appeared to me in a vision and helped me out of it. Maybe she would know something now.

I touched the hilt of the sword.

Aerin? I was speaking in my mind. She could read my mind. She'd hear me.

Hello, Caspar. What is happening? I sense a lot of magic.

We're in the ley lines, I said. *I'm trying to travel to the North Pole.*

To find the elves? Aerin asked.

Yes. The giants want to attack, but I think we can win them over. Still, I can't take Layla there to try until I go there first and get a visual.

But your body is weak, Aerin said.

It is. I'm afraid I'll pass out once I arrive. I thought, you know, maybe you could help me out?

I can keep you company, Aerin said. *But you need to be ready to wake up before you actually will. You aren't asleep. You're still alert.*

I think the magic flowing into me is sustaining me, I said. *I fear that once I leave the ley lines—if I can even figure out when I've arrived and should leave—my body will fail.*

Why do you suspect that you get so tired after casting? Aerin asked.

I don't know. Probably because that's a lot of power the human body isn't used to. I figured it just taxes my system.

But magic also heals you, right? Aerin said. *Have you tried healing yourself after casting?*

When I'm that exhausted, I can barely stay awake, much less cast more magic, I said. *That would be like running out of fuel on the side of the road, with the only solution being to drive another mile farther to the closest gas station.*

You only run out of gas if you don't stop to fuel up before you go empty, Caspar.

So you're saying I should stop and fuel up? I asked.

You're on the ley lines, Aerin said. *You have elemental power within you already. Maybe you just need to take breaks from time to time. Let yourself recharge a little before you dive back into the ley lines.*

But if I'm not at a river, if the ley line is in the land, how can I be sure that I'll be able to get back into it?

You wield the power of earth, Caspar. Ask the earthen elemental to open itself up to you, to swallow you back into the ley lines.

I sighed. The giants are probably already at the North Pole. If I don't get there soon...

If you get there and you pass out straight away, you aren't going to be of any use, Aerin said.

I'm afraid that they'll just attack, I said. I told them to wait for me. I just don't know how long they will wait. And what if the elves see them and attack them first?

Their bodies can withstand a lot more than yours, Caspar, Aerin said. *They might not be as magically powerful as you are, but their bodies are more resilient. They'll always be able to endure the ley lines longer than you can.*

So you're saying I need to take a break.

I don't think you have a choice, Aerin said.

I don't even know where I'll emerge, I said. For all I know, I'll pop up in the middle of the ocean.

Thankfully, you have the element of water at your disposal, Aerin said.

But people are waiting for me, including Rina and the drow.

Then use your fairy portals, Aerin said. *Once you jump out of the ley line you'll be able to visualize your location. Go get them, take them to wherever you emerge, and then resume your journey through the ley lines.*

All right, I agreed. So what do I do? Just leave the ley lines and hope I'm somewhere that I can bring the rest to? I can't bring them into the ocean, even if I do have access to the element of water.

Then find a place, an island, any place nearby you can bring them. This isn't rocket science, Caspar.

All right, I said, still clinging to the hilt of Aeron's blade. *Here goes nothing.*

I pulled myself out of the ley line. Earth pressed against my face. It was heavy. Like I was buried alive. But I wasn't six feet under. The ley lines were deeper than that. I called on the element of earth, and I erupted on the surface in a shower of soil.

I spat the dirt out of my mouth. I touched the hilt of Aerin's blade. "I made it. Not sure where I am. There are a lot of trees. Maybe Canada?"

Most likely, Aerin said. Not like when I was in the ley lines and we were speaking mind-to-mind.

"So now what?"

You should get some rest before you fairy portal your way back to our friends. Make sure they bring enough supplies to set up camp here while you make the rest of the journey northward.

I sighed. "At least it isn't so hot here."

It was close to dusk. The sun was setting on the horizon. I didn't have a lot of time to find a place to rest while I recovered. I heard a rustling in the leaves in the distance.

"What was that?" I asked, touching Aerin's blade.

I don't have eyes. How would I know?

I snorted. "Whatever it is, it's big."

You're in Canada, right?

"I'd assume so. Can't know for certain."

It could be a bear.

"You have to be shitting me. A bear?"

Maybe. If it is a bear, remember, don't run. You should never run from a bear but stand your ground.

"I could fly."

As tired as you are, you might pass out in mid-air.

"Should I play dead?"

I think they say you should if it's a grizzly. But if it's a black bear, never play dead. Or is it the other way around?

"Wow. That's super helpful, Aerin."

How am I supposed to know? I haven't ever been to this part of the world. We have different species of bears in India, where I spent most of my life.

The bear appeared in front of me. It was large. Brown. Not sure if it was a grizzly or what. It looked at me and roared.

I almost peed my pants. It wouldn't have mattered. They were already wet from the trip into the Mississippi.

Remember. Stand your ground.

"Fuck that!" I said. I surveyed the area I needed to be able to visualize the space. Otherwise, all of this would be for nothing. Then, drawing on fairy magic, I formed a portal to the place I'd left back in Missouri, at the confluence of the two rivers and ley lines.

I jumped through.

And I heard gunfire. I looked up and saw the shield Layla had cast over the group.

"Thank God, you're back!" Layla shouted. "You need to get us out of here!"

"Are you fucking serious? It's either machine guns or bears." At least if I took us back into Canada, we'd outnumber the bears.

I formed another portal. Layla maintained her shield as the drow, Elrand, and Jag ran through my fairy gateway.

I grabbed Layla's hand. "Have your bow ready. There's a bear waiting for us on the other side."

"Are you joking?" Layla said.

"I didn't make it all the way to the North Pole," I said. "I ran out of energy. I can barely keep my focus as it is."

Layla nodded, grabbed my hand, and we jumped through the portal together.

CHAPTER FOURTEEN

My legs gave out as I hit the ground back in the Canadian forest. I was spent.

"Come on, you big bully!" Jag shouted at the bear.

Layla stepped over to him and touched his hand, lowering his fists. Then she looked at the bear. "Hello, there."

The bear whimpered.

"You're hurt?" Layla asked.

The bear nodded.

Was Layla seriously talking to this bear? I suppose it made sense. She'd said that the druids of old could speak to animals, and the sort of magic she'd learned, the kind that allowed both of us to hear Agnus speak, was of the same kind.

Speaking of Agnus, where was he? I looked around and saw him curled up in Rina's arms. I nodded at her, communicating my appreciation. Rina smiled back as she scratched Agnus behind the ears.

Agnus purred. "That's right, babe. Just like that."

I rolled my eyes. Now he was hitting on Jag's girlfriend. Probably not a smart move considering that Jag's biceps were almost as large as my cat's entire body.

The bear extended his paw toward Layla. She took it and pulled a thorn out of it. The bear yelped, pulling his paw back.

"There you go," Layla said. "Let me touch the wound. I can take away the pain."

The bear reluctantly extended his paw again. Layla took it in her hand and channeled golden healing magic into it. It was the element of aether, the one I used when I healed people.

"He's a sweetie," Layla said.

I had to pick up my jaw from the forest floor. "He wanted to eat me."

"Not really," Layla said. "He was in pain and afraid. Wounded animals can be extra aggressive because they're vulnerable."

"I'll have to take your word for…"

"Caspar, are you okay?" Layla asked.

My head was throbbing and spinning at the same time. "I'm… I…"

I grabbed Aerin's sword. If I fell unconscious, at least I knew she'd be there to keep me company. I rested my head on my hands, lying on the ground. My eyes fell shut. I couldn't keep them open any longer.

Something cool touched my forehead.

I opened my eyes. I was back in my old apartment in St. Louis. Aerin was leaning over me with a moist towel in her hand, dragging it across my brow.

"We're not really here, are we?" I said.

Aerin smiled. "Like the last time, this is in your mind. But are you really here? What's real anyway?"

"We're going to do philosophy now?" I said.

Aerin giggled and smiled at me. She was beautiful. I wasn't in love with her. Not like I was with Layla. But I'd be lying if I said I didn't find her attractive. Of course, this was more like a dream, or a vision, than reality. If everything I saw was in my mind, her appearance was probably drawn more from recollection than fact.

She was spirit now, after all. She didn't have a body. She was bound to her blade and, now that I wielded it, we were bound together in a unique and oddly intimate way. Not in the sexual sense, but on a deeper level. She could read my mind. I didn't seem to be able to do the same with her—maybe because she didn't have a body, she didn't have a brain to read.

Still, I felt strangely closer to her now that she was dead than she and I ever were when she was alive. Again, not like with Layla. This was like the kind of closeness that Danny LaRusso had with Mister Miyagi in the Karate Kid movies. She was in my head, like a sage, a spiritual guide.

Very weird for me since I was usually the one people went to for spiritual advice. I was so accustomed to being "Pastor Caspar" that for years I didn't have a spiritual advisor of my own. Not until Rusty, my AA sponsor. Philip filled that role briefly during my last few months of ministry, I suppose. Now, Aerin took that mantle. Not that she was a theologian or a priestess of any sort. She wasn't a particularly spiritual person when she was alive, and her beliefs weren't like mine. She believed in reincarnation, for example. Not my worldview.

But she knew me in a way that no one else could. When I touched her blade—or perhaps I should say *our* blade—she could see right into my soul. She could see what I didn't see. Things about myself I either wasn't aware of or tried to deny.

"You're doing well, Caspar."

I snorted. "All I can hope is that Gronk hasn't taken the giants and slaughtered the elves by now."

"I'm sure he hasn't," Aerin said.

I shrugged. "I don't know."

"Your body is resting," Aerin said. "Perhaps this is a chance to gather your wits. What will you do if the giants are already in a battle with the elves when you arrive?"

I sighed. "I don't know. Try to stop it, I guess."

"What if it's the elves who attacked the giants, and not the other way around?"

"I don't know," I said. "From what I understand, these elves are civilians."

"Who've lived their whole lives thinking of giants as orcs, as a threat to their existence."

"And if a clan of giants is marching near where they think they've found temporary refuge in this world…" I didn't want to finish the thought.

"I'm just saying you should be prepared," Aerin said. "I don't know that's what has happened or that it will happen. All I know is that whatever happens, you need to remember who you are."

"The chosen one?"

"The one who unifies people who otherwise could never be joined as one," Aerin said. "That's the mark of every good leader, of everyone who ever changed the world. They've all had an uncanny ability to bring people who otherwise wouldn't ever have anything to do with one another together."

I snorted. "There is neither Jew nor Greek, slave nor free, male nor female."

"Jesus?" Aerin asked.

"St. Paul, actually. But he credited Jesus' revolutionary ministry which crossed cultures, transgressed the social barriers of his time, and embraced even the outcasts of the time."

"I suppose I knew that," Aerin said. "Though, it never struck me that unity was a hallmark of your religion, Caspar."

I sighed. "Because people are constantly fighting over dogma. Over social issues and what should or shouldn't be tolerated or labeled as sin. People are more concerned with being right than righteous."

"Seems like a shallow, insecure way to practice a religion," Aerin said.

I chuckled. "That's funny."

"Why do you say that?" she asked.

"Because there's a thing in Christian circles. Everyone thinks their theology is deep. It's easier, I think, to simply discount someone's thoughts as shallow or trite than to deal with what they're saying. Then, they slap a label on it. Like, that's just liberal theology. It's leftist thought. Or, on the opposite end of the spectrum, they're just extremists, fundamentalists."

"Label and dismiss," Aerin said, shaking her head.

"Exactly," I said. "Funny thing is, I used to think my convictions were shallow, hollow, poorly thought out. Then, over time, as my thought deepened, I found that I was somehow in the same waters that I thought were shallow before. I suppose one man's kiddie pool is another man's ocean. I thought I was traversing the Pacific, looking out at those who were splashing around in shallow puddles with disdain. It never occurred to me that I might have had our positions backward."

"We're all on a journey," Aerin said. "Doesn't do anyone any favors to make any assumptions about where someone else is on theirs."

"The journey is in many ways the point," I said. "Once you think you've arrived, that you've figured it all out, that's when you're probably more lost than ever."

"That's deep," Aerin said.

"Someone else would call it shallow." I laughed. "Much easier to dismiss ideas you don't like if you can just assign them a label, discount it, and move on."

"It's a defense mechanism," Aerin said. "Only those who are insecure in their convictions have reason to be terrified of being wrong and are so buttheaded about being right."

"That's the thing," I said. "I had to accept a while back that I didn't have to be right to be happy. I didn't have to know everything about God, to know God. Once I gave myself permission to be wrong, to realize that the world wouldn't stop spinning if I thought about something the wrong way, I finally found freedom. Learned that more in AA than in the church. The need to be right all the time is a form of bondage. When someone says something I disagree with and I find myself getting angry about it, I've learned to stop trying to dissect their arguments and win the debate and instead ask why their position threatens me so much."

"How is that working out for you now?" Aerin asked.

"What do you mean?"

Aerin shrugged. "I don't think that it's just in the domain of religion where dogma has its pitfalls. The giants can't see things from the elves' point of view. The elves don't understand the giants. The few who know the truth, like Brightborn, are consumed with a lust for power and use people's narrow-mindedness as a way to manipulate them."

I sat up on the edge of what, in this vision, was my couch in my old apartment. "Brightborn and I are the same."

"In some ways, you are," Aerin said.

"Neither he nor I care much about being right," I said. "We both recognize that trying to force the world into our dogmas won't get us where we want to go."

"There are important differences between him and you," Aerin said. "You value truth even though you can never be sure you've totally comprehended it. You pursue it as if some master is riding on your back, dangling the truth in front of you like a carrot on a stick. You won't necessarily get the carrot, yet you've come to appreciate what the master is doing. You're moving forward. You're pursuing truth, and the pursuit is its own reward. But Brightborn, well, he knows that everyone is pursuing their own carrot. He's stopped walking toward his. Instead, he's set his sight on others who cling to their dogmas, their vision of the truth, so that he can manipulate them to his advantage."

"He knows it's all bullshit," I said. "That's why he's trying to manipulate the prophecy. He's trying to put Layla forth as the chosen one for some reason."

"Because it fits his narrative. He believes the elves are

destined to rule the world. The chosen one has to be an elf, even if it's one who opposes him."

"But he doesn't put any stock in the prophecy," I said. "He has no faith in it, but he uses the fact that other people do believe to force them to do his bidding."

"See, you both realize that you cannot attain the full truth," Aerin said. "The mysteries of spiritual things are beyond mortal comprehension. But while you adore the mystery, he disparages it. He manipulates people's fervent belief to get them to do what he wants."

"So if I'm supposed to unite the peoples, I need people to see through what he's doing," I said.

"Some will follow him, Caspar," Aerin said. "You may have to fight against them to defend the innocent, to protect the world. But always remember that your enemy believes they are on the side of truth. No one fights a war while imagining themselves the villains."

"Even those whom I must fight I should hope to save," I said. "But how can I do that without coming across as the very thing I hate? As if I'm the one who thinks he's right, that they're wrong?"

"By showing mercy when you can. By wielding the sword only in defense, never in aggression. By standing ready and willing to open your arms to embrace even those who raise their blades against you."

"Even if it means they'll just stab me in the back?" I said.

Aerin nodded. "*Especially* when that's the case. As the chosen one, you are not meant to win a war by winning battles. You will win the war by winning hearts."

"I think that is harder to do than it would be to defeat an enemy with force," I said.

Aerin nodded. "Which is why most men resort to strength of arms to win their wars. It's the easier way. It's simpler to kill another person than it is to change their heart and mind. But many mighty empires have fallen during the course of the world.

Those who changed the world by affecting hearts, we remember their names, and people follow them still. Who changed the world more, Caesar or Christ? Who continues to inspire peace today, Alexander or the Buddha? Is it the battle tactics of Grant that Americans recall and revere when they think of the US Civil War or the resolve and inspiration of Lincoln?"

"I get the point," I said. "Sometimes I wonder why in the world the prophecy selected some no-name preacher from the Midwest to save the world rather than a warrior."

"Stop trying to be something you aren't," Aerin said. "You have your warriors to do what must be done. But it is not the strength of arms you have at your disposal that will defeat Brightborn. The prophecy selected you precisely because you *aren't* what you think you need to be to defeat him."

I sighed. "I still don't know what to do. When we get to the North Pole. Then what?"

Aerin smiled. "There's a phrase in your mind that I've heard you remind yourself of time and time again, Caspar. You do the next right thing, next. That's all you can do."

CHAPTER FIFTEEN

I opened my eyes. This time, it wasn't Aerin looking at me. It was Layla. In my vision, all I did was walk through my apartment doors into a light that was where the hallway was supposed to be, and I woke up.

"You awake?" Layla asked.

I nodded. "I feel better. Refreshed."

Layla smiled and kissed my forehead. I sat up and looked around. The bear was snoring not far from where we were sitting. Agnus was curled up on his paw. "We have a pet bear now?"

Layla shrugged. "He's a sweetie. If you open yourself to him, I'm sure you'll be able to speak to him, too."

"Does he have a name?" I asked.

Layla cocked her head. "I don't know. What is a good name for a bear?"

I shrugged. "Yogi?"

Layla rolled her eyes. "We're not calling him Yogi the Bear."

"I don't know," I said. "You name him. I've never named a bear before."

"And I have?" Layla asked.

I laughed. "You're the one who has been communicating with him."

"How about Clarence?" Layla said.

"Why Clarence?"

Layla shrugged. "I don't know. He just seems like a Clarence to me."

I chuckled. "Maybe you should run that past him after he's awake. We should probably let sleeping bears lie."

"He'll like Clarence," Layla said. "It's a dignified name, don't you think?"

"I suppose."

"Everything okay, Caspar?"

I nodded. "I talked to Aerin while I was asleep. She just gave me a lot to think about."

"I see." Layla turned her head and stared off into the depths of the forest.

"You don't have to be jealous of Aerin, Layla," I said. "You weren't when she was alive. You don't have anything to be jealous of now."

Layla grinned and kissed me on the cheek. "I know. It's not jealousy. Sometimes, though, it feels like when you talk to her, something about you comes to life."

"She can read my mind, Layla. She can speak to things that are going on in my head that I'm not even aware I'm thinking. Think of her as a mystic therapist. A spiritual guide."

"I suppose that's acceptable. In these visions you have with her… You aren't, you know, doing anything with her?"

"Good Lord, Layla. Of course not. Nothing like that."

"Just had to ask."

"You didn't have to ask. You can trust me, Layla. Even in my dreams, I don't desire anyone other than you."

Layla kissed me on the lips. "I know, Caspar."

"How's everyone else doing?" I asked.

"Sleeping," Layla said. "After the attack back at the rivers, everyone's spent."

"Including you, I suspect," I said. "That shield you cast was impressive. It had to be exhausting."

"It was," Layla admitted. "But I couldn't sleep until I knew you were okay."

I nodded. "Thank you, Layla. I need to go back into the ley lines. The giants are already at the North Pole. I'm sort of anxious about what might be happening there while I'm still here."

"I understand," Layla said. "At least we should be safe here."

"Did you manage to get any supplies from Dwight before they attacked?" I asked.

Layla grinned. "Actually, yeah. We have some coats. I have one for you, too."

I nodded. "I didn't even notice what everyone was carrying when I made the portal here. I was so focused on keeping everyone alive."

Layla reached over and grabbed a thick winter coat from a pile of things she'd assembled. I tried it on. It fit perfectly. It was one of those coats that looked like it was made of garbage bags. Not what I would have picked, but going coat shopping in the middle of the summer meant having to settle for whatever could be found.

"Thanks for this," I said. "Just don't throw me out with the garbage."

Layla giggled. "I think Dwight grabbed these things from the Goodwill. You should see Jag's coat. It has fur."

I laughed. "Jag has a fur coat?"

"He looks fabulous," Layla said. "Not in the way that he thinks. It's a woman's coat, but it was the only thing, according to Dwight, they had that would fit him."

"Is Dwight okay?" I asked. "I hope he didn't get caught."

"He came and went before the military showed up to attack," Layla said.

"So it was the military?" I asked. "Our military?"

Layla nodded. "If we couldn't be sure before, we can say for certain now that Brightborn has the US government in his pocket."

"Well, I'm pretty sure we're in Canada," I said. "Hopefully, you'll be safe here until I get back."

Layla took my hand. "We'll be fine, Caspar. Hopefully, you have enough energy now to make it all the way to the pole."

I nodded. "I sure hope so. I'd rather not have to do this again. I have a sinking feeling that the giants and elves aren't sitting around campfires and singing Kumbaya together. I can only hope that the giants have managed to keep their distance and the elves don't know that they're there yet, but I doubt that's the case."

"You're probably right," Layla said. "You should get going."

I kissed Layla softly on the lips, then called on the power of earth and plunged myself through the ground like an earthworm. Digging my way through the soil as it parted around me, I entered the ley line.

This time, it was easier. I suppose it's like anything else. The more experience I had entering ley lines, the easier it would be. I could only hope that I'd gained more endurance, too, and that I'd finish my journey with enough energy left to do whatever the situation demanded when I arrived. Ideally, I'd show up, give my greetings to a bunch of bored giants, and then I'd come back and portal everyone else to join them.

Could I be that lucky? Not likely.

CHAPTER SIXTEEN

The current of magic flowing alongside me started to spin and then changed directions. That had to be the pole. The magic was spinning the same way a compass might if someone stood there with one.

I exited the ley lines and blasted into ice-cold waters and broken chunks of ice. It might have been a solid glacier of ice if the giants hadn't busted through it. I drew on the element of fire, not because it would do much in water but because keeping it in focus tended to warm me up. The water was so cold my joints ached. It was so cold that I could feel my nipples rubbing against my shirt and water-soaked coat. Funny thing about cold. It makes your nipples get bigger, but something else… I'll just say it had the opposite effect.

The element of fire helped. I'd have to bring in some air and blow-dry myself off as soon as I made it to the surface. I used the element of water to create a current and shot myself out of the water. I flew into the air and landed ungracefully on the ice shelf. I looked around and saw a hundred or more figures, fully covered in thick parkas, stood around me. Three of them had the drawstrings on their bows pulled back, with arrows in place, ready to fire. The bows were like Layla's. They were elves. But what had happened to the giants?

"Just like the ugly one said, a human."

"The ugly one? Aren't they all ugly?"

"You know what I mean."

"Yep, I'm human," I said. "Nice to meet you all, by the way."

One of the two elves who'd been talking walked up to me and tried to take my sword. I jumped back. "Don't touch that."

"What is your name, human?" the elf said. His head was mostly shrouded by his hood and scarf. Only his long white beard flowing out from beneath it suggested he was anything but a spring chicken.

"Caspar Cruciger," I said. "The husband of Layla Brightborn."

The man nodded, then turned and began conversing in hushed tones with three other elves. Meanwhile, the crowd around me had grown from around a hundred to maybe twice as many. As I looked around, more elves were closing in on our position. The giants didn't attack, if for no other reason than that they were sorely outnumbered.

The man returned, looked at me curiously, and took down his hood. "Welcome to our temporary abode, Caspar. We'd like to speak with you if you're amenable to it."

I nodded. "Where are my friends? The giants who came here?"

"They are safe," the elf said. "At least for now. But I should warn you that there are some who are quite uncomfortable with their presence here."

"What about King Brightborn?" I asked. "Is he here?"

The elf shook his head. "We've not seen him since we first arrived on this world. Good riddance, if you ask me. But not everyone is asking me. My opinion is not universal."

"And you are?" I asked.

"My name is Aelfrich."

"Are you the leader here?"

Aelfrich shrugged. "Depends who you ask, and those who'd

call me their leader, I'd prefer they didn't."

"Why is that?" I asked.

Aelfrich put his hand on my shoulder. "Come with me. We'll talk more once we get inside."

"Inside?"

Aelfrich gestured in front of him. I hadn't noticed—three giant spires, like the ones I'd seen in the Elf Kingdom on New Albion blending into the glaciers towering around us. "How'd you get these here?"

"We built them the same way we would back home," Aelfrich said. "The magic here is nearly limitless. Anything we could do at home, it seems we can do here even more efficiently."

"Impressive," I said. "I bet you'd like to find a warmer climate, though."

"About that," Aelfrich said, "join me inside, and we can speak frankly. It is by luck that it was my men who came upon you when you emerged from the ley lines. Had it been the others…"

"The others?"

"Like I said. Inside."

Aelfrich placed his hand on a square panel at the base of one of the spires. The doors slid open, parting from the center, and I stepped inside.

"Caspar!" Brag'mok said, his large feet thumping on the ground as he ran to me. Gronk and a couple of the other giants whose names I couldn't remember stood at the opposite end of the atrium. The walls towered around us. The single floor gradually spiraled upward to the top of the spire. It wasn't as large as the spires I'd seen on New Albion, but the architecture was similar. Clean and simple. Not particularly ornate, but its design had flourishes here or there. Letters, what I presumed to be in elvish, were written in a gold script on some of the pearly white walls.

"You guys are here?" I asked.

"We are,' Brag'mok said. "If it wasn't for Aelfrich here, the others would have overwhelmed us."

"The others?" I asked.

"Come, Caspar," Aelfrich said. "Why don't you take a seat?"

Aelfric gestured to the chairs set against one of the walls. I sat in one of them and Aelfrich sat in the other, while Brag'mok stood behind me. Gronk and the others watched from a distance.

"Some time ago," Aelfrich said, "We all believed. We were led to believe that the king had died and Hector had risen from the dead to claim the role of the chosen one."

"Hector," I said. "That's right. He was the king's right-hand man. The fairies were impersonating him and the king to make it look like the king was assassinated. "

"The fairies caused upheaval in the kingdom. They were trying to spark a revolution. At least, that's what we were led to believe."

"I remember," I said. "Meanwhile, Brightborn was behind it all."

"He wanted to come back as though he'd risen from the dead, present himself as an eternal hero. Most of the people bought it. We hadn't had fairies act so boldly on New Albion in centuries. But those of us who knew of Brightborn's activities on Earth, what he was planning to do, knew better. However, the spirit of revolution was in the air, and the people got a taste for it. There were many elves who refused to let it go. I became a figurehead of the movement for no other reason than my age and experience on Earth as a former visitor acquainted with the principles of democracy."

"Brightborn didn't move to squash the revolution?" I asked.

Aelfrich shrugged. "Our world was failing at the time. Magic returned about the time he seemingly came back from the dead."

"Yeah," I said. "I did that."

"So we've come to learn," Aelfrich said. "Thanks for trying. Sadly, that was a part of the king's scheme all along. He needed more magic to finish off the giants. Most of them, anyway. He spurred a war that was supposed to end all wars. The end result?

New Albion was depleted, uninhabitable by the time the conflict was over."

"So you had the choice to either follow him to Earth or die on New Albion once the rest of the magic faded," I said.

Aelfrich nodded. "You asked why the king didn't try to quash the spirit of revolution. Brightborn is a calculating man. Brutal, yes. A tyrant? Certainly. But he does not use violence indiscriminately. Every move he makes, he's thought out long in advance. He thinks through how every subtle gesture he makes, every strategic decision, will be evaluated by others. Brightborn didn't try to end the revolution because he knew a civil war was the last thing the elves could weather while resettling back on Earth. He believed that if he saved us from our failing planet and showed us a future unencumbered by our past that the revolution would die out on its own. Were he to try to end the revolution, it would have only entrenched those who opposed him. In truth, I'm not sure he thought he'd be able to defeat us. At the time, I'd wager, we were almost as powerful as the loyalists."

"But coming to Earth didn't end the revolution," I said.

Aelfrich shook his head. "Of course not! The spirit of revolution lives on."

"But not all of the elves here agree," I said.

Aelfrich shook his head. "We are divided. The goals of our revolution have changed."

"And those goals are?"

"We aren't sure," Aelfrich said. "That's why we aren't fighting amongst ourselves. We're coexisting, divided, but still one community. Half of the elves are waiting to learn what Brightborn had planned because they still follow him, and the other half are unable to decide how or in what way they can oppose him. The position of the revolutionaries is uncertain. We lack direction. Thus, fighting amongst ourselves at the moment would be pointless. Not until we know what we'd be fighting for or against."

"You've really been in the dark about what he's doing since you came to Earth?" I asked.

Aelfrich nodded. "Ironic, considering that at this time of the year, the sun never sets here."

I chuckled. "Yeah. I forgot about that. At least it's not as cold as it would be during the winter when the sun never rises."

"Speaking of being cold, aren't you freezing?" Aelfrich asked. "You're all wet. I know the spire is warmer than the outside, but still."

I shrugged. "I have the element of fire coursing through me at the moment. It's keeping me warm. But you're right. The wet clothes are uncomfortable."

Aelfrich cupped his hands around his mouth. "Darling, Catreen. Would you mind getting our guest a change of clothes? Just grab him something of mine. I think we're roughly the same size."

"Your wife?" I asked.

"One of them, yes," Aelfrich said.

I nodded. I knew that the elves weren't opposed to polygamy on moral grounds. It was why Layla reluctantly agreed to the marriage between herself, Aerin, and me. Undesirable, but not unthinkable.

I didn't see Catreen when Aelfrich called to her. She answered from one of the rooms a few turns up the spiraled floor above us.

"She'll have something for you shortly," Aelfrich said. "However, I must warn you, while you're here, you shouldn't fraternize with the loyalists. That we're protecting you and the giants is patently offensive to them. Among other things, they are firm believers in elvish supremacy."

"I need to bring the rest of my people," I said. "They're not safe. We were attacked in Missouri."

"Where the gate used to be?" Aelfric asked. "Who attacked?"

I nodded. "The government. They've come under Brightborn's influence."

Aelfrich shook his head. "Well, that figures."

"Layla is among them," I said. "Will that pose a problem?"

Aelfrich bit his lip. "We'd best bring them here in secret. The last time Layla was in New Albion was before the revolution began. There are those among the loyalists who would see her tried for treason and delivered to her father accordingly."

"He's been trying to put her forward to the elven legion as if she was the chosen one all along," I said.

Aelfrich cocked his head. "Interesting. He knows that the elvish people have a great deal of faith in the prophecy. He is something of an agnostic himself, as I'm sure many of your political leaders are. However, it is wise to put on a show of piety for the people's sake."

"That's more familiar to me than you realize, given my country's politics," I said.

"Here you go, sir," an elf woman said.

"Thank you, Catreen. It was Catreen, right?"

"Indeed, sir."

"Just Caspar is fine," I said.

"Yes, sir."

I nodded my appreciation as I took the clothes that Catreen handed me before walking away.

"Apologies for that," Aelfrich said. "Our women are not used to addressing men they do not know by their first names."

I snorted. "Quite the opposite of the drow."

"The drow, you say?"

I nodded. "They are with us, too. I need to bring them here with Layla."

"I see," Aelfrich said, narrowing his eyes and stroking his beard in thought. "I should say, I'm curious to meet one. Again, it might be best to keep their presence hidden from the loyalists. To have you and a few giants among us is one thing. Your numbers are few, but if they start to grow, the loyalists will become uneasy."

"Well, we plan to get Brightborn's attention. He's been hiding, working behind the scenes. As revolutionaries, perhaps you might be able to help us locate him so we can stop him?"

"I'll have to hear more about his plans," Aelfrich said. "But certainly, that is a possibility. We may be able to help. He sends a legionary here almost weekly to keep tabs on us. I should say, their visits have become less frequent lately."

"They lost the fairies," I said. "They could make portals before. Now, they have to travel by the old-fashioned way."

Aelfrich's eyes widened. "You don't say? How did that happen?"

I smirked. "I made an alliance with the fairies who'd been living on New Albion. They came to Earth and, with the aid of the Furies, we overthrew the Unseelie and bound them to the realm of the fae."

"A shrewd move," Aelfrich said. "I can respect that. One revolutionary to another."

I chuckled. "I've never thought of myself as a revolutionary, to tell the truth."

"You told me that your government sees you as a threat, did you not?" Aelfrich said.

"I suppose they do."

"And you're trying to undermine the powers that be, to overthrow their rule?" Aelfrich continued.

"I'm trying to save our democracy," I said. "The freedom of *all* people. I'm not trying to overthrow anyone so much as trying to restore what I fear we're losing."

"Freedom is often the cry of revolutionaries," Aelfrich said. "Like it or not, you are a revolutionary. Should you be the one many believe you to be, the chosen one of the prophecy, the revolution you spark will be more than one of freedom. The prophecy predicts that you will usher in an age of unity."

"It does," I said. "I suppose you're right. As the French used to say, *vive la révolution!*"

CHAPTER SEVENTEEN

Aelfrich was surprisingly hospitable. The elves had developed quite the arctic fishing enterprise in the short time since they'd arrived. So, that's what was for dinner. They didn't prepare it the way I was accustomed to. It was a new recipe to them, too. While they had fish on New Albion, they didn't have the same kinds. It wasn't seasoned, just seared by a group of elves who had an affinity for fire magic.

Most of the elves could wield one of the elements. Only a few, like Layla, could wield two or three. None of them could wield all five. I was an anomaly—one of the many factors that signaled my identity as the chosen one of the elven prophecy.

The fish was lightly charred, not so much that it tasted burned, but enough that it added smokiness to the flavor. It wasn't bad. I tried to communicate the urgency of bringing the rest to join us while I ate fast. They were probably safe in the Canadian forest, but I wasn't sure how many wilderness survival skills they had. I was a Boy Scout. I'd earned the wilderness survival merit badge, which required making it through a night in the woods, under the stars, in a lean-to makeshift shelter. Even so, I wasn't sure I'd last long without magic. Thankfully, Elrand was with them. He was more adept at magic than the rest. If they needed water, even fire, he could provide it.

Still, Layla was probably on edge, worried about me at this point. She would assume the worst when I didn't return immediately after I arrived. Either that I'd gotten lost, didn't survive the journey, or had been captured or killed upon arrival.

"We have three spires," Aelfrich said, picking his fish apart with his fingers and tossing a piece into his mouth. "The other two are occupied by loyalists. How many people are we talking about here?"

"A hundred or so. You have thousands of people here. Surely our numbers won't be a problem?"

"We have the accommodations," Aelfrich said. "The problem is the reaction their presence in our spire could cause amongst the loyalists. I'd propose we construct another spire for your people."

"That's a lot of effort to go to considering that we're not going to stay here long."

Aelfrich shrugged. "We don't intend to stay here long, either. Certainly, we'd like to leave by winter. It is not such an ordeal as you'd think to create a structure like these. If you'd like, I could teach you how to do it."

"That would be fantastic," I said. "Frankly, we haven't had accommodations so pleasant for months. We've been hiding out in a junkyard veiled by the fairies for a while now. At the North Pole or not, I imagine the people would appreciate better housing."

Brag'mok and Gronk looked at each other. They were seated across the room, lounging on the floor next to the table where dinner had been served. The elves dined like the Romans used to, reclined and lounging next to tables that were low to the ground. It was humorous to see the giants' massive bodies crammed next to each other at the table. They weren't completely accepting of elvish culture, but they were playing nice. The rest of the giants were eating elsewhere in the spire. By the contorted looks on their faces, neither Brag'mok nor Gronk were big fans of elf-baked fish.

"Let us finish eating," Aelfrich said. "Then I'll take you to create your new shelter. You have all the magic that's needed. It usually takes a team of elves to forge a spire."

We finished eating, and Aelfrich took me out onto the ice. It was rough. I didn't have the shoes for it, but I managed well enough. I stopped channeling fire to keep me warm since, thankfully, one of Aelfrich's wives had dried out my coat. It was cold. Not as cold as you might think. It was summer, after all. Still, having come from brutal Missouri Summer temperatures, it was jarring. Funny how the body adjusts to temperatures over the course of a winter season. Those first few days in the thirties seem bitterly cold, but by the end of the winter, the thirties aren't too bad at all. I shivered as we trekked through the ice.

"I'd like to set up a spire far enough from the rest that no one will likely come upon your location. None of the loyalists, anyway," Aelfrich said.

"I appreciate it, Aelfrich. Mind if I ask why you've been so welcoming?"

The elf chuckled. "I suppose because you've given the revolution the most hope we've had since leaving New Albion. If we're going to get rid of Brightborn, you're the most important ally we'll have. Especially if the rest of Earth's governments are already in league with him."

We hiked across the ice for several miles. It probably wasn't as far as it felt. When you don't have a sure footing and you're cold, every step is a chore.

"This should do," Aelfrich said, pulling a small box from his cloak. He flipped a latch and opened it. Several crystals of various lengths were set in impressions that looked as though they'd been formed to fit the crystals perfectly. "These crystals contain the imprints of architectural plans for any number of spires that might be constructed through the use of elemental magic."

"How do they work, exactly?" I asked.

"Each crystal contains the complete structure of a given spire. This one," Aelfrich said, holding one of them up, "is the crystal that was used to construct the spire where we dined earlier."

"Any suggestions for one that might fit our purposes well?" I asked.

"You won't need one as large as ours; your numbers are fewer. Not to mention, a shorter structure won't be as obvious in case any loyalists wander out here looking."

"Probably true," I said.

Aelfrich grabbed one of the crystals. It was shorter than most of them. "It will also be easier for you to do since this will be your first time. It takes a lot of energy to do this. I imagine you're already quite tired."

I nodded. "It's been a rough few days."

Aelfrich handed me the crystal. "All you need to do is channel the elements through the crystal in their proper order."

This was familiar territory for me. "What is that order?" I asked.

"Usually, you'd use earth first. However, there isn't any soil here. We learned quickly that the earth you'd evoke would come from the seafloor and would break through the ice, which would compromise the structure. You need to construct the shell of the spire from water. Then, you'll need to channel air through the crystal to chill the water form as it emerges."

I cocked my head. "Your spire didn't look like it was made of ice. It was rather warm inside."

"The ice will form a mold. You have aether, do you not?"

"Of course," I said, nodding.

"Life itself was once forged from water," Aelfrich said. "The sea is full of life. Fill the mold of ice with aether. Cast fire upon it to melt the ice, and the aether will form something like bone, or ivory, as the primary material for the structure. Ensure that you cast your magic directly through the crystal. Any magic apart from the crystal, like if you overcharge the crystal or send other magic into the structure, can impact the final form of the spire."

I took the crystal in my hand. I touched the hilt of Aerin's' blade. I didn't have a belt to slip it through on the elven clothes that I was wearing. Instead, there was a string, a cinching my waistband to hold it in place. Aelfrich didn't know about Aerin, so I didn't speak out loud, but I made sure she could hear my thoughts.

You can do this, Caspar.

I nodded. I didn't need her encouragement so much as I wanted to check in and give her an opportunity to speak. Since arriving at the North Pole, everything had gone more smoothly than I'd anticipated. Almost *too* smoothly. Sure, there were some loyalists we'd have to deal with. But I hadn't imagined that we'd be welcomed with open arms like this. If anything was amiss, I wanted to give Aerin a chance to say something. She had a keen eye for things like this, even if she could only perceive what was happening through me if I touched my blade and funneled what was happening to her through my memories.

It took more focus than I was accustomed to. Lately, the magic I was doing required a lot of *bang* and *pow*. Major flows of energy. Stopping the earthquake, for example. This task, as Aelfrich described it, required precision. It would require a lot of magic, and it needed a steady stream of each element in its proper order. At least, I figured, once I finished, I'd have a place to sleep.

A tower of water formed as I delicately pushed the element through the crystal. The water spun like a typhoon as it rose. The element flowed from my fingertips into the crystal, then it was redirected by the crystal in a predetermined path. Even as the water spun, it took on the definite shape of a tower, the water remaining within the confines of the form it was intended to take.

I added air, and the water slowed and then froze into a

column of ice. It wasn't as tall as the other spires, but it was just as wide.

"You're doing great," Aelfrich said. "Now, add aether. It will give the whole structure a golden glow. Once the aether has filled the shell, add fire."

I nodded and drew on aether. My fingertips glittered with golden magic, which I directed into the crystal. It shot forth with an intelligence I couldn't control. It was following the blueprint written into the crystal. When it had filled the ice shell, I did the same with fire. The warmth coursing through my body was an extra perk. Once the ice melted, the aether within solidified, making the whole structure glisten like a polished pearl.

"Amazing," Aelfrich said. "For one man to do this alone is incredible."

I shrugged. "It didn't feel like I was doing it. It was almost like someone else was directing my magic."

"The brilliance of crystals," Aelfrich smiled. "With limited magic on New Albion, we didn't have a lot to waste with training. This technology was developed a few centuries back. It meant that any elf, presuming he could wield the proper element required for a spell with the requisite focus, could do the kinds of spells that only master sorcerers used to do."

"So this works with other spells, too?" I asked. "Not just making buildings or towers?"

Aelfrich nodded. "It's how we gained an advantage over the orcs back on New Albion. It's also why, I imagine, the king will soon begin recruiting from the loyalists into his legions. Any elf who can wield any magic can be an asset. All the king has to do is give the elves the proper crystals that correspond with their elemental proficiencies and they'll be able to wield whatever battle magic he requires."

"Well, that certainly poses a challenge," I said. "I don't have a guide to follow. No crystals or blueprints for my spells. I've had to figure things out as I go."

"Unfortunately, only the king holds the crystals that contain battle spells," Aelfrich said. "All I have access to are domestic crystals that help establish our community outposts. I suppose, if the king gets his way, he'll be remaking the whole world this way."

I nodded as I looked at the spire I'd made. "This thing is beautiful."

"Would you like to go inside?" Aelfrich asked.

"Definitely!"

"First, we need to use your palm print to program the doors. The first person to use the sensor will become the administrator of the spire. If you'd like anyone else to have access, all you have to do is have them press their hand to the sensor and then place yours over the same place immediately after. It has to be quick, or it won't work."

We walked over to the doors. I put my hand on the sensor. It glowed dimly beneath my touch, and the doors opened.

"Let me show you how to program it for everyone else," Aelfrich said.

I nodded as Aelfrich put his hand on the sensor. "Now put yours there, Caspar."

I put my hand over the sensor while it still glistened in an outline of Aelfrich's palm. Then it pulsed with a golden glow that faded away.

"That's it!" Aelfrich said. "Now, I hope you don't mind that I can access your spire. Be careful who you allow access. Once someone's palm is programmed into it, you can't get rid of it. The only way would be to destroy and remake the spire, which can be a real pain in the ears."

"In the ears?" I asked.

"Just an elven expression. It doesn't hurt our ears."

I snorted. "Yeah, we call it a pain in the ass. Similar expression."

"Probably even less pleasant than a pain in the ears," Aelfrich said, grinning.

"Metaphorically speaking. No one wants a literal pain in the ass."

Aelfrich chuckled and rested his hand on my shoulder. "I'll leave you to it. Feel free to bring Layla, the drow, and the rest of your people when you're ready. I'll go ahead and send the orcs in this direction with some supplies. Food and such."

"Thank you, Aelfrich. I appreciate the hospitality."

Aelfrich nodded with a kind smile as he stepped toward the door heading out. He placed his hand on another panel. "Just press. You don't need to program the one that lets you out."

"Got it!" I said, nodding.

"Your appearance is no mistake," Aelfrich said. "Our movement was starting to lose its steam. We lacked direction. Your arrival gives us hope for a path forward, a vision for establishing a new home here among you."

I nodded. "Before that's possible, I'm afraid we'll have to take down Brightborn."

"There's no telling how soon the king will send another legionary to visit," Aelfrich paused, "if he doesn't come himself. If he does, well, that would be convenient. Otherwise, perhaps, you can exercise some subterfuge and follow his emissary when he leaves."

"Sounds like a plan," I said. "Thanks again, Aelfrich."

CHAPTER EIGHTEEN

I waited for the giants before heading back to Canada to gather the rest of my posse. My army? My crew? I don't know what to call them. My "group" sounds a little too touristy. My "people" made it sound ethnic, but we were about as diverse a bunch as you could find. My homies? Well, they weren't all from my hometown. The Caspar Crew might work, but I didn't want to make it about me. So, the Elven Prophecy Posse would have to do.

Brag'mok, Gronk, and the rest of the giants showed up, knocking on the door. I opened it, programmed the sensor to accept their palm prints, and welcomed them inside.

"You made this?" Brag'mok asked.

I nodded, a prideful grin spread across my face. "Pretty cool, right?"

"Actually, it's a lot warmer than outside," Gronk said.

I laughed. "Right. Cool is just an expression. Whatever. I think it's nice! Better than the junkyard."

Brag'mok shrugged. "We had supplies there to work with. Nothing like that here. Just a lot of ice."

"Ice, ice, baby," I sang, "Too cold. Too cold."

The giants cocked their heads in perplexity.

I waved off their confusion. "Sorry, you probably don't know that song."

"Why would someone sing about how cold ice is? Isn't that a bit…mundane?" Gronk asked.

I nodded. "The guy went by Vanilla Ice. It was on brand, I suspect."

"Flavored ice?" Brag'mok asked. "Sounds delicious."

I shrugged. "I think he called himself that because he's white. I don't know for sure."

"Humans are weird," Gronk said.

I snorted. "Yeah, tell me about it."

"We've got this," Brag'mok said. "You're free to go get everyone else if you're ready."

"All right," I said. "Keep the space in front of the spire clear. That's where I'll bring them."

"I don't think anyone is eager to go outside again any time soon," Gronk said. "At first, the ice and snow were a novelty. We didn't get this kind of weather on New Albion. Now, well, it pretty much sucks."

"I get that," I said. "I haven't enjoyed snow since the days it used to mean days off school. Once I started having to drive in it, well, it became a nuisance. I don't like being cold."

Brag'mok removed his armor and set it aside. "Nice and warm in here. Is it normal for your nipples to get hard in the cold?"

I smiled. "Totally normal."

Brag'mok poked at his pectorals. "Looks like they're back to normal. Doesn't feel good rubbing against metal armor."

"You should try a wool sweater," I said. "It's the worst."

"We'll be waiting for you," Gronk said. "We brought some fish with us. We'll try to catch some more. I imagine everyone will be hungry."

"Probably," I said. "They've been lingering in the wilderness since I left. I imagine they're starving."

I formed a fairy portal and, visualizing the space in the woods I'd left, I connected it and jumped through. Ideally, I'd be able to keep the portal open and bring everyone back to the spire without having to make a second one. That was the hope, at least.

I found the drow gathered around a small fire. Layla had her feet up on a log, lounging against Clarence's large, furry body. Agnus was curled up in her lap. Jag was standing in front of everyone telling... Ghost stories?

"It was a cool night," Jag said, his voice hushed. "A night a lot like tonight!"

I smirked. Surely he'd seen me come through the portal, but, you know, the show must go on.

"But it wasn't in the forest. It was on a highway. Ten years ago, on this very night. In a dense fog just like this. I saw the worst accident I'd ever seen. There was this sound, like a trash truck falling off the Empire State Building. When they finally pulled the driver's body from the twisted, burning wreck, it looked like... *THIS!*"

Jag put his hands to the side of his head, his thumbs in his ears, and stuck out his tongue. With wide eyes, he snarled and shook his head back and forth.

I scratched my head. No one reacted to his attempt at a scare. The story wasn't all that frightening.

Jag continued, "If anyone asks you about that night and where you came from, tell them Large Marge sent ya!"

I giggled. Now I knew where his story came from. *Pee Wee's Big Adventure.*

Rina raised her hand.

"Yes, Rina?" Jag asked.

"That makes no sense. Who is Large Marge, and why is she sending us? And what does the highway have to do with anything? We're in the woods. Wouldn't it be scarier if you told a story about the woods?"

Jag shrugged. "It's the only ghost story I know. Give me a break!"

I cleared my throat. Everyone turned and looked.

"All right, stop!" I said. "Collaborate and listen."

Layla looked up and sprung to her feet. "Vanilla Ice, Caspar? I was worried sick, and you show up serenading us with bad rap lyrics?"

"Sorry," I said. "I came from the North Pole. *Ice Ice Baby* was stuck in my head, for obvious reasons."

"How did it go?" Layla asked. "Are the giants okay?"

"They're fine," I said. "No one's fighting. And the elves were kind. A fellow by the name of Aelfrich welcomed me. Helped me construct a spire where we can stay while we wait for Brightborn or one of his legionaries to show up."

Layla frowned. "Aelfrich, you said?"

I nodded. "Yeah. I'm guessing you know him?"

"Of course I do," Layla said. "I used to call him Uncle Aelfrich. He and my father used to be best friends."

"Used to be?" I asked. "It sounds like he's leading the revolution now. There's a divide between the elves. Ever since your father faked his death and people got a taste for the idea of change."

Layla scratched her head. "I don't know. I mean, it's been so long since I was there. I suppose that tracks. I would never have pegged Aelfrich for the leader of something like that. He was always so conservative. Restrained, even. But he and my father had a falling out several years ago. I didn't think it reached the point that Aelfrich would try a coup."

"A falling out over what exactly?" I asked.

Layla shrugged. "I never knew. Adult stuff, I was told. All I knew was that he wouldn't be joining us for festivals anymore."

"Even something small can plant seeds of bitterness and resentment that grow over time," I said. "I suppose it isn't surprising that a small disagreement years ago might lead Aelfrich to the path of revolution."

Layla shook her head. "It's a shame. They used to be best friends. It's too bad that my dad is such a dick. Sounds like Aelfrich could have been a good influence over him."

I smiled. "Yeah. Damn dicks. How many problems in the world come back to dicks."

Layla shrugged. "Assholes and pussies share some of the blame, too."

I laughed. "Yeah, if we were all just torsos without lower halves, we'd not only lack effective metaphors for people with undesirable behaviors, we'd have a more peaceable world."

"Probably because it's hard to treat people poorly when you can't go anywhere," Layla said. "You know, legs and all."

I nodded. "Not to mention, we'd still need some way to get rid of waste. So, even if we didn't have assholes, we'd develop something else to serve the function."

Layla cocked her head. "Are we still talking about my father, or are we entertaining hypotheticals pertaining to dismembered bodies?"

I shrugged. "Both. But it's helpful. Even if your father wasn't doing what he is doing, chances would be that someone else would take his position or be doing something just as horrendous. Same goes for us, too. If we weren't here, trying to save the world, I'd like to think someone else would step up to do it."

"True," Layla said. "Eventually. But we have the advantage of foresight. We know about the prophecy."

"Do you think everyone's ready to get up and head to the pole?" I said.

Layla chuckled. "Do you want to wake up Clarence and tell him that you're taking him to the arctic?"

I shook my head. "Clarence? Hell, I don't want to tell Agnus that, much less a five-hundred-pound grizzly."

"What's the urgency, then?" Layla asked. "We're good here. A bit hungry, but we'll be fine until morning. Let everyone get their sleep."

"Sleep? Are you sure that's what you want to do right now?"

"Oh honey," Layla said, wrapping her arms around me. "I was talking about *them*. I have other plans for you."

CHAPTER NINETEEN

Waking up first thing in the morning to a bear moseying his way around camp is unsettling, to say the least. I wasn't sure I'd ever become accustomed to Clarence. I had to take Layla's word for it that we should, by virtue of aether, have a connection to animals. They wouldn't be a threat. Certainly not mammals. Technically, I could probably even communicate with snakes.

It made sense from the perspective of the book of Genesis. In the beginning, there was harmony between humans and animals. Originally, mankind was to have dominion over them. Not in an oppressive way, not to exploit them. Rather, humans were supposed to relate to animals the way that God related to us.

The idea was that by having other creatures to care for, we would understand how God cares for us selflessly. It would ultimately deepen our relationship with Him.

Quite brilliant, until the snake started talking and the shit hit the fan. Even then, it wasn't until after the great flood that God grudgingly permitted humans to eat meat. Truth be told, from a biblical perspective, humans were originally created to be vegetarians. We don't talk about that much. Telling people isn't great for evangelism. People like their burgers and barbecue.

The point is that aether is connected to the source of life, the breath of God that was exhaled into the first man's nostrils in the beginning. It made sense that this same breath that called all creatures into existence would give us a kinship, a connection most human beings long ago lost. The druids of old figured that out. They may not have had the Bible, but they had the revelation of nature herself—a book that is every bit as divinely inspired as any religious text. Perhaps it's harder to read than the Bible. But in some ways, as much as people screw up the Bible when they try to interpret it, I'm not so sure that people miss the mark much more when looking to see the hand of God in nature.

Funny thing is, the deeper I get into magic, the more I find myself depending on my faith, on my God. I was playing with magic that most people in the church would think of as witchery or sorcery. I was following a prophecy not contained in the Bible. But at the end of the day, my core beliefs—the fundamentals about *who* I believed in, not just what I believed—gave me the strength to move forward. I didn't *know* what to believe anymore, but I did know who I was following, and, in my experience, God has never let me down.

"Caspar!" Jag called.

He and Rina, I'd noticed the night before, were curled up on the opposite side of the simmering campfire in the middle of the clearing where everyone was staying.

I rolled over, stretching my arms overhead and yawning.

"What's up, Jag?"

"You up for a morning workout? You know, before we head north. I assume that's what we're doing, right?"

I chuckled. "You know what, Jag? That sounds good. But what are we going to do? We're out in the middle of the wilderness."

A shit-eating grin split Jag's face. I'd seen that smile before, back when he was training me at the gym, and I asked him what we were going to do for our day's sessions. That grin portended pain and suffering.

Whatever he had planned, it was going to suck.

But what the hell. We were the only two awake aside from Clarence, and if we needed to shower afterward, I could always evoke water magic to make it happen. Not that I wanted to shower with Jag in the middle of the woods. If anyone walked in on us, it would be awkward. But logistics aside, I was sure I could figure out a way to do it that would keep any jokes regarding our heterosexuality off the table.

I chuckled to myself, thinking about it. "So, what do you have in mind, Jag?"

"Follow me."

Jag headed off into the woods and found a giant log. He patted it.

"We're not lifting that," I said. "*Sans* magic, there's no way. The thing probably weighs a ton!"

"I didn't say we'd lift it, Casp. We're going to stand on it and do squats."

"Without weight?" I said.

Jag chuckled. "Not hard on solid ground, huh? But when you're trying to keep your balance and do a squat in perfect form, it really hits the glutes."

I snorted. "Just what I needed. Something to hit me in the glutes."

Jag shrugged. "Everyone's glutes need a good punishing from time to time."

I laughed. "I'm going to pretend you didn't say that. Because this conversation is about to get weird."

"You're the one who's hearing weirdness in what I'm saying, Casp. Just try it."

Jag and I both climbed up on the log. It was nearly parallel to the ground. So, there was that. Trying to balance on an uneven log and do squats at the same time would be nearly impossible. Jag raised his hands over his head and pushed his butt back, making sure his knees didn't cross the front of his toes. He lowered his ass to the log, then pressing through his heels, stood again.

"Just like that! Now, you try!"

I raised my hands in the air. I knew the fundamentals of a sound squat. I'd just mentally checked off all the boxes while watching Jag do it. The log was round, which forced more of my weight into the arches of my feet than I was accustomed to. The main thing is that you don't want to push with your toes. When you stand, according to Jag, you need to press with your whole foot, which is usually accomplished by focusing on pushing with the heels. The rest of the foot gets involved, but when you focus on the heels, it prevents you from shifting the weight too far forward.

I lowered my butt just fine.

"There you go! Now explode up!"

I exhaled as I pressed my legs and started to stand. But the curved log's surface made pushing through my heels more difficult than I anticipated. The thought of falling off into poison ivy, or oak, or whatever was growing on the forest floor, made my muscles fire in ways I'd never experienced. Little muscles I didn't realize existed were recruited to maintain my balance as I pressed through the movement. I stood up without falling!

"I did it!" I said, raising my fist into the air.

Then my foot slipped out from underneath me, and I slipped off one side of the log. I twisted, trying to catch myself…

And catch myself I did—with my balls.

"Fuck!" I squealed at a higher pitch than I'd vocalized since before puberty kicked in.

"Owwww!" Jag said. "Nut shot! Ten points."

"Not funny!" I said in the key of high C.

"Lesson number one," Jag said. "Just because you've completed the exercise doesn't mean you can let your guard down. You have to maintain balance throughout the movement. Balance and focus."

"I'm not doing that again!" I said.

"Do ten in a row," Jag said.

"Dude, I'm not paying you right now. You're not my trainer at the moment so you can't tell me what to do."

"Once your trainer, always your trainer," Jag said.

"That's not a thing."

"How would you know? You've never been a trainer."

I sighed. "I trained Agnus how to use a box."

"No, you didn't," Jag said. "Training a cat to use a box is as simple as showing them where it is. It's nothing like training a dog to go outside. Or a preacher to do a squat."

I snorted. "So now I'm on the level with training dogs? Thanks, Jag."

"Oh now," Jag said. "Training preachers to do anything, I've found, is much harder than training dogs. But perhaps more rewarding in the end."

I shook my head. "Aren't you supposed to give your dog treats, at least, when he finishes what he does? When have you ever given me treats?"

Jag laughed. "What do you give a preacher as a treat? Communion wafers? Good job with those twenty push-ups. Take and eat, the body of Christ."

I chuckled. "Do ten more, and you get to drink the blood, too."

"Nope," Jag said. "No alcohol while you're training. It screws with your metabolic rate."

I shrugged. "Some churches use grape juice."

"Unnecessary sugar," Jag said. "While we're at it, you'd better make sure those communion wafers are low carb."

I rolled my eyes. "You've got to be kidding, right?"

"Yeah, pretty much. But you're just delaying the inevitable. You're going back on that log and doing ten more squats. Come on, I'll do them with you."

"But my balls!" I protested.

"Your balls will be fine. Get on the log!"

I hopped up and stood side-by-side with Jag, and we did ten squats in concert. I was, oddly enough, more focused than before. Something about a blow to the 'nads will do that to you. I wasn't sure my future hopes for fatherhood could weather another rack.

"We did it!" I exclaimed, careful not to throw my fist in the air this time so I wouldn't lose my balance.

"We did!" Jag said. "Now lie down on the log. Place your hands on your chest like so. Ten push-ups."

"You've got to be shitting me," I said.

"Nope. Good thing, because if I was, it would be a lot more uncomfortable for both of us than these push-ups."

I chuckled. "I wasn't being literal, Jag."

"Nope. But I was. We're doing push-ups with balance. Narrow hand positions will bring in a little more triceps than usual. Let's do it!"

CHAPTER TWENTY

When we were done with balance exercises, we took a jog through the woods, hurdling over fallen branches. I was still in elf clothes, which were surprisingly comfortable. Silky smooth, especially on my still-tender fellas down below. They also let in an odd breeze that I wasn't accustomed to in that region of my body.

I imagined that this was what it must've felt like when Adam frolicked in the Garden of Eden…except he had a hot Eve to prance around with. I had Jag. A hulking amateur bodybuilder who smelled like socks. Not the same.

I cast a cloud over us. It wasn't too hard. Just a little draw from the element of water, bringing together the moisture in the air. If I drew it in more densely, I'd produce a floating glob of water, but I was getting better at focusing my abilities. Keeping the water molecules at a slightly greater distance produced clouds rather than the water blobs. I made sure to make it big enough so we wouldn't bump knees while we showered off.

We both showered—our backs to each other to prevent any awkwardness—under the rain cloud I'd summoned. No shampoo or soap. Plain water would have to do. It was also chilly. Maybe, eventually, I'd learn to use fire to warm up my water. It would take careful focus and delicate balance to pull it off. I was getting better with my abilities, but I was afraid that right now, I'd either douse the fire with water and spoil it or overheat the water, either scalding us or turning it into steam. Lukewarm water, matching the ambient temperature, felt especially cold when a breeze was added to it.

Yes, I could wield air. However, causing a gust of wind and thwarting the breeze already in the air were two different things. At least it wasn't as cold as the North Pole.

One fact about exercise, you have to keep up your calories. There wasn't a lot of food immediately available in the Canadian forest. If we were forced to stay there, Layla's bow skills could be combined with her affinity with animals to help us hunt some game. So far, though, they hadn't resorted to that.

By the looks on people's faces as I returned to the camp, they were glad I was back. They'd had enough of the forest. I wasn't sure that moving them to a glacier was a step up in the world, but at least we had accommodations there and easier access to food. Even if it was fish. Besides, we needed to be ready. Once Brightborn came, even if he just sent an emissary, we needed to stop him.

Targigoth and Trixie were likely wherever he was, too. I had to assume that was the case. If it wasn't, surely they'd have returned to us by now. Trixie had to know where I was. I'd been casting a lot of magic lately. She'd be able to sense it. The fact that she hadn't shown up yet made me mildly anxious. One would think she'd at least pop in to give me an update regarding whatever the hell she and Targigoth were up to.

"There he is!" Rina shouted, stepping away from the three drow elves that she was speaking with.

I waved. "I'm here. Everyone ready for an arctic adventure?"

Layla hooked her arm in mine. "As ready as ever!"

I snorted. "Everyone, make sure you're bundled up. We have a lodging there that's warm. But we'll be portaling onto the middle of a glacier."

Rina nodded, then turned and shouted out her orders to the other drow, and they started gathering their things.

I felt pressure on my shin and looked down. "Hey, Agnus. How are you doing, buddy?"

"Just dandy, you beetle-headed flap-ear'd knave."

"Still on the Shakespeare kick, I see," I said as I bent over and scooped my cat into my arms. My original hope to create one portal and leave it open didn't pan out. I had to remake my portal, which I did quite easily since visualizing the space in front of the spire was as easy as imaging a polar bear in a snowstorm. I did make sure to keep the spire in my eye's mind, however, lest my portal dumped us into some random snowy wasteland.

"You coming, Clarence?" Layla asked.

Clarence growled.

"It's probably a bit cold for him," I said. "He's not a polar bear."

"You can stay inside," Layla said.

I raised my eyebrows. "I suppose. But he has to pee outside."

Clarence rumbled. I don't know how Layla translated his sounds into something sensible. She had more practice working with animals than I did. To date, I'd only used my abilities to hear Agnus and a mouse that was hassling me back at the church where I used to be the pastor.

Clarence made a low-pitched grumbling sound.

"Believe it or not, he likes the idea of going to the North Pole. He said that he's eager to leave so he can hibernate. His sleep was cut short here because winter ended early. Climate change, I guess. He wanted you to know he won't eat or pee much when he's hibernating. So he won't mess up your precious spire."

I bit my lip. "All right. But we may have to leave at any time. So long as he understands that he might have to wake up and get his furry ass in gear at any moment, I suppose that's fine."

Clarence made another sound—something between a grunt and a growl—and Layla nodded, ensuring me that he was fine with it.

I went through the portal first to make sure that there weren't any loyalists on the other side waiting to attack or any other undesirable surprises.

Thankfully, no arrows came flying our way. I didn't see anyone nearby. Only the spire I'd masterfully constructed looking back at me in all its splendor. Yeah, I was prouder of it than I should have been. After all, it wasn't like I'd created the plans in the crystal. I just gave the crystal the raw material needed to make it. Still, it was pretty cool knowing that I'd done it. Especially since prior to this, the most complicated structure I'd ever built was a birdhouse.

About thirty seconds later, the rest of the crowd came through the portal. Layla was first, then Jag, and finally Rina, Elrand, and the other drow. Altogether, of course, the drow far outnumbered the rest of us.

I helped everyone program their palms into the spire. Not just the folks in charge. The way I saw it, every one of the drow was temporarily calling this place her home. Anyone who wanted to come and go could do so at their leisure.

"Welcome!" Brag'mok said as the crowd poured through the doors.

"Hey, Brag'mok," Layla said. "Looks like we avoided a battle."

"For now," Gronk interjected. "I'm still not certain about this plan. If Brightborn doesn't turn up soon, lingering here won't be any better than sitting around the junkyard with nothing to do."

"Fair enough," I said. "But at least we have an option to pursue. Aelfrich said we should avoid the loyalists at all costs. I wonder if we might be able to spy on them a little more discreetly."

Layla nodded. "If they are true loyalists, they'll have to at least acknowledge me. I am a Brightborn, after all."

"But Aelfrich said a good number of them believe you abandoned them," I said. "They think you betrayed your father. So even you will have to remain discreet."

"Well, I should like to meet Aelfrich myself," Layla said. "It has been too long, and I have a few questions for him."

CHAPTER TWENTY-ONE

As everyone settled in, Layla and I headed out to the other elven spires where I'd encountered Aelfrich. He'd insisted that Layla be kept hidden from the loyalists, so she pulled her parka over her head and wrapped a scarf around her face.

I knocked on the spire. No answer. I didn't dare check the other ones. The last thing I needed was to start a fight. The whole area looked like a ghost town. Almost like when I'd visited the original royal quarter in New Albion, where I'd met Echor.

"How weird," I said.

"Where could they have gone?" Layla asked.

I shrugged. "I doubt they went far. I could always fly up and try to get a bird's eye view. If they're anywhere nearby, I'd surely see them. What's strange, though, is that every one of the elves is gone. The revolutionaries and loyalists alike."

"My father had to have something to do with it."

"I don't know, Layla. He doesn't have fairy power. Could he create a portal and take all the elves away?"

Layla shook her head. "I don't think so. Unless you think Trixie…"

"She wouldn't be in league with him. She *couldn't* be. She defeated the other fairies and had them locked away."

"I know, Caspar. I'm not saying that's what happened. She and her fairies know better than anyone how terrifying my father can be. The Seelie fairies came from New Albion. But what if they captured her? She and the rest of the fairies left with Targigoth."

I snorted. "None of this fits. There has to be a reason why Trixie and Targigoth didn't tell us what they were up to. But they wouldn't betray us. Those are the last two who would ever have reason to side with your father."

"Fly away, junior birdman," Layla said. "I guess looking around can't hurt."

I bit my lip. "Junior birdman?"

"Fly away, upside-down!"

"How do you even know that song?" I asked. "We used to sing it in the Scouts."

Layla shrugged. "Weird, the things I've picked up here or there studying human culture."

I chuckled, gathered aether and air, and extending my arms in front of me, I shot into the sky.

I flew all around, circling the whole glacier. I didn't see a single living soul other than a walrus, a group of seals, and several flocks of seabirds.

I was just about to give up and fly back to Layla when I noticed a small circle. I descended and landed in the middle of it. Ten stones, breaking through the ice. They looked similar to the ones that Elrand had used as a temple near his cabin in the woods. There was some magic about them, a warmth that suggested that they'd been used recently. I recognized each of the elements latent in each of the five stones, respectively. But I didn't know how to reverse-engineer whatever magic had been done to figure it out. If anyone knew, it would be Elrand.

I flew back to Layla and told her what I'd seen, and we went and retrieved Elrand from the spire.

"A stone circle, you say? Fantastic! This is quite exciting!"

"Is it?" I asked. "It seems like the elves just abandoned us here, or they were abducted. It's more worrisome than exciting if you ask me."

"Of course," Elrand said. "It's just fascinating that after centuries the same magic from our common ancestors, the ancient druids, has been passed along in both the elven and drow traditions."

Layla scratched her head. "I thought the drow didn't do magic?"

"They don't," Elrand said. "But they study it. They know the academics of magic, the traditions of our ancestors. It's how I was able to learn to wield earthen magic."

"Is there any way you can figure out what they were doing there?" I asked.

Elrand bit his lip. "Possibly. The ancients believed that stones not only serve to help channel and amplify magic but that they absorb energies and impressions of events that occur near and around them."

"Like a video recorder?" Layla asked.

"A lot like that," Elrand said. "The molecular structure of certain stones can absorb energy. Any time living creatures, especially humans or elves, do something that's charged with energy, it leaves an impression of what happened behind."

"Charged with what kind of energy?" I asked.

"Not necessarily magic," Elrand said. "It's energy that remains within the soul of the living, aether if you will, that is released with intense emotion."

"So if they were celebrating something, for example, the stones would get an impression?" Layla asked.

"Or, if they were furious, terrified, anxious, or even sad. Any intense emotion, other than perhaps boredom, would do it."

"Well, I doubt that the elves from those spires all came to that circle and sat on their thumbs bored out of their minds," I said.

"I agree," Elrand said. "Take me to the circle. Perhaps we can coax the stones to tell the tale."

Elrand sat in the middle of the stone circle. He removed his coat, then took off his shoes and socks, pressing his bare feet into the ice. I touched my hand to Aerin's blade just in case she had something to say about what was happening. I was making a habit of that when situations that had consequences occurred. She usually stayed quiet. She'd speak up if she had something important to say.

This time, she had nothing. I held my hand there just in case.

"There's no soil here," Elrand said. "Just ice. Usually, going barefoot like this helps with grounding. Connecting my spirit to the earth. This is different. Water, even ice, is more volatile than earth. But if I can connect the stones and envelop them with aether, I might be able to do this."

"Do you need any extra power?" I asked.

Elrand nodded. "Come sit opposite me."

I sat and crossed my legs.

"Remove your shoes," Elrand said. "Ground yourself to the ice."

I didn't want to put my feet on the ice. My little tootsies would get cold! Since we were using magic, I couldn't call forth fire to keep them warm either. Any extra magic might interfere with what Elrand was attempting.

"All I need is aether," Elrand said. "Just a trickle more than I'm already channeling."

I focused and let the vivifying power of aether flow through me, adding it to Elrand's aether already coursing through the ice and spinning around the stone circle.

"These stones hold more memories than I anticipated," Elrand said. "They were not always here. This stone circle was brought here from New Albion with the rest of the elves."

"These are not stones native to New Albion," Layla said from outside the perimeter of the circle.

"That is because these stones were not originally from New Albion. They came with the ancients. The memories stored within are rich."

"How far back do they go?" I asked.

"I cannot say," Elrand admitted. "Perhaps all the way to Taliesin, the prophet himself. But extracting such memories, the further back in time something is in a stone's structure, the more difficult it is to access."

"Start with what's most recent," I said. "Let's see if we can figure out what happened to the elves first. Then, perhaps, we can try to learn more from the stones."

Elrand nodded and squinted his eyes in focus, and a golden mist sizzled off the stones.

"Come, we are seated in the middle of the vision. Let us step outside the circle and observe what tale the stones might tell."

While we were sitting there, it was almost impossible to tell what was happening. The visions didn't come with audio tracks. We'd have to piece what we saw together based on the images alone.

Three men, their bodies shrouded by long, black, cloaks stood in the circle. They were channeling aether like we had done moments before. Like us, they were summoning a vision. We were about to see a vision inside of a vision, which I hoped wouldn't be another vision of someone having a vision, of someone having a vision.

Sort of like looking into a mirror reflecting another mirror. Thankfully, that wasn't what they were evoking. Seven images appeared, and they discounted them all and continued funneling more magic into the stones.

"What are they doing?" I asked.

"They're trying to go back to the beginning, to the moment the elven prophecy was first revealed to Taliesin."

"How can you be sure?" I asked.

Elrand shrugged. "Because that's what I'd do if I had these

stones. Imagine if you had an item that could reveal to you a vision of Christ—along with other things. Would you be looking for the other things?"

"I suppose that makes sense," I said. "Maybe because they can't get their scroll to open?"

"Possibly," Elrand agreed. "Or, perchance, they're looking for the greater mystery."

"Which is?" I asked.

"Which deity revealed the prophecy to Taliesin, to begin with. The only way to unravel, or defeat, a prophecy is to challenge the god who put it forth."

I shrugged. "So you think it's the loyalists, not the revolutionaries, who are trying to discern this information?"

"I don't know," Elrand said. "We don't know anything for certain. All we can do is wager a guess and keep watching. This vision we're seeing is fresh. It happened only a matter of hours ago. If the elves went anywhere, this should give us an idea where they went."

I watched as the three elves channeled more magic into the stones, their bodies convulsing with the power they were evoking. It was more than they were accustomed to wielding, more than they had probably accessed before they had come to Earth and the place where the ley lines intersected. I hadn't even considered how much power that gave the elves here access to, but they clearly knew it. That must've been why Brightborn had sent them to the North Pole. I'd figured it was because it was discreet. But that didn't make sense. Surely there'd be a more hospitable place where the elves could remain hidden. An island in the tropics or something.

Finally, another vision appeared, the one that they wanted. The three figures stepped aside as another man appeared. His form was more translucent than the three. It was a vision of a vision, after all.

The frail man with a scraggly beard leaned on a staff and

stood before three chests. The chests were open and filled with scrolls.

"The scrolls of the prophecy," Elrand said.

"Three sets," Layla said. "For the elves, the drow, and the giants."

The man, who I presumed was Taliesin, had a single piece of parchment unrolled. He held a quill in his hand. He looked at the ground.

A snake slithered up his leg.

I shivered. A snake? Why'd it have to be a snake?

The serpent curled around his body and then whispered something into Taliesin's ear.

Taliesin started to write.

The final prophecy was dictated by a serpent? There was only one talking serpent I'd ever heard of, and he wasn't a friendly fellow. He was the one who tempted Adam and Eve. The devil, in creaturely form.

Suddenly a bright light flashed in the middle of the circle, disrupting the vision—a portal. Trixie flew through it, followed by Targigoth. They closed the portal then opened another one. With his hand extended, Targigoth lowered it over the three men. Then Targigoth and Trixie opened another portal, a separate one to someplace else, and disappeared.

The vision disappeared.

"I can't believe this," I said. "The prophecy I've been following was dictated by the devil?"

"We don't know that," Elrand said.

"We saw a serpent," Layla said. "That doesn't mean it's Satan, Caspar. I thought you said you didn't like snakes because they bite, not because of what the Bible says about them."

I snorted. "Talking snakes are different! That wasn't God whispering in Taliesin's ear, Layla. Whatever it was that snake whispered, that's what he wrote on the scroll."

"We don't know what was happening in that vision," Elrand

said. "Or even if it was the same serpent that revealed all the prophecies. Taliesin might have called forth wisdom from many creatures, the wisest of many different species."

I didn't hear him. "If I'm the chosen one of a prophecy dictated by the devil, that doesn't make me a hero. Brightborn might be talking about one-world government and shit like that. But if I'm the one chosen by Satan, that can only mean one thing. It means I was chosen to be the Antichrist."

CHAPTER TWENTY-TWO

"Stop it, Caspar. You aren't the fucking Antichrist."

"You don't know that I'm not, Layla."

"You don't know that you are!"

"I know what I saw!" I shouted, removing my belt and leaning Aerin's sword in the corner of the room in the spire that we'd recently called home.

Agnus greeted my right calf with a headbutt.

"I think it's awesome," Agnus said. "A most notable coward, an infinite and endless liar and hourly promise-breaker, the owner of not one good quality."

"I'm not in the mood for your Shakespeare bullshit, Agnus."

Agnus snorted. "All's well that ends well."

"If I'm the Antichrist, this isn't going to end well. I know what the Bible says ends up happening to the Antichrist."

"It was the name of the play," Agnus said. "*All's Well that Ends Well*. Never mind. Don't be stupid, Caspar. If you were the Antichrist, you'd know it."

"He's right," Layla said. "I don't know your Bible like you do, but I highly doubt you're the one whose appearance is supposed to harken the end of the world. We don't even know who that snake was. It was more likely than not just a common snake, a pet, like Agnus."

"I'm not a pet!" Agnus protested.

"You know what I mean. Druids were known to have an affinity for animals. Just as we do with Agnus, and like I do with Clarence."

"Speaking of him, where is the bear?"

"Snoring in a room off the first floor," Agnus said. "While you guys were off doing whatever it was that got you so worked up, he found a dark corner and got his hibernation on."

"Got his hibernation on?" I asked.

"I don't know the technical term for going into hibernation!" Agnus said.

"I think that might be it. Just going into hibernation," Layla said, smirking.

"Whatever," I said. "It doesn't matter. Targigoth and Trixie showed up before Taliesin could write what he was about to jot down on the scroll. I don't think that timing was accidental."

"They didn't want them to see what was on the scroll. Do you think they got the scroll themselves and knew?" Layla asked.

I shook my head. "It's possible. I wish they'd told me what they were planning. It looks like they also got rid of all the other elves. They sent them off somewhere."

"Perhaps it wasn't so that they could prevent them from discerning the prophecy, but so that you'd have an opportunity to do it yourself," Layla said.

I snorted. "Aerin said something similar when I set the sword in the corner. She whispered to me that I could do what they never finished. But if the devil was involved, I don't know if I want to."

"You're starting to sound like those assholes who are in charge of your old denomination," Layla said.

I huffed. "Am not."

"Leaping to conclusions that something you don't understand must be of the devil?" Layla said. "Sounds like what they did when they saw you healing people. It didn't jibe with their world-view. Must've been from the devil."

I sighed. "I see your point."

"The only way to know for certain what we saw is to go back. We need to see that vision for ourselves. We need to know what Taliesin wrote on the scroll."

"I can try," I said. "That was a ton of magic they were drawing through the ley lines, and there were three of them."

"But none of them were as powerful as you, Caspar," Elrand said.

"Maybe not. But again, there were three of them. I might be stronger than any one of them, but not all three."

Layla shrugged. "You have Elrand and me, not to mention the giants. Gronk is a sorcerer, isn't he?"

"I suppose so," I said. "A sorcerer warrior."

"The giants can withstand a lot of magic without it taking a toll on their bodies."

"Yeah, but they can't wield it as powerfully as you or Elrand, certainly not as potently as me."

Layla cocked her head. "Still, Caspar, weren't you recently saying you needed to keep everyone involved?"

I nodded. "Everyone needs to be involved. Whatever is revealed, they can't be waiting for you and me to relay it to the rest. I might be the chosen one, or the Antichrist, or whatever the hell the prophecy suggests that I am, but I can't expect people to just follow me blindly. I need everyone's help, their expertise and input. Not to mention, if people are going to follow me and I am what I suspect, well, they deserve to know the truth."

"That you're concerned about the truth, Caspar, tells me that the very thing you're worried about could never be," Layla said.

"As Agnus put it, quoting Shakespeare, isn't the Antichrist an infinite and endless liar, an hourly promise-breaker? That you want them to know the truth, even if it isn't pleasant, suggests to me that you're wrong about what the vision indicates you're supposed to be."

I sighed. "I hope you're right."

CHAPTER TWENTY-THREE

We gathered everyone around the stone circle. Everyone except Clarence, who was sleeping, and Agnus, who wouldn't be bothered. It was too damn cold.

Elrand suggested we sit in a circle, five of us to correlate with the given stones. That meant Layla, Elrand, Rina, Gronk, and me. That meant all of us were represented. Technically, Elrand and Rina both represented the drow, but because he was a dude and the drow didn't hold males in high esteem, he was more of a lone ranger, a hedge drow whose assistance was needed on account of his magical proficiency.

I was sitting between Layla and Gronk. Rina was sitting on the other side of Gronk, and Elrand closed off the circle. Holding Layla's hand, I couldn't help but smile as I noticed how unique and diverse our circle was. I wanted to sing Kumbaya, but most of them wouldn't get the significance of it.

"All right," Elrand said. "Everyone needs to focus aether. It's the one kind of magic that all of us can wield. We need to allow the stones to absorb it. The magic will spin counter-clockwise if it works, as I observed before, like turning a clock backward. Once we are at the beginning of the vision of Taliesin, I will let go of Rina's and Layla's hands. All of you should follow suit and walk slowly to the perimeter outside the stone circle so as not to disturb the energies. If we do it properly, we should be able to observe the vision until the magic we've given it runs out. Ideally, it will be enough to see everything we need."

We all focused our minds. I was the strongest, from a pure power perspective. I don't know how you measure magic. Amperes, joules, girth?

It didn't matter. With our hands joined our aether joined as one—one people, one spirit—the whole idea gave me goose-bumps. I resisted the urge to get sentimental about it as the golden energy started to swirl counter-clockwise around the stones. Each stone maintained a tether to the cone of magic swelling around us.

Flashes of memories popped up in our midst. Strangely, there weren't many involving elves in New Albion. There were a few visions of elven kings—I could tell they were kings based on the regalia they wore that matched Brightborn's—attempting unsuccessfully to manipulate the stones. But the visions only appeared to be connected to four of the five stones. Each stone shone a light on the image, like a projection, but the fifth stone was not involved.

"Perhaps the other stone," Elrand said, "was not on New Albion at all."

"I've never seen these stones before," Layla said.

"One stone," Elrand said. "Still on Earth so that the other four might not be fully utilized, that they might not evoke the memory of Taliesin until the time when the elves returned to Abred."

"Abred?" I asked.

"Another word for Earth," Layla said.

I nodded. "So using these stones upon their return to Earth has always been a part of the elves' plans?"

"Possibly," Elrand said.

"If it was, I didn't know anything about it," Layla said. "Of course, I didn't know that my ancestors had been hoping to come back to conquer Earth for centuries, either."

The aether swirled around us, rewinding its projections of time. It wasn't a continuous recording, in reverse. It was more like when you use the rewind button on the remote and what you're watching takes small jumps backward. If it worked like when we saw it before, it would play forward in a more continuous, smooth fashion once we stepped out of the circle and the magical energies turned clockwise again.

The druid I'd presumed to be Taliesin, the old man we'd seen before, appeared, his image flashing around us. Once he disappeared, Elrand stood, breaking the circle. We all followed suit, letting go of each other's hands, and stepped back to the perimeter of the circle.

I walked right into one of the stones. "Doh!"

Layla giggled.

Thankfully, my clumsiness didn't screw up the image we'd evoked. I stepped aside and outside the perimeter of the circle.

Elrand touched one of the stones. The swirling cone of aether slowed and then started turning in the opposite direction.

The vision started to play forward at a regular, real-world pace. Again, the vision played without any audio to help make sense of the sounds that were coming out of the famed prophet and bard's mouth as he spoke his incantations.

He was seated on a stump, in the middle of the stones, and had a single, flat stone that he used as a desk, itself resting across two smaller stumps. He had the three chests. He sat within the stone circle, evoking magic not unlike what we'd done. As the visions played, he took his quill to parchment and scribbled on his scrolls.

There wasn't a serpent anywhere to be seen. Taliesin wasn't gleaning the content of the prophecies from the snake. At least not yet. He was using the stones to look *forward* in time. How in the world…

Once again, we started seeing visions within the vision. I saw…myself.

If there was any doubt before now that I was the chosen one, that was thoroughly blown out of the water.

Taliesin saw me in the alley that fateful night when I tried to rescue Layla from B'iff. When I got stabbed by the Blade of Echoes.

He wrote something down—presumably, the first prophecy—on one scroll and then two others to match before rolling them up, sealing them with a wax seal that he used his magic, aether mixed with fire, to melt. The seals, I learned, the prophet had made precisely to only open at certain times when the events started to unfold.

I saw Agnus appear. The second prophecy was about my familiar. A guide. Someone whose wisdom would aid me on my path. Taliesin saw the moment Agnus first spoke to me. I chuckled, watching it from a distance. That look on my face, you'd think I'd seen a ghost. Again, Taliesin wrote three copies of what he saw and placed them in each of the chests.

More visions flashed by, corresponding to each of the prophecies that had been fulfilled. I saw the moment Layla and I kissed—that was the third prophecy. I saw B'iff die again, destroying the Blade of Echoes, the fulfillment of the fourth prophecy. I saw myself, in New Albion, recharging the ley lines, the fifth prophecy. Then, there was the sixth prophecy. I remembered it well because it was so ominous. "He shall attain the power of another. And with it shall come not peace, but a sword, and more blood shall be shed upon the worlds than has ever been in a single day since the worlds were hewn from the abyss." I remembered that one because I thought I'd fulfilled it when I recharged the ley lines, but that was only the fifth. The sixth was the death of the giants. Taliesin saw hundreds slaughtered, one flash of death after another. We saw it, too. Gronk and Brag'mok, who was also with us outside the circle, grunted, and the rest of the giants roared in agony at the sight of it. Taliesin wrote the dreadful words, at least that's what I presumed he wrote since he was penning a language I'd never learned, and sealed the three scrolls before resting them in their chests.

Then the seventh. We'd seen the serpent speak to Taliesin before, but we hadn't seen the whole vision.

I saw the giants entering the portal to come to Earth. I was there when it happened. I recalled it like it was yesterday. That was their version of the seventh prophecy. Taliesin recorded it, sealed it, and placed the scroll in one of the chests. Then, I saw Aerin fall on her blade–sealing her spirit to the same sword that now hung from my waist. Taliesin recorded his interpretation of what he witnessed and sealed the seventh drow prophecy before placing it in their chest.

There was one final prophecy to reveal. He searched the future. He looked to the past. Taliesin pinched his chin in a quandary. He wasn't sure what the seventh prophecy would say concerning the elves. He spun the magic cone around him clockwise with a fury until he saw the entire Earth. I imagined he might have been mildly surprised to see that the world was, in fact, round. A single snake was wrapped around the world. It was translucent and green. Spanning the equator, the snake had his tail in his mouth as if he was holding the whole world together.

Was this a literal vision? Was there really a snake wrapped around the planet? They believed in Jormunganr in Norse mythology. I knew the tale of Thor and the Midgard serpent. Could it be true? Whether it was or wasn't, in Taliesin's vision, the serpent released his tail. The whole world turned brown, the green lands becoming barren in the blink of an eye. The seas dried up.

Then the planet burst into flames.

The serpent, which had only been in Taliesin's vision before, slithered on the ground and made its way up the ancient prophet's leg. This was what we'd seen.

When it spoke to Taliesin, he withdrew another quill from his pocket. Not the same one he'd used before. This one was not a common white feather. It had a golden hue. When he wrote, the letters appeared in violet. But we couldn't read it. I certainly couldn't. Even if it had merely been written in an ancient tongue, which Elrand or Layla might have been able to figure that out, the letters he wrote disappeared as quickly as he wrote them. One letter was gone as soon as he finished the next.

If the ancient druid was aware of it, he didn't show it. He exhibited no signs of surprise as he wrote. His countenance remained calm, his posture relaxed.

Taliesin took the scroll, sealed it as he had done with the others, and put it in the last chest, the elves' chest. Then, he took the serpent by its neck, tossed it into the middle of the circle, and crushed its head with his heel.

It reminded me of another prophecy, what I'd always believed to be the first prophecy predicting the coming of Christ in the third chapter of Genesis:

I will put enmity between thee, Serpent, and the woman. Between thy seed and her seed; it shall bruise thy head, and thou shalt bruise his heel.

CHAPTER TWENTY-FOUR

I stood there staring blankly at the space between the stones where the vision had played out. What had we just witnessed? We saw how Taliesin discerned the prophecy. An ancient druid, at a time of persecution, rose to the occasion and peered into the future to give his people a prophecy that would carry them through exile with a message of hope. How he'd done that, I didn't have a clue.

Surely, Brightborn's agenda wasn't what Taliesin had in mind. Did he realize that it would be a leader of his own people who the chosen one would have to defeat? More than that, did he realize that the chosen would come from the race that had persecuted him and the ancient druids, forcing the elves and giants to leave Earth to begin with?

What was I supposed to make of the snake? Elements of Norse mythology had blended seamlessly with a Judeo-Christian prophecy in the vision. I wasn't sure how to interpret that. As I understood it, the serpent Jormunganr held the world together in Norse mythology. When the serpent let go of its tail, that was supposed to signal the beginning of Ragnarök, what I've always known as the Apocalypse. Then, when Taliesin stomped on the head of the serpent at the end of the vision, I couldn't help but make the connection to my faith. A seed of man, Genesis prophecies, would crush the serpent's head even as it struck at his heel. In my tradition, we understood the seed of the woman to be Christ. When the serpent struck him at the crucifixion, he was wounded, but Christ ultimately dealt the serpent a death blow by rising from the grave and defeating death itself.

Now, how in the world would I put all these ideas together in a way that made any sense? Was the only way to achieve victory to destroy the thing that held the world together? That seemed nonsensical. I couldn't wrap my mind around the idea that a literal snake was wrapped around the globe, holding it together. But there had to be some significance to these visions.

Layla put her hand on my back. "Are you okay?"

I nodded. "I wish we knew what he wrote on that scroll."

No sooner did I say it than a bright light flashed in the middle of the circle, and a fairy portal opened. Trixie flew through, followed by Targigoth.

"You're back!" I exclaimed.

"We're baaaaaaack!" Trixie sang as she buzzed around my head.

Targigoth stepped forward. He had a scroll in his hand. He had *the* scroll in his hand.

"You guys got the prophecy?" I asked.

"We did, we did, we did!" Trixie said.

Targigoth nodded and handed it to Layla.

"Do you know where Brightborn is?" Layla asked, taking the scroll in her hands.

Targigoth sighed. "The elves are all together. They are fighting among themselves. A group of elves who oppose the king launched an assault against him the moment we brought them together."

"That's when we snagged the prophecy!" Trixie said, beaming with pride.

"Why didn't you guys think to tell us what you were up to?" I asked.

"I asked her not to reveal our plans," Targigoth said. "It is the duty of a high priest to ensure the safety of the prophecies. In lieu of an elf priest on Earth who could guard the prophecy, I felt duty-bound to recover it myself."

"It was foolish!" Gronk said.

"I think it was brave," Layla said, staring at the prophecy. "And it's not entirely true that the elves don't have a priest here to open the scroll."

Targigoth cocked his head. "You've brought Echor back to Earth?"

"Not exactly," Layla said. "He bestowed the priestly rites upon me when we took him back to New Albion. I am the elven high priest."

"You kept this from us?" Targigoth asked.

Layla scratched her head. "Anyone who knew would have dangerous information. My father was already seeking me, but if he knew I was given the priestly rites, there's no telling what he'd do."

Gronk snorted. "He probably would have shown himself. He would have been looking for you, and we could have avoided all of this."

"Or," I said. "He would have slaughtered everyone to get to Layla."

"This is likely," Brag'mok said. "Gronk, I agree with Caspar. Any information that Brightborn doesn't have is an advantage we must retain."

"Exactly," I said, nodding.

"It worked to our advantage after all," Trixie said. "Brightborn forged a new gate to New Albion. He went seeking Echor. Had he known that Layla was the new priest, we never would have found him."

"You found him on New Albion?" I asked.

Trixie shook her head. "We fairies found him as he forged his new gate. We assumed it was a trap. That he was trying to lure us through the gate. We are vulnerable in New Albion. Especially now that the magic there is almost entirely gone. We would have been defenseless against him."

"Where is this gate, exactly?" I asked.

"It is where the original gate was," Targigoth said. "The one first forged when our ancestors fled the earth."

"At the Ring of Brodgar?" Layla asked.

Targigoth nodded.

"The ring of what?" I asked.

"One of the many stone henges in Brittany," Layla said. "It is between the lochs of Stenness and Harray on a small isthmus in Orkney, Scotland."

"I still have no idea where that is," I said.

"Of course you don't," Elrand said. "You're an American."

"What's that supposed to mean?" I asked.

Elrand shrugged. "Most Americans think of themselves as the center of the world. No offense. But in other parts of the world where national borders are more numerous, and the countries are smaller, people tend to be more aware of geography outside of their own nations."

I bit my lip. "Well, I can't exactly argue with that. So is this like Stonehenge?"

"Similar," Layla said. "But only about a third of the stones remain."

"Not anymore," Targigoth said. "Brightborn has reconstructed the henge and used it to open another portal where the ley lines intersect, back to New Albion."

"He went there to get Echor?" I asked.

Targigoth nodded. "I'm sorry to say the elf was unable to open the prophecy. Now, we know why. Brightborn executed him on the spot."

"He killed Echor?" Layla asked. "Oh, my God!"

Targigoth nodded. "Severed his head from his shoulders right in the center of the henge and sent his body back to New Albion."

"But before he died, the king tortured him," Trixie said. "Echor revealed that it might be possible to discern the prophecy using these five stones."

"And they already had these stones set up and ready?" I asked.

Targigoth grunted. "Brightborn believed these stones could be a weapon. We don't know how he found the final stone, but he did. The henge was built here, but not to reveal the prophecy. He believed he could use it to make the world submit to his rule."

"This stone circle could do that?" I asked.

Elrand nodded. "We used aether here. Other powers could be united to the circle and channeled in various ways. Still, I can't imagine any earthly power being used as such a weapon. Even fire, while devastating, is limited by water."

I'd had my hand resting on Aerin's blade during the entire conversation. So far, she hadn't said a thing. Now she piped up.

Celestial power. The gifts I was supposed to give to you, and now Layla possesses.

"It's your power, Layla," I said. "Aerin says that must be it."

"But I'd never use the power that way," Layla said. "My father surely knows that."

The celestial power precedes all of existence. With it, great things can be made. But anything that exists can be eradicated as well.

"Aerin says that your magic can create things out of nothing, and it can also take things that exist and destroy them in an instant."

Layla shook her head. "I don't know how to do that."

"All that Brightborn would have to do is ensure that the power Layla possesses is cast within the circle," Elrand said. "Then the magic could be guided through the stones and channeled by his other sorcerers."

Layla took two steps back. "I shouldn't be here. If he came back..."

"We knew that his plans had something to do with Layla," Trixie said. "Brightborn ordered his elves here to try to discern the prophecy and then to bind you. He knew you'd be arriving soon. When Caspar came, the elves knew Layla wouldn't be far behind. So we thought it best to beat him to it, and since we weren't sure how soon you'd be arriving, all we could think to do was remove the elves from the area."

"Remove them to where?" I asked.

"They're safe," Trixie said. "Not all of the elves are guilty."

"Some of them opposed the king," Targigoth said. "We thought it would distract Brightborn if we sent the elves to the Ring of Brodgar."

"Could you take me there?" I asked. "Could you take all of us there?"

"We could," Trixie said. "But I don't know that we should."

"She's right," Elrand said. "Any stone circle would do, not just this one, provided that the king was able to get Layla inside of it. He could bind her to the circle, despite her power, and draw the power out of her."

Layla held out the scroll, the final scroll of the elven prophecy. "I don't think we should do anything until we know what the final prophecy reveals."

"I agree," I said. "The vision of Taliesin wasn't exactly clear. We aren't sure what it meant. Until we know what prophecy Taliesin wrote following that vision, we'd be foolish to make any moves at all."

CHAPTER TWENTY-FIVE

I'd helped open the giants' and drow's prophecies. I knew the process. Layla held the scroll in her hands. I focused my mind on channeling each of the five elements into the seal. The colors of each element swirled together on the seal as the wax, previously invulnerable, started to peel away from the parchment. A loud trumpet blared, though there was no trumpeter in sight. The seal shattered into a shower of sparks, like fireworks, all around us.

Layla unrolled the scroll. Then she furrowed her brow and cocked her head. "I don't get it."

"What is it?" I asked.

Elrand stepped up behind her and looked at the scroll. His eyes widened in surprise. "It's blank."

"What?" I asked.

"The scroll," Layla said. "There's nothing on it."

I snorted. "Let me see it."

Layla handed me the scroll. Sure enough, it was as blank as a chalkboard on the first day of school. "We saw the words disappear as he wrote them in the vision," I said, scratching my head. "It looks like what we witnessed wasn't an illusion."

"But what does this mean?" Layla asked.

"He didn't put that scroll in the chest for no reason," I said. "I'd suggest your father erased the words if we hadn't just seen Taliesin write it that way. But he did write *something*."

"After the serpent spoke to him," Elrand said. "You've already identified two mythological traditions with respect to the serpent's significance. But that does not consider, in this case, the meaning that Taliesin himself who was neither a Nord nor a Jew or Christian might have thought of the serpent who spoke to him."

I shrugged. "The symbolism seemed pretty overt."

"The symbols you discerned are associated with ends of the world," Elrand said. "The Midgard serpent reflects Ragnarök. The serpent in the Garden of Eden represents the fall of mankind, and all the world, from glory. Did you know that there are no snakes in Ireland?"

"Didn't St. Patrick chase all the snakes from there?" I asked.

"Just a story," Elrand said. "In truth, there haven't been snakes in Ireland since the ice age. But Scotland and Wales have their venomous adder. England has three breeds of serpents, including the adder."

"Interesting lesson about my least favorite creature on Earth," I said. "What does that tell us about the prophecy and the vision?"

"The story of St. Patrick casting snakes out of Ireland represents an import of the Judeo-Christian association of the serpent with evil. The Nords believed a serpent held the world together. But the Celts believed that serpents slithered up from the center of the earth and possessed great wisdom, all the secrets of the earth herself. For the druids, the serpent was an Earth Healer. That it shed its skin each season suggested to the druids that the earth they represented was meant to be reborn, to shed its old skin."

"So, snakes are good?" I asked, raising my eyebrows.

Elrand nodded. "To the druids, yes."

"Then why would Taliesin stomp on its head?" I said.

"Perhaps as a warning," Elrand said. "Maybe he knew you'd see this vision. Perhaps that was what the serpent told him."

"A warning of what?" I asked.

Elrand shook his head. "We're getting into the domain of interpretation. Anything I suggest is only a best guess."

"I understand that," I said. "I can relate to the difficulty of interpreting visions. I've tried preaching the book of Revelation before. Saying much of anything about it with absolute certainty, other than the outcome at the end, is dubious."

"The crushing of the serpent for the Celts might have been seen as an ominous sign," Layla said. "The end of the cycle of rebirth. But in Caspar's belief system, it would symbolize hope. Taliesin saw Caspar in his visions. He knew that Caspar came from a different world, with different beliefs. What if Taliesin was mingling his beliefs with Caspar's, offering *both* a warning and a sign of hope?"

"Even the Genesis prophecy is both a warning and hopeful," I said. "It does warn that the serpent would strike at the heel of the prophesied seed of the woman, but it also indicates the serpent's defeat."

"But none of this tells us why Taliesin left the page blank," Layla said.

I pinched my chin. "He *didn't* leave it blank. What he wrote disappeared as he wrote it. He must've known that was the case. Did he mean for us to discern it, somehow, as if he'd penned it with invisible ink?"

Layla nodded. "Perhaps he realized that the prophecy might fall into the wrong hands. That we, I mean the elves who owned the prophecy, were the threat to overcome. In contrast, the giant and drow prophecies weren't hidden this way."

I bit my lip. "He wrote it with a different quill. Golden rather than white, and the ink he wrote with was purple. Like the celestial magic you got from the rings, Layla."

I'd almost forgotten that I was resting my hand on the hilt of

Aerin's sword. *The celestial power in the rings should be able to draw on the magic writ upon the scroll. She won't need to channel magic. The magic is there. If she swipes her hand over the page, it should illuminate the ink.*

"Aerin says that she thinks if you just swipe over the paper with your hand, it should reveal what was written. Sort of like a secret decoder ring."

"A secret decoder ring?" Layla asked, raising one eyebrow.

"Never mind," I said. "It's a geek thing. Just run your hand across the parchment. See if it works."

I held the scroll for Layla as she ran her hand across the paper. Sure enough, letters appeared beneath her touch. They disappeared quickly, which meant that we'd have to decipher it one word at a time.

"It's working!" Layla said.

Elrand looked at it carefully and sounded out the words as Layla glided her hand across the paper. Her hands were small, but that didn't matter. It was the rings that exposed the celestial ink hidden in the parchment, not her hand.

Everything Elrand said sounded like gibberish. Almost like he was speaking in tongues at one of those charismatic churches that believe in that kind of thing. I didn't embrace that particular practice. I didn't see the basis for it, at least the way they did it, in the scriptures. But it did strike me that many of the Christians who did embrace it drew on Paul's statement regarding the tongues of men and angels in First Corinthians, and they often justified their practice by arguing that they were speaking in angelic tongues since the word "tongues" in Greek means "languages."

I thought it was a way to justify babble-speak but, now, I wasn't so sure. If this wasn't an angelic language, it was written in angelic ink.

I pressed my lips together. I didn't want to interrupt Elrand while he was working on translating the words. When he finished reading, he stepped back and chuckled.

"What is it?" I asked. "What does it say?"

"The best I can translate it is: 'There is no fate. The future is what you make of it, Naayak.'"

"The future is what I make of it?" I asked.

Elrand nodded. "It's interesting that he addressed you directly in this prophecy, Caspar."

I bit my lip. "Why would he want to hide this from the elves? It's not exactly revealing."

"Because the obscurity means that you are not guaranteed a victory," Layla said. "My father is not destined to fail. If he read that, it would only embolden him."

I snorted. "Now that I know it, I'm not sure whether I should be happy that nothing else is destined to happen or anxious about it. Before, I was always holding onto the idea that I was supposed to unite the peoples in the end."

"That has not changed," Elrand said. "You are to unite the peoples. How you go about it, however, it seems, is your choice alone."

CHAPTER TWENTY-SIX

Was I supposed to be relieved? The only thing that prophecy did was put more pressure squarely on my shoulders. The future of the world was in my hands. I was supposed to unite the peoples. That's what everyone believed, what the first prophecy supposedly said. Unite them how? Uniting people in death and the destruction of the world was a sort of unity. I couldn't accept that that was what it meant.

If nothing was left to fate, was it up to me from the start? Were these prophecies foretelling the future alone, or were they signposts identifying the challenges that would befall me, along the way, no more than tokens of advice to lead me toward this point? Was I supposed to learn that nothing was decided, that no future was certain unless I got my shit together? Brightborn might actually win?

It wasn't the first time I'd encountered the fate versus free will dilemma. It was a matter that had divided Christian theologians for two thousand years. The Bible affirms both that God has foreknowledge of predestination while at the same time holding humans responsible for their own decisions. Divine agency and human agency—both are affirmed in the scriptures. Theologians have historically tended to fall off one side of the horse or the other. Either God predestines everything, and there's nothing we can do about it. Or, humans have free will, and while God knows the future, he doesn't direct it. Neither of these options accounts for all the biblical passages involved.

For me, the whole issue was resolved by the belief that humans have limited understanding. From our perspective, everything we do is based on our choices, our decisions, our will. From God's perspective, the whole script of human history is known. He's outside of time and knows what we will choose at every turn. Therefore, human decisions that occur within time are already known to him.

Not satisfying? Probably not. But when I read the scriptures about predestination, there isn't any hint in those passages that people should be up in arms about their will or freedom being violated. Those passages occur in moments when comfort was needed, when shit is hitting the fan and people are prone to worry about their eternal security. At those moments, God tells them, "Don't worry, I've chosen you from the beginning. No one can take you from my hand." In other instances, when humans are lackadaisical or are justifying their actions, God exhorts them to consider their choices. He reminds human beings that they are responsible for loving one another. They can't just rest on "destiny" and figure whatever will happen, will happen. They need to take action and do what they're meant to do.

Sorting out the philosophical tension between God's foreknowledge and human freedom isn't the point. The Bible intends to exhort and encourage. The rest? Well, it's a mystery, and for the most part, I'm fine with that.

That tension meant that I couldn't rest on my laurels. I had responsibility for what was going to happen next. But I couldn't despair, and I couldn't allow myself to be overwhelmed by fear and uncertainty. The future was coming. The only thing I could do about the future was the next right thing. I had to do my best, now. Tomorrow would worry about itself. Or, it wouldn't. If it didn't, well, I wouldn't be there to stress over it—and no one else would be, either–.

"So, what do we do now?" Layla asked as we stood around the stone circle.

Targigoth stepped up and put his hand on my shoulder. "How about we go inside and get warm before we worry about the next steps?"

"Wise," Elrand said. "This is information we should spend some time considering before we make any rash decisions."

I nodded and, drawing on a little fire magic, I shrugged. "I don't know. Feels warm out here to me. I'm good!"

Layla rolled her eyes. "Not everyone is a walking furnace, Caspar."

I chuckled. "I know. I think we should go in, warm up, and make a plan. The one thing I do know is that now that we know where Brightborn is and what he's planning to do, we shouldn't sit around thinking about it too long."

We all piled into the spire I'd made. It was nice and warm inside, so I stopped channeling fire. Everyone was thrilled with the place. It was my version of Superman's Fortress of Solitude. Yeah, it wasn't a mystically powered temple with the collective wisdom of my hologram ancestors. But it was a castle in the arctic, and it did feel peaceful inside.

We knew we had to move fast. But we didn't want to be reckless. We didn't know for sure what Brightborn was doing now that the other elves were there.

Most of the giants and drow were settling in, exploring the spire. It probably wasn't a good idea to settle in since this safe haven was likely temporary. However, even if we did launch an assault on Brightborn, unless we ended the war all at once, I wasn't sure where else we could go. The government saw us as traitors. Would that change if we won? Probably not. If anything, it would get worse. For now, this was the only place in the world where we could rest, even if we'd only be able to stay there a short while.

In the middle of the spire was a round table that stood a few inches off the floor. I rested Aerin's blade on the table. Lounging on the floor with a sword at my side wasn't comfortable. I rested my hand on it so she'd have a voice as all the other leaders gathered around. The giants were represented by Targigoth, Gronk, and Brag'mok. The drow were represented by Rina, Elrand, and technically, Aerin. Jag and I were the only humans, and Layla was the lone elf. Trixie, perched on my shoulder. The other fairies were buzzing around outside the spire and anywhere else they wanted to go. They could move across the world at will, and Trixie could summon them in an instant when she needed them.

"There's only one thing we know," I said. "That's that whatever we do next might decide the future. Not just for us, but for the world."

"No pressure," Jag said.

I smiled. "None at all."

"All I know," Targigoth said, "is that when we took the elves to the stone circle where Brightborn was, he wasn't particularly thrilled."

"The elves are divided," I said. "From what I understand, he's been avoiding the conflict among them, hoping that the revolution would die out on its own once they came to Earth."

"For once, Brightborn was wrong," Brag'mok said.

"If there is a strong resistance," Layla said. "We can use that."

"I agree," I said. "Aelfrich should be an asset. The elves are already divided. If we can join our forces with the revolutionaries, we might have to force Brightborn to fight against his own."

"Elves will die," Layla said. "He's going to avoid fighting at all costs. We might have good numbers, but we are still very few compared to the whole population of humans on Earth."

"If the people of Earth turned against Brightborn," Rina said, "it's hard to imagine he'd be able to defeat them all, even with his power."

"But they can wield the elements," Layla said. "Brightborn and the legion could evoke natural disasters—earthquakes, tornados, hurricanes, tsunamis. The havoc he could cause if the world turned against him would be immense."

"Still," Rina said, "some well-placed bombs could take out the elves."

I shook my head. "We can't let it come to that. This isn't about elves versus humanity or elves versus giants anymore. This is about those who love freedom, who love the Earth, and those who out of fear would cede their liberties to Brightborn on a false promise that he could save the planet."

"You could save the planet," Elrand said. "You've already demonstrated that."

I nodded. "Hopefully, I managed to convince people of that. But as far as we know, Brightborn still has the governments in his back pocket. We have to proceed on that assumption given that my own government sent its military against us."

"They did that to us after you already demonstrated what you could do, after you put your video out there, which the government surely saw," Rina said.

What if you go alone? You and Layla?

I raised my finger. "Hold on, Aerin is talking."

"Alone?" I asked.

Think about it, Aerin said. *Brightborn knows that his political situation is about as stable as a meth lab. The revolutionaries will see Layla and rally to her, more than likely. But if you have an army with you, they'll be more likely to fight.*

"You think we could avoid a battle that way?"

If you want to save lives, you have to win over the rest of the elves. Brightborn is the real threat. If he falls, Layla is his only heir.

I grunted. "Assassinate him?"

If it comes to that. He's been wanting to put forward Layla as the chosen one all this time. You have Trixie. You have fairy portals. If he pulls any shenanigans, you can portal your cute little butts out of there in a jiffy.

"Our cute butts?" I asked, raising my eyebrow as confused stares were trained on me around the table.

Aerin giggled. *I was being nice. I could have said you'd be able to portal your nasty asses out of there, you know.*

I chuckled. "Aerin thinks that Layla and I should go alone. We need more information. As boastful as Brightborn is, he's been confronted with a political powder keg that could explode in his face at any moment. If we want to avoid death, and I'd rather not see any more giants or elves fall, especially since so few remain, we need to use the leverage we have to give him a chance to abdicate."

"You seriously think that Brightborn will abdicate to Layla?" Brag'mok asked.

I shook my head. "I'm not sure."

"He won't," Layla said. "But worst-case scenario, it will force him to show his true colors. It will give us a chance to present our case to the rest of the elves. Even the loyalists will reconsider their position when they realize he'd sooner put his entire people in danger when he should be trying to forge a new home for them here on Earth. I can only hope that it's enough."

CHAPTER TWENTY-SEVEN

It was Layla and me. Technically, Layla, Aerin, and me. Of course, as far as anyone knew, it would just be us two. Trixie could send us to the henge where Brightborn and the elves were. If things got too hot, I'd take us back to the North Pole.

Layla had her bow and a quiver full of celestially charged arrows. The magic in her arrows, if they struck someone, would spread through the target. Layla had been struck by a blade with the same power infused in it before, and there was no way to stop the spread. The only way to save her was to give her the enchanted rings that Aerin had brought to St. Louis intended for me.

The move had screwed up Aerin's plans, but ultimately, it had saved Layla's life. So far, the power had saved her more than once. She was able to use that ability to portal similar to the way I portaled with fairy power. She'd used her power to escape her father twice. From what we understood, her power was capable of a lot more than we'd anticipated. We were only beginning to discover what she could do with it. Including how it could be used as a weapon if Brightborn was able to capture her in the stone circle that we'd used at the North Pole.

Trixie took us outside the Ring of Brodgar. We didn't want to risk the possibility that Brightborn was using the stone circle to open another gate to New Albion or doing who knows what else. If Layla's power could be used as a weapon in the stone circle at the pole, we figured it best she avoided popping up in the middle of any stone circle.

It was striking how green everything was, especially in the middle of the summer. Back in Missouri, most of the green would be burned out by now. It was surprisingly temperate, it felt more like a spring day than the hot summer ones we'd experienced back at the junkyard ranch, and it wasn't as bitterly cold as the North Pole.

For once, we were comfortable. Temperature-wise. I was pretty certain discomforts were about to abound.

Except that we didn't see anyone.

Trixie buzzed around us. "Any clue where they went?" I asked.

Trixie continued flying around. She licked her finger and stuck it into the air as if she was discerning the direction of the wind. That likely wasn't what she was doing. She was trying to sense magic. If the elves were using any, she'd know where they were. Of course, Brightborn knew that we had the fairies. He would be careful. But not all the elves who were with Brightborn were *with* Brightborn.

"This way!" Trixie said, taking off through the air.

Layla and I looked at each other and shrugged. We started walking in the direction Trixie had gone.

Then she buzzed back into view.

"Sorry!" Trixie giggled. "I forgot you're so slow!"

"Yeah, feet are like that," I said. "Can't move as fast as those hummingbird wings you have."

Trixie smiled. "Well, I could take you there."

I shook my head. "I'd rather get a look at them from a distance. I'd like to know what we're facing before we're in the middle of them."

Trixie scratched her head. "I can take you to a place like that. Somewhere they won't see you."

"We won't have to walk?" Layla asked.

"Not a step!" Trixie promised.

"Then sign us up!" I exclaimed.

Trixie made another portal. We emerged in a thicket on the other side in the middle of the woods. There was a wide-open grove below. We were around fifty feet away from Brightborn, who sat on a stone, flanked on either side by a half dozen elven legionaries. We were far enough away that they wouldn't see us hidden behind the trees but close enough that we could mostly tell what was happening. The downside was we weren't close enough to hear what they were saying.

"Where are the rest of the elves who were at the North Pole?" I whispered as Trixie perched herself on my shoulder.

"Not far from here. But someone here used magic. This is what I found," Trixie whispered back.

"My father used magic?" Layla asked, also hushing her voice.

"Not him," Trixie said. "The other one."

"The legionaries?" I asked.

"No, the other other one," Trixie said. "The one approaching through the trees."

I narrowed my eyes as Aelfrich appeared at the edge of the clearing.

Brightborn and Aelfrich approached each other. Brightborn nodded curtly in acknowledgment of his fellow elf's presence. Aelfrich nodded back. Not a particularly warm greeting. It wasn't adversarial, either. It was formal.

Layla had said the two men were once close friends before they'd had a falling out. She was too young at the time to remember what issue had divided the two men. I suppose if you've had a grudge against someone for years, a cordial but cold greeting would be appropriate. I wasn't one for grudges. I'd had to let go of that mindset as part of my AA program. My sobriety depended on it. But people who didn't have the advantage of having to learn such principles for the sake of sobering up did hold grudges over unresolved resentments.

Brightborn and Aelfrich were chatting politely. Then Aelfrich pointed at Brightborn and raised his voice.

Brightborn could have ordered his legionaries to arrest him, but he didn't. He shook his head, then threw his hand in the air and turned around. Foolish, I thought, to turn your back on a revolutionary. Of course, Brightborn had the legion there. If Aelfrich tried something, they'd stick their spears in his gut before he had a chance to lay a hand on the king.

A bright light flashed from somewhere behind us as Aelfrich stomped away from the elven king. Aelfrich and the king both turned to look. Layla and I looked, too.

A great golden cone of magic was swirling in the distance.

"Trixie," I said, my voice still hushed. "Is that in the direction of the henge?"

"That is the henge," Trixie said. "They are creating a portal."

"To New Albion?" Layla asked.

"I don't know," Trixie said. "I can't tell where it connects to."

Aelfrich was running in our direction. Whoever was casting the portal, he wasn't happy about it, judging by his furrowed brow and pursed lips.

"Quick, Trixie," I said. "Take us over there. Get us out of here."

Aelfrich would see our portal, but he wouldn't see us. Not that I was worried if he did. He was on our side. He was a friend. But he was moving with a purpose, and the last thing he needed was to be taken off-guard by finding Layla and me hiding in the woods.

Trixie summoned a fairy portal. I could have done it, but she could take us anywhere without seeing it first. The portals I could make were derivative of her magic, anyway. She could do it more efficiently than I could. Since she was here, having me do it would be like cooking your family's Thanksgiving dinner if Emeril Lagasse was your brother-in-law.

Trixie took us to the edge of the Ring of Brodgar. The gateway was huge. This stone circle was almost a football field's length in diameter.

"Caspar!"

I turned. Aelfrich was standing there.

I glanced a Trixie. "Really?"

"Sorry!" Trixie shrugged. "I thought you wanted to see what was happening."

"What are you doing here?" Aelfrich asked.

"Trying to get to Brightborn," I said. "We have the prophecy. We know what it says. We thought we could put pressure on him."

Aelfrich scratched his head. "Come on. That portal. We have to go."

"Why?" Layla asked. "Where are they going?"

"Back to the pole!" Aelfrich said. "The loyalists are attacking. While we were here trying to sort out our differences with the king, they snuck around and plan to go back to attack your spire."

"Well, shit," I said. "Shouldn't you go get the rest of your revolutionaries?"

Aelfrich bit his lip. "You've got a fairy, and you can cast fairy portals. You can bring them to us. But we must go now. Come with me, Princess Brightborn."

Layla started to step forward, and then she stopped. "Wait, why do you want me to go into that stone circle?"

"We have to get there in time to warn your people," Aelfrich said.

"We'd show up at the same place as everyone else," Layla said. "They're already gone. They'd get there before we would. There'd be no point. Why are you trying to separate Caspar and me?"

Aelfrich clenched his fists. "I don't have time for this. Just get in the circle. I'll explain when I get there."

"No," I said. "I can send her there with a portal of my own."

"Just grab her!" Brightborn shouted from behind. "We need her rings inside the circle!"

"Fuck!" I shouted, drawing on the power of air. I sent a gust at Aelfrich, blasting him into the magical cone. I turned to send another toward Brightborn. He raised his sword as I sent more air his way. My spell parted at his blade. I shot fire at him. The same thing happened. He kept walking toward us.

"Caspar, get us out of here!" Layla shouted.

"But you wanted to talk to him," I said.

"Not now!" Layla said. "This was a trap. We have to go!"

I nodded. "Trixie! Let's get out of here!"

Faster than I could, the fairy queen cast a portal over us and returned us to the spire I'd made at the North Pole.

CHAPTER TWENTY-EIGHT

I shook my head as Layla and I walked into the spire. "So, he was the loyalist all along."

"Do you think there even *were* revolutionaries?" Layla asked.

I nodded. "The ones he insisted I not show myself to. That was why. They would have told me the truth. He and his people were loyal to your father the whole time."

"They didn't look like they were in agreement about much when they talked in the woods," Layla said.

I shook my head. "They knew we were there. Somehow. They were keeping up the ruse to get us to leave. They hoped we'd follow them into that portal. But it wasn't a portal to New Albion, or to anywhere else."

Layla frowned. "My father was trying to get us in there so he could use the power in my rings."

"But to attack what?" I asked.

"I don't know…"

The front door to the spire opened as Layla and I stood at the entrance speaking.

"Caspar!" Brag'mok said. "You're back! Quick, we must prepare for battle."

"For battle?" I asked. "What's going on?"

"A bunch of elves appeared at the stone circle," Brag'mok said. "They're armed and marching in our direction."

"Shit," I said. "I think I know what your father was trying to do. That was a portal here, the whole time. He was going to use your magic to destroy our spire."

"Along with the drow and the rest of the giants," Layla said.

I nodded. "He'd wipe out our whole army. Using your magic! Then, all he'd have to deal with would be us."

"Where are the drow?" she asked Brag'mok.

"Already armed with their bows and patrolling outside the spire. I was patrolling alone at a distance. I must go and prepare Gronk and the rest of the giants."

I nodded. "Armor up. It appears we won't be able to avoid a fight this time."

Layla already had her bow; she'd taken it with her to Scotland. I had Aerin's blade. If I allowed Aerin to wield it through me, I could hold my own against any of the elves. Plus, I had all my elemental badassery at my disposal. I'd light a literal fire under their asses if push came to shove.

Clanging metal sounded through the spire as the giants marched down the spiral ramp. Their armor, although made from old car parts, looked formidable. We had to get out there fast. Rina and the drow were fine warriors, but they'd never fought elves before. The giants, well, that's all they'd ever known.

Gronk stepped up beside Layla and me. Brag'mok followed not far behind as we hurried to the front door of the spire.

I pressed my hand on the pad, the one on the inside that was supposed to activate the door.

It didn't open.

"What the hell?" I asked. "This one wasn't even supposed to be programmed at all. Anyone could get out. That's what Aelfrich said…"

"What Aelfrich said?" Layla sighed. "This wasn't just a spire, a place of lodging that he helped you build, Caspar."

I shook my head. "It was a trap."

"The drow are out there alone," Layla said. "Can they fend off the elves without us?"

"They are good," Brag'mok said. "But the elves have greater numbers."

"Dammit!" I screamed, pounding my fists on the door.

"Use your magic," Layla said. "You built this place with the elements."

I tried to draw on aether—but it didn't respond. Air gave me nothing. Neither water nor fire nor earth responded. "It isn't working! I can't draw on my magic."

"Dampeners," Brag'mok said. "The elves had magic dampeners back on New Albion."

"Often deployed against our sorcerers," Gronk added.

"Can we shut them down?" I asked.

"I highly doubt Aelfrich set them up on the inside or anywhere you could get to them from in here," Gronk said.

"And we can't get out. If we could, I wouldn't need to destroy the dampeners to begin with."

"Fucking *Dad*!" Layla shouted. "*Such* an asshole!"

I sighed. "He's always two steps ahead of us, luring us into his traps. He couldn't get you into that stone circle to use your power, so he resorted to locking us in this God-forsaken prison."

"So he can take out the drow without fighting us," Layla said.

"Um, Caspar?" Jag said, stepping out of one of the rooms. "I know war isn't my strong suit. But what's that green stuff coming out of the walls?"

"He wasn't trying to isolate the drow," Layla said. "He locked us inside to poison us!"

Elrand stepped out of the same room Jag had come from. "It's not a deadly poison. I think it's—"

"*Heeeeeeey! Heeeey, baby!*" Agnus sang as he staggered out of the room. "*I wanna know know know know. If you'll be my kitty!*"

"He weighs a lot less than we do," Elrand said. "I think the stuff just screws with your head."

"I'm almost six years sober," I said. "I'm not inhaling that crap."

"I don't think it counts against your sobriety date when an evil king, aka my dad, forces you to inhale," Layla said.

I sighed. "Why is he trying to get us high?"

"Because we'll be easily manipulated," Layla said. "We won't be able to fight. He still wants to keep me alive, and he can't kill you without killing me, Caspar. Our souls are bound."

I coughed. "Can your magic break us out of here?"

Layla bit her lip. She evoked celestial power, but it fizzled on her fingertips. "Looks like the dampeners impact that stuff, too."

"*Who let the cat out! Meow, meow, meow!*"

"Yup, Agnus is high."

"I am!" Agnus agreed.

My head started to spin.

"*I was just a lickin' my balls,*" Agnus sang, "*and then I got high.*"

Layla sighed. "Well, at least it isn't Shakespeare."

"Poor guy doesn't have a litter box in here," I said. "He might be high, but if he has to go and he doesn't have a good place to bury his waste, he'll be pissed."

Layla giggled. "Bad pun, Caspar."

"Pun not intended for once," I said.

Brag'mok and Gronk threw their bodies against the door. "We have to get out before this stuff gets to us. We're bigger than you. We'll last longer."

"Hey," I said to Layla. "Did you ever realize that you can feel your teeth when you're high?"

"What are you talking about, Caspar?" Layla asked, rubbing her finger across her teeth.

"No," I said, giggling. "Not like *that*, you silly, pretty person, er, elf person, you. Like, in your mouth. It's like you're more aware of them. Less aware of anything else. But not *those* teeth. It's like I can sense them there."

Layla was licking her lips, dragging them across her teeth. "I don't know what you're talking about! They feel the same to me!"

I laughed, curling up on the floor. "You know, you know what I mean. Your tooths. They're in your mouths. And it's like they are just totally announcing their presence. Here we are, yo! We're your teeth! Don't forget to floss us, you lazy son of a bitch!"

"I hate flossing!" Layla said. "Such a pain in the butt!"

I giggled and snorted. "You floss your butt? That's not how you're supposed to do it, babe!"

"Babe?" Layla asked. "You never call me babe, babe!"

Brag'mok threw his body against the door again.

"Hey, dude! Don't run into walls. S'not smart!"

Brag'mok ignored my sound advice and threw his shoulder against the door again. There was a loud thud but nothing budged.

"I hope those drow bitches are kicking the elves' asses!" I said.

"You shh-shh-shouldn't call them bitches, Caspar. It's missogy misogynisss. It's miso soup."

"I like soup!" I said. "Soup is good! Who doesn't like soup? No one! Because it's amazing!"

"What's the difference between stew and soup anyway?" Layla asked. "I can't ever figure it out, you know?"

Agnus started pawing at the door. "Brightborn! You starveling, you eel-skin, you dried neat's tongue, you bull's pizzle, you stock-fis-o for breath to tither what is like thee! You tailor's yard, you sheath, you bow case, you vile standing tuck!"

"Hey, Agnus!" I said. "You're high! That makes no sense!"

Agnus hissed. "It's the Bard, asshole! I know what I'm saying!"

I snorted. "The bard, yeah. Taliesin was a bard, too, wasn't he?"

"Lard bard, what a card!" Layla said.

I cracked up. "You're a poet, did you know it?"

Brag'mok and Gronk took another charge at the door. Agnus stumbled out of their way. Then they tripped over their own feet and fell to the ground barely sliding into the door.

I laughed and clapped. "Ten out of ten! Perfect form!"

"Let's see you do it!" Brag'mok said. "If you're so smooth, you smooth criminal you!"

"Hey!" I said. "How'd you know that song? *Braggie are you okay? Are you okay? Are you okay, Braggie?*"

"Don't call me Braggie!"

"That's what his momma used to call him," Gronk said, smacking his leg.

"Get out of the way," I said. "I'm taking out that door!"

"Casper!" Layla bent double with laughter. "If the giants couldn't break it down, you can't do it!"

"It's not the size of the ship, babe, it's the motion of the ocean!" I declared.

"Huh?" Layla asked. "That doesn't make sense?"

I shrugged, my shoulder feeling like it belonged to someone else. "I heard someone say that once. I think it's what men who have small wieners say to make them feel better about it."

"So you say it a lot?" Layla asked.

"Yeah. I mean, what? Hey!"

"You're gonna hurt yourself, Caspar!" Layla said.

"Will not!" I said. "Watch this! Here I come to save the *day!*"

I extended my fist and charged at the door. The door parted and I dove right through it, crashing into the ice at Aelfrich's feet.

He was laughing. "Legion. Bind them all while they're still incapacitated."

"You buttface!" I shouted. "My friends! Where are my friends!"

"The drow?" Aelfrich asked. "They're fine. Technically, they are elves. The king insisted they be spared. You know, races that can use magic are in short supply, so they've been sent elsewhere."

I clutched at him and missed, my hands clasping thin air. "Did you send them to Disneyland? I want to go to Disneyland!"

Aelfrich rolled his eyes. "We'll talk once you've sobered up. Well, the king will talk to you. He has big plans for you and Layla."

"My daddy sucks!" Layla said. "He sucks *bad!*"

"I'll be sure to tell him you said that," Aelfrich said.

The legionaries walked through the doorway with their spears in hand. They had ropes and started tying up Brag'mok, Gronk, Layla, and were making their way to the rest of the giants who were lounging all over the spire.

My hand brushed the sword at my side.

Don't let them take the blade! You need to grab it. You might be out of it, Caspar, but I'm here.

"I… Whaaaat?"

Just grab the blade. I will take care of this.

I shrugged and grabbed Aerin's blade, and the next thing I knew, I'd sprung to my feet. A legionary thrust his spear at me. Aerin had control of my body. She knocked it aside, spun around, and sliced his throat.

"Get him!" Aelfrich said.

Two more legionaries charged me. Aerin flipped me back and kicked one of the elves under the chin before plunging her sword into the chest of the other.

Aelfrich took two steps back. "How are you… You should be…"

"I *am* out of it, bitch!" I shouted maniacally. "High as a kite! Makes it easier for her to take over!"

The next thing I knew, Aerin's sword was clashing with Aelfrich's spear. He swung at my legs, and I found myself jumping over it. I was in the backseat in my own body as Aerin swung at his head. He ducked. It was pretty cool. Aerin was fighting like a badass, and I was along for the ride. Totally high, but totally kicking elf butt.

Aelfrich was good. Two more elves came to back him up. He and Aerin were a pretty even match. But once he had the other legionaries at his side, we'd probably be done for.

The bear, Aerin said. *Your abilities are like a druid's. Don't think too hard, Caspar. He can hear you.*

"The bear?" I asked.

"The what?" Aelfrich asked, taking another jab at me with his spear, which Aerin avoided by bending my body to one side in a way I was pretty sure I'd feel the next day.

"Hey, Clarence!" I shouted. "Dinner time!"

Aelfrich was confused until he heard a roar. The bear jumped out of one of the rooms and charged at the two elves who were backing up Aelfrich.

Aerin guided my hand as she twisted my body and knelt to cut his leg out from under him. The blow didn't dismember him. But it cut a tendon, forcing a scream in agony from Aelfrich as he dropped to the ground.

"We're not going to kill him?" I asked.

We need to interrogate him, Aerin said.

I nodded as Aerin picked up one of the ropes that the elves had used to tied up the giants and bound Aelfrich's wrists.

Aerin looked around through my eyes.

The rest of the elves are fleeing back to their portal. Let them go. We'll go after them later.

I nodded. "Thanks, Aerin. That was badass."

Aerin shook my head. *It had to be done. I do not enjoy killing. It is not badass. It is a tragedy.*

"I agree! But still, you kicked ass."

Sober up, Caspar. I'll keep the reins until you're back to yourself.

"Is Layla okay?" I asked.

She's okay. She will be, anyway. Let's finish tying Aelfrich up, then I'll take down the dampeners. You should summon some water. You're going to have one hell of a headache once this stuff wears off.

"But he took the drow. He said they sent them somewhere…"

Which is why, once you sober up, we're going to need to interrogate Aelfrich.

183

CHAPTER TWENTY-NINE

Interrogating Aelfrich was going to require the sort of barbarism that was featured in the murder motel in the *Hostel* movies.

"Make sure he's tied up tightly," I said.

Jag tightened the ropes around his wrists and ankles. We didn't have chairs; otherwise, I'd have tied him to one. Whatever. Aelfrich's comfort was the least of my concerns.

I'd never interrogated anyone before. Not my style. I'd been interrogated a few times by church authorities. My old bishop Matthias had made a habit of emotional torture in the form of threats to my career and salvation. In the first case, he'd lost his career, so whatever. In the second, I didn't need a dickhead's assurance as a foundation for my eternal security.

"I've got this," Jag said. "Let me do the dirty work. You do the talking."

I looked at Layla, whose incredulity was betrayed by her wide-eyed stare. What in the world was Jag going to do to the elf?

Jag took off Aelfrich's loafers, which were not the best for navigating frozen icebergs, but he'd made do.

"What are you doing?" I asked.

"Just wait," he said. "This is going to be brutal."

Then Jag started tickling Aelfrich's soles. The elf started laughing.

"Really, Jag?" Layla asked. "Tickling his feet?"

"The worst torture in the world!" Jag exclaimed, beaming with a sadistic pride, the same expression he used to make when he tortured me at the gym, as his fingers danced between the elf's heel and arch.

Aelfrich giggled, "Stop it!"

"Tell us where the drow were taken!" I demanded. "Or prepare for more tickling!"

I glanced at Brag'mok and Gronk, whose brows were both furrowed. They were utterly confused.

"No! *Tee-hee*! I won't tell you! He'd kill m..*oohhh aaah hahahaha!*"

"If you don't tell us, I'll let him tickle you to *death!*" I promised.

"Th-th-that's not poss—*ahaha*—sible!"

"Try me," Jag said, flexing his muscles while he tickled the elf's insoles.

It may have been the strangest thing I'd ever seen. A hulking bodybuilder tickling another dude's feet? Who wants to see something like that? But I had to admit, it was better than violence. I didn't have the stomach for it. Worst-case scenario, he wouldn't break, and we'd have to resort to more extreme interrogation methods. But on the off chance that tickling the elf got him to tell us where the drow were, as weird as it was, it was worth a shot.

"If you don't tell us where the drow were sent, I'll have one of these giants tickle your armpits, too!" I said.

"Why them?" Aelfrich complained. "If I ha-ha-have to be t-t-t-tickled, can't sh-she do it?"

"I'm not tickling you, Aelfrich," Layla said. "You knew me as a little girl. Stop being a creeper."

Aelfrich bit his lip and grunted in a vain attempt to suppress his giggles.

"Tell him what he wants to know!" Jag demanded. "Or I'll shove my fist up your ass and yank out your colon!"

I cocked my head. "Talk about going from zero to a hundred on the torture scale."

"He has my girlfriend, and I'm losing my fucking patience!" Jag screamed. "Tell us *now!*"

I'd never seen Jag so red and furious. It was jarring how he'd gone so quickly from tickling to disembowelment. You'd think there'd be something in between that, like waterboarding, mild pain, burning, or whatever. But I understood it. I was one to bottle up my emotions and let them explode. It was one of the many character defects I'd had to sort out in the twelve steps. It had often led me to drinking. Now, it might lead Jag to homicide…um…elficide if he wasn't careful.

I rested my hand on Jag's shoulder. "Why don't you take a break, buddy?"

Jag looked up to the top of the spire and screamed at the top of his lungs.

"Now, Aelfrich," I said as Jag stormed off to one of the rooms. "We can let him come back and do whatever he wants to do. Or we can have a cordial, candid conversation between adults. Where are my friends?"

"Up your ass and to the left!" Aelfrich sneered.

I looked at the elf with feigned alarm. "That sounds serious. I might have to see a doctor about that. Unless you want to check, you know, to be sure."

I undid my belt, turned around, and pointed my butt at Aelfrich's face.

"No! *No!* NO!" Aelfrich said. "Not the butt. Please, anything but the butt!"

I snorted, tightening my belt again. "So, where are they, Aelfrich?"

My arm brushed the hilt of my sword.

You suck at this, Caspar. A butt in the face, really?

I smirked internally. She was right, but I wasn't inclined to inflict pain.

You don't want to hurt the guy, Aerin said, reading my mind. *But Brightborn has my sisters held hostage. You remember what he did to the last drow he captured. Sometimes you have to do things you don't want to do. Things that aren't really who you are.*

I shook my head. I hoped she wasn't right. But I felt like we were making progress. Even if tickling and butts in faces didn't draw the information out of him, he was breaking. I could feel it.

The dampeners are down, Aerin said. *You don't have to hurt him. Just frighten him. Water. Fire. You have more than enough magic at your disposal to get the information you need. Do what you have to do. You need my sisters, and they need you before Brightborn harms them.*

She was right. Just because Aelfrich said that they were safe, it didn't mean that he was telling the truth. It could be true that Brightborn wouldn't harm those who could wield magic since they might be a valuable part of his new world order. However, that didn't mean he wouldn't make their lives miserable. I had visions of him stabling them, breeding with them to populate his new elvish world. A grand 'ole time for king nasty, not so much for the drow.

I extended my hand and formed a bulb of water in my palm. I kicked Aelfrich back with my foot, pinched his nose, and tilted his head back.

"I have to warn you, I'm not exactly sure how this waterboarding shit works," I said. "So if you drown, oops. Sorry about that."

"I won't tell you a thing!" Aelfrich shouted.

I blasted my ball of water down his throat. He gagged, panic filling his eyes.

I formed a ball of fire in my hand. "Too bland. I know. How about we make it a little … spicier!"

"Stop!" Aelfrich said. "Don't do that!"

I closed my hand and extinguished the flames. I wasn't going to do it. But he didn't know that.

"Look," Aelfrich said, "Brightborn and I have our differences, but he's right. This planet is headed for destruction."

"Maybe," I said, snapping my fingers and reforming the tongue of flame on the tip of my thumb. "But I didn't ask you to justify why you're loyal to the king, Aelfrich. I asked you where the drow are."

"He's trying to save your planet!"

"Like he saved ours?" Layla interjected. "He destroyed our home, Aelfrich! All for the sake of his stupid war!"

"A war he fought to come here to save this world," Aelfrich said.

"Bullshit!" Layla shouted. "He did it because of his ego. He did it for power!"

I placed Aerin's blade at Aelfrich's throat. My hands started to shake. Yes, I'd killed before, but not by choice. I'd been forced to do it when I'd killed Hector with the Blade of Echoes. When I'd been forced to kill Fred with magic to save Layla. Never like this. Never in a calculated way.

"This blade won't just kill you," I said. "You know what this blade can do, don't you?"

"It's the blade of the drow princess, the one that holds her soul," Aelfrich said.

I nodded. "It separates souls from their bodies. It doesn't just kill you. It damns you, Aelfrich."

Honestly, I didn't know if what I was saying was true, but it sounded good. I did know that when I'd wielded it in Pruitt-Igoe the blade had separated the Unseelie fairies from their hosts. I knew that the blade had captured Aerin's soul when she'd enchanted it and struck herself with it.

Lord, I didn't want this dude to be stuck in the blade, too. Surely, that wouldn't happen. The dust Aerin had used was no longer on the blade, and I'd already used it—well, Aerin had—to slice down a few elves just recently.

I didn't count those on the list of people I'd killed. That was Aerin. I was just there, high on gas, watching her do it.

"I don't know exactly where he has the drow or where he intends to take them," Aelfrich said. "He can travel between stone henges, like the one here and the Ring of Brodgar."

I scratched my head. "How many rings like that are there?"

Layla shrugged. "Dozens."

"You're sure about this, Aelfrich?" I asked.

"I swear it!" Aelfrich said. "That's all I know! Brightborn doesn't share much. He holds his cards close to the chest. But I know he's moving. I haven't been to many of his spots. I've been here, most of the time, trying to convince the revolutionaries—"

"So there are revolutionaries?" Layla interjected.

Aelfrich cringed in regret at saying too much, then sighed. "Of course. The elves I led you to believe were the loyalists."

"I already suspected as much," I said. "That's why you told me not to show myself to them. Because they would have embraced Layla and me."

Aelfrich bit his lip.

Get to the elves first. They might be able to help you narrow down where the drow are if they've been observing Aelfrich.

I nodded, agreeing with the sentiment Aerin passed along through our soul-bound connection via the sword.

"All right, then we go join up with the revolutionaries. We know where they're at. We were just there."

Aelfrich snorted. "What are you going to do with me?"

I bit my lip. "I don't know. Probably nothing. I'll let the revolutionaries decide what happens to you."

Aelfrich stared at me with his eyes wide in horror. For the revolutionaries, whatever he'd done siding with Brightborn was personal. I doubted they had the same reservations I did when it came to violence.

CHAPTER THIRTY

We left the spire, aka stoner trap, and with Trixie buzzing around me, we all gathered close together. You'd think, with a relatively small group of giants, we wouldn't take up that much space. But they were giants, after all. Plus Jag, and Clarence, who'd grudgingly dragged his paws out into the cold. Layla held Agnus, who was muttering something under his breath—probably curses and more Elizabethan insults.

Trixie opened a portal back to the Ring of Brodgar. It might have been the largest portal I'd seen. Certainly, it was bigger than any I had made. It rivaled the old gateway at the confluence between the rivers and ley lines that used to lead between Earth and New Albion on the full moon.

Yeah, I was glad that Trixie was handling the gate travel. I could open a small portal and bring everyone through it in single file, or if they rubbed shoulders and held hands, double file. But Trixie could pull a giant portal over us and send us all there at the same time. It reminded me of elementary school when we used to play with a giant parachute out on the playground. Some of the kids would stand around holding it. When they threw it up and we ran underneath it, the parachute mushrooming over us, it gave me the same otherworldly sensation I felt as this giant fairy portal enveloped us.

Brag'mok and Gronk had Aelfric hog-tied, dangling from one of the fallen elves' spears. They were carrying him between them. Jag reached up periodically to tickle the elf's tootsies. A little weird, if you ask me. Jag was just a little *too* fixated on tickling feet. It made me wonder what his internet browser history might look like—not that I really wanted to know.

Either way, it was a harmless form of torture. In my book, Aelfrich deserved it. Not only did he take away my drow army, with one of Brightborn's legions, but he'd deceived me and gotten me high after nearly six years of sobriety.

It wasn't like I could talk about it with my sponsor. I suppose at the end of the day, if it didn't lead me back into drinking, it wouldn't be the end of the world. I was trying to save the world. Why was I so worried about sobriety date coins? Probably because if I ever drank again, it *would* be the end of the world. At least, the end of the world insofar as Caspar Cruciger remained a productive or even a tolerable citizen of it.

We appeared again in the Ring of Brodgar. To my surprise, we found ourselves surrounded by elves, hundreds of them with spears pointed at us.

But once they saw we had Aelfrich bound and tied, one of the elves, a slender male with a vague resemblance to Orlando Bloom as Legolas from *The Lord of the Rings* movies, approached with his bow in hand. He raised his hand and lowered it again. As he did, the rest of the elves lowered their spears.

"Princess," the elf said, making eye contact with Layla.

Layla cocked her head. "Illarion?"

The elf smiled wide. "You remember me?"

"Holy crap!" Layla said. "You're all grown up!"

Layla hugged the young elf and kissed him on the cheek.

"Illarion, this is my husband Caspar."

"It's an honor, Naayak," Illarion said, bowing his head. "Your reputation has fueled our rebellion. Were it not for your successes, I fear the spark of our revolution might not have tendered even a small flame."

I smiled. "So, you two know each other, I presume?"

Layla nodded. "I used to babysit his troublesome ass."

Illarion laughed. "If you couldn't tell, I've graduated from the trouble department."

Layla shook her head. "I'm surprised my father hasn't killed you!'

"Oh, he wants to," Illarion said. "But look at our numbers. Your father is still holding out hope that he might win us over. Those loyal to the throne outnumber us, but we have most of the youngest and fiercest fighters from New Albion. If he tried to kill me, this revolution would turn into an outright revolt. He's so distracted with piddly stuff like world domination that he can't be bothered to worry about us."

"So, he thinks once he takes over this world, he can throw lavish gifts at you, and you'll be so grateful that you'll submit to him again?" I asked.

Illarion nodded. "Yeah, but that's not what this movement is about. We're tired of fighting wars that do nothing but serve our king's ego."

I nodded. "I get that."

"It's not that we're against fighting," Illarion said. "We'll fight for our freedom. That's all we want. But if Brightborn succeeds with his plans, it won't only be the elves who will lose their freedom. This whole world will suffer."

"Well, we have Aelfrich," Layla said.

"I saw," Illarion said. "To be carried around by two orcs like that. It must be humiliating for him."

Layla giggled. "Yeah. But those 'orcs' are fighting with us. We'd love for you to join us, but you need to refer to them as giants. They get a little testy when you call them orcs."

Illarion nodded. "You want us to join you? Princess, we were hoping to crown you as our new queen."

"Queen?" Layla asked. "My father isn't dead. I can't be queen."

Illarion reached into a cloth sack that he had strapped around his back and retrieved a bronzed crown. "This belongs to you."

Layla's jaw dropped. "My mother's crown? How did you get that?"

Illarion grinned. "I'll just say, we went on a quest."

I snorted. "A quest? Like in video games?"

"What are video games?" Illarion asked.

Layla waved her hand. "Never mind. Illarion, I thought this was lost forever. After my mother…" She trailed off, sadness overtaking her.

I rested my hand on Layla's shoulder. Her mother had supposedly been abducted by a band of roving "orcs" at some point in the past. They'd taken her and her crown. Layla didn't talk about it much, but it was one of those early pains that she'd never totally get over.

When you're older and a parent dies, it sucks. It's scary. It feels strange, like you're alone for the first time in your life now you don't have them there as a safety net. It doesn't matter how old you are when that happens. I can't imagine how hard that must've been for her to go through that at such a young age, particularly given that her dad was a royal prick.

"If I wear this crown," Layla said, "my father will think it's treasonous."

"Doesn't he already think that, Layla?" I asked. "But he's been trying to convince the legion that you are the chosen one."

"I think that's propaganda," Layla said. "He knows I wouldn't embrace that role. He knows I believe you're the chosen one. My dad believes in elf supremacy."

"I agree," Illarion said. "Brightborn has never believed in the prophecy. But he knows that most of his legion does. He has to give them something, a reason to believe that his one-world government is the unity that the prophecy dictates. What better way to secure their support than to convince his legions that his heir, the one who will eventually succeed to his throne and take his place, is the chosen one?"

I nodded. "That makes sense. It's a way to justify his actions. He's playing the role of John the Baptist."

"Who?" Illarion asked.

"Preparing the way for one who is greater than him," I said. "Not that he thinks Layla is greater than he is."

"He doesn't think anyone is greater than him," Layla said, chuckling. "But he can use me to make our people think that's the case. Like I'm undergoing a time of trial and testing to prepare me to take his throne."

"Sounds like bullshit," Jag said, walking over and extending his hand.

Illarion cocked his head. "Yes, sir. You have a hand. Why would I touch yours if you've been touching bull shit?"

Layla giggled. "Handshaking is a custom in human society, Illarion. Like bowing. It's a polite way to greet someone. And 'bullshit' is an expression. It means nonsense."

Illarion scratched his head and grabbed Jag's hand. Jag squeezed it.

"Ouch!" Illarion said.

"Sorry. You're supposed to squeeze."

"Jag," I said. "Everyone knows you're a real man. You don't have to squeeze their hands extra hard to prove it."

Jag's face reddened. "Just didn't want him to think I was handing him a fish. I hate dead fish handshakes."

I chuckled. "Jag is a friend of mine."

Illarion nodded and looked at Layla. "So you'll wear the crown?"

Layla looked at it. "Nothing would piss off my dad more. So, sure. If you'll fight with us."

"Of course we will," Illarion said. "We've just been looking for an opportunity to join with you."

"You might want to do something with Aelfrich," I said. "He's kind of a bitch."

Layla giggled at Illarion's nonplussed expression. "That means a complainer. Not literally a female dog."

"Ah," Illarion said, shaking his head. "You humans have odd idioms."

I snorted. "That's nothing. Just wait until you meet my cat."

CHAPTER THIRTY-ONE

Illarion unbound Aelfrich and tossed him into a wicker cage. I don't know where they got it from. They'd probably made it.

"Will that hold him?" I asked. "He can use magic, you know."

Illarion smiled and showed me a small bag full of what looked like salt crystals. That pink salt they say is supposed to be good for you.

"What is that?"

"It will dampen his magic. Not as sophisticated as the dampeners the king has. Those are pricy. But the concept is the same. The crystals refract magical energies. Any spell cast within a circle made from them gets diffused, and the spell loses almost all its power."

"So, if you made a circle of that stuff around me…"

"You'd be as plain as any old human," Illarion said, smiling.

I grinned. "I wouldn't be plain. I'd still have my fantastic personality!"

Illarion smiled and looked at Layla. "Where'd you find this human? He's funny!"

"I think the prophet found him first," Layla said. "I'm just stuck with him!"

"Yeah, yeah, yeah," I said. "Stuck with me. You know, Illarion, she just wants me for my body."

"She does?"

"He's joking again, Illarion," Layla said.

The elf didn't look impressed with the joke. "Ah."

"So, we've got Aelfrich locked up," I said. "What does this coronation ceremony look like?"

Layla sighed. "It's pretentious and full of a lot of hoopla and regal shit."

Illarion shrugged. "That pretty much sums it up."

"Can't you just put on the crown and be done with it?" I asked.

Illarion shook his head. "We elves hold our traditions in high regard. It would be unthinkable to bypass the rituals. It's unorthodox enough as it is that the heir of a reining king would don a crown."

"My mother's crown…" Layla had a faraway look. "Where did you find it, anyway?"

Illarion scratched the back of his right arm with his left hand. "Layla, I…"

Layla cocked her head. "What is it, Illarion? What don't you want to tell me?"

Illarion sighed. "It was in the Royal Cavern of Oweynagat."

Layla stared at Illarion blankly. "No. Why would it… No, it couldn't be!"

"What is it?" I asked, discerning distress in Layla's voice.

"The Cavern of Oweynagat. It's a place of both birth and death. It's where royals are born and where we're laid to rest. If my mother was buried there with her crown and I didn't know it…"

"Your mother was not abducted by or…giants," Illarion said. "Based on the condition of her corpse, we believe she was beheaded."

"By my father," Layla said, her voice shaky and hushed. "I can't believe it. Why would he kill my mother?"

Illarion rested his hand on Layla's shoulder. "Let me show you something. I'll be right back."

Illarion stepped into a small tent. There were several in the area where the elves of the revolution had set up camp. They weren't as sophisticated as the store-bought tents we'd set up at the junkyard ranch for the drow. Those had zippers and floors. These looked like they'd been pitched with sticks and canvas. Functional, perhaps, but not at all fancy.

Still, in the temperate climate of Scotland in the summer, they were functional. The tents would keep the rain off their heads.

Illarion stepped back out of his tent with a small codex in his hands. It didn't have the age of the scrolls of the prophecy. The paper didn't look old at all. The style of the book, however, reminded me of early manuscripts of Christian scriptures I'd seen in biblical museums. Illarion handed this to Layla.

She opened it, her eyes wide, as she read the words. "My mom wrote this?"

Illarion nodded. "She did."

"This is some seditious stuff!" Layla exclaimed.

"From the reigning queen, no less," Illarion agreed. "It's her manifesto for revolution—how the elves should rise up and embrace a new peaceable way of life. It was a prescription for a peaceful revolution, a way to overthrow the king, her husband, and establish a governance where all people have a say and all people are valued."

Layla flipped through some of the pages. "She advised peace with the giants. I mean, she used the word orcs, but I don't know many elves who've tried to argue that the giants could be allies, partners in creating a better way of life on New Albion."

Illarion nodded. "We discovered that your mother tried to disseminate this manifesto for revolution throughout New Albion. She had copies made. They were set to be distributed, but the elf trusted to deliver them read a copy and reported his findings to the king. The next thing anyone knew, from what I've been able to learn, your mother had been abducted by orcs."

Layla wiped tears from her eyes. "I knew my dad was cruel. I knew he was a heartless son of a bitch. But he killed his own wife, his daughter's mother, because she threatened his power."

I rubbed Layla's back. "If you take that crown, you'll carry her mantle forward. It may not be a revolution on New Albion like she envisioned, but you can lead these elves to overthrow your father. You can be the one who helps them find a place in this world that is in harmony with the nations."

Layla shook her head. "But my father already has the world's most powerful governments wrapped around his finger."

"Until he doesn't," I said. "I'm not saying forging a new life here if we defeat your father will be easy. But you can do it, Layla."

Layla shook her head. "I can't. But *we* can, Caspar. If I'm going to send a message of unity, if you're going to unite the peoples as the prophecy declared, our marriage can be a sign to the rest of the world. We might be different races, but we are one people."

Illarion grabbed a purple robe out of his tent and draped it over Layla's shoulders. "It's a bit long, but it could work. It's just for the ceremony."

"You had royal robes just stuffed away in a tent?" I asked. "Weren't you all just at the North Pole and brought here suddenly by Trixie and Targigoth?"

Illarion chuckled. "They came and took us, along with Aelfrich and the loyalists. But it wasn't the first time we'd been here. We didn't stay at the North Pole all the time. Too cold!"

"So you've been traveling back and forth all this time?" Layla asked.

"Brightborn sent us to the North Pole to try to activate those stones," Illarion said.

"Why'd you go?" I asked, "and why'd he want you to go? Surely Brightborn realizes you oppose him?"

"He does and he doesn't," Illarion said. "He dismisses our movement because we're young. He imagines we'll grow out of it. We've played it carefully. We offer our help when we can. We only resist when we must. Besides, he insists on dealing with the revolutionaries and loyalists as one and the same. When he sends us anywhere or gives a universal order, he directs it to all of us. It's his way of discounting our movement to make it less appealing, I suppose. But when it comes to revolutions, as the late queen advised in her manifesto, the time to resist must be chosen carefully. We must not resist for the sake of resistance. We must wait for the chance to rebel when our resistance can make lasting change."

Layla chuckled. "I wish I was older and could have known that side of my mom. It sounds like she was brilliant."

"The manifesto is yours," Illarion said. "I mean, you're about to be crowned."

Layla bit her lip. "Do you think it's really in my mother's spirit that I be considered a queen? Kind of monarchial, don't you think?"

"The thing about being queen," Illarion said. "If you say that you won't be dictatorial, you can do that."

"You could establish a parliamentary system," I said. "Like the Brits or the Canadians."

"You wouldn't have to be a typical ruler," Illarion said. "You would serve as a figurehead to rally around as we stand together against Brightborn."

Layla pressed her lips together. "All right. Well, we need to do this fast. We need to rescue the drow."

"Once you're crowned, the rest of us will follow you wherever you'd like to lead us," Illarion said.

"See," Layla said, "that's what I'm saying. I don't want people to follow me out of fear like they do my father. If anyone is going to follow me, they should do so because they want to."

"They will want to, Layla," Illarion said. "We've been hoping for this day for a long time. Ever since you left and rumors of your opposition to the king started to trickle through the gossip mills of New Albion."

"Then let's get this done," I said. "I don't want to wait any longer. There's no telling which stone circle Brightborn has taken the drow to or where he's imprisoned them. Trixie is trying to find them now, but I don't think Brightborn will give them up if he can avoid it."

The revolutionary elves and the giants came together to see Layla get crowned. It was quite something to see the giants embrace these elves and for the elves to welcome them likewise. It had taken a lot for the giants to accept Layla and the drow, but these were New Albion elves, citizens of the kingdom that the giants had been at war with. The kingdom under Brightborn's leadership had murdered thousands of giants. Not just giants generally, but *these* giants' families and friends.

However, the giants knew that these elves were different. For centuries the giants had hoped some bold elves would rise up to defy the brutal elvish monarchy. Now, despite being too late to make a difference on New Albion, these elves were nonetheless ready for change. Change was inevitable now that they were on Earth.

There were two ways they could look at it. On the one hand, with so much change already, did anyone need more change? On the other hand, since change was already in the air, why not refashion their lives on Earth the way they wanted to live, no longer bound to the ways of life on New Albion.

Illarion said some things in ancient elvish. I didn't know what he was saying, but I imagined it was platitudes and formalities about the momentous occasion. It sounded like a liturgy. I knew that cadence in his voice. We had liturgies, responsive readings, in the church. You can tell when someone's reading or reciting something like that. It's a little wooden. Words are carefully chosen. It sounds…not disingenuous but devoid of real excitement or passion.

When I was a minister, I went out of my way to add a little enthusiasm to our liturgies. We were saying words that should elicit marvel, a thrill, unbridled joy. It didn't make sense to me that so many ministers recited the liturgies as if every service was a funeral.

Most of the words that Illarion spoke sounded like that. It wasn't his fault. This wasn't a ceremony that anyone had seen since Brightborn had been king for longer than most of them had been alive, but the words were nonetheless familiar. Memorized, perhaps, as a part of elvish education.

Only when Illarion took the crown in his hands did I detect any enthusiasm in his words. And when I did, it was an outpouring of excitement.

Standing behind Layla, he put the crown on her head, choking on his words as if holding back tears. "The day has come! Long live the Queen! Long live our future!"

The elves erupted in cheers. The giants cheered, too. For them, as it was for the revolutionaries, Layla's coronation meant a challenge to centuries of elven brutality.

Would she succeed? Would I succeed as the chosen one? It was impossible to know for sure. The prophecy made it clear that nothing was known, no future was certain.

However, we were ready to move forward, and if we had to fight our way through the legion to save the drow, that's what we'd do.

CHAPTER THIRTY-TWO

"How many more stone circles are there?" I asked Illarion.

"There are dozens," the elf said. "All I know is that he must be near one of them. And with all the drow and the rest of the loyalist elves and his legion nearby, they shouldn't be hard to find."

I sighed. I was getting tired. We'd tried the famous Stonehenge in Wiltshire, England. We teleported to the henge in Avebury. We explored the region surrounding the Callanish Stones, the Castlerigg Stone Circle, the Boscawen-Un, the Rollright Stones, Mitchell's Fold, the Tregeseal East stone circle, and a few others whose names I couldn't remember. Each time, I summoned air and aether and flew around the area. Trixie did the same, checking for magic, looking for anything that might linger in the air, any residual magic in the stones that signaled that Brightborn had been there, that anyone had traveled there.

So far, we were zero for…I don't know how many. I'd lost count. Until recently, I didn't even know about any of these stone circles aside from Stonehenge. It was something, seeing these temples the ancient druids used before they were forced to flee from our world. If these stones could tell tales like the stone circle did at the North Pole, I could spend the rest of my life hanging out in stone circles, evoking aether and observing centuries of magic, events erased from the records of history.

As a history geek, the potential that these stone monoliths represented made me giddy. I had to swallow that excitement. We had to find the drow. Even Aerin didn't have a clue where they could be.

I collapsed in the middle of one of the circles.

"You all right?" Layla asked.

"Too much flying for one day. I'm spent," I said.

"I don't know what other circle they could have traveled to," Illarion said.

"I think we should go back to the camp at the Ring of Brodgar," I said. "The giants are still there, along with the rest of the elves. We can get some rest and try again. Even if we found them, now, in this condition, I wouldn't be any help facing off with them."

If Layla noticed the dejection in my voice, she didn't acknowledge it. She simply put her hand on my back and kissed me on my cheek. She understood.

It's funny. I'd had the weight of the world on my shoulders for some time. But when people I felt responsible for were in danger, people I could identify, faces I knew, it felt twice as heavy.

Trixie took us back to the Ring of Brodgar. Illarion showed Layla and me to a tent.

"Not exactly fit for a queen and her husband," Illarion said. "But it's the best we have."

"It's perfect, Illarion," Layla said. We found Agnus and Clarence. Layla wanted both of them to join us. Agnus? That was fine, but Clarence? Don't get me wrong. I liked the bear. He'd saved us in the spire at the pole. But sharing a small tent with a bear who'd fill half of it wasn't exactly a prescription for a good night's rest.

Clarence curled up outside. I imagined he was tired, having had his hibernation interrupted again.

Agnus nuzzled my hand as I tucked my arm under my head and pulled one of the blankets that Illarion had left in the tent over my head.

"How'd it go?" Agnus asked.

"What, not insults today?" I asked, yawning.

"Not in the mood. Not after what has happened."

I nodded. "You're getting soft, buddy."

"The drow are hot. What can I say? Those pointy ears…mmm, sexy like mine."

"You mean like mine?" Layla asked.

"Meow," Agnus said. No, he didn't actually meow. He said, "Meow." As in, "Me-*ow*, I love me some elf ears."

"We tried every stone circle," I said. "No luck."

"*Every* stone circle?" Agnes asked. "Did you try Elrand's circle back in Missouri?"

I bit my lip. No, we hadn't. It was such an obvious one that it hadn't occurred to me. "How would Brightborn even know about that one?"

"Worth a shot," Layla said. "We could send Trixie to check it out while you get your rest."

I nodded. "Hey, Trixie!"

A few seconds later, Trixie came buzzing into my tent, her green glow illuminating the inside. "Hey, there, Caspar! What's up?"

I winced. As tired as I was, her chipper voice gave me an instant headache. "Agnus had a great idea. He said we should check around Elrand's circle."

"Interesting," Trixie said. "I sensed magic there, but I figured it was just latent magic in the stones."

"It might be," I said. "But they have Elrand with the rest of the drow. I wonder if he's trying to signal us by using some subtle magic to try to get your attention."

"That would make sense," Layla said.

I pushed my blanket aside and got to my knees, ready to act.

Layla put her hand on my chest and gently pushed me down. "Caspar, you said it yourself. Even if we found them now, you wouldn't be in any condition for a confrontation. Let Trixie check it out. It might be, like she thought, residual magic. If it is Brightborn and the drow, nothing of note is going to change between now and the morning. Trixie will let us know, and we can launch a surprise assault first thing in the morning."

I nodded, my vision swimming with exhaustion. "All right. I guess you're right. Just be careful, Trixie. Make sure they don't see you. Like Layla said, if they are there, we don't want them to know that we know that's where they went. We want to take them by surprise."

"You've got it, Caspar!" Trixie said.

My head fell back on my arm, which was doubling as a pillow given our simple sleeping situation. "I think the planet could be exploding and Trixie would still sound happy."

"Maybe that's because after living in hiding from the elves, she finally has a purpose," Layla said. "She's been blessed as queen of the fairies by the Furies, and she's helping you save the world that the fairies were always meant to protect. Seems to me her happiness is well-founded."

"I suppose," I said. "When this is over, maybe I'll be able to sit down long enough to experience happiness."

"I'm happy," Layla said. "Anxious about a lot concerning the future, yes, but happy, no less."

I smiled as Layla draped her arm over my curled-up body. "Yeah, I am, too, strangely enough. What's really weird is I'm happier since we figured out the final prophecy."

"Now that you know it all depends on you rather than fate?" Layla asked.

"Yeah," I said. "You'd think it would add to the pressure. At first, I think, it did. But you know, I don't feel trapped by the whole notion of inevitability anymore. I don't have to worry that an ominous prophecy is going to tell me that millions of people will die or someone I love is going to be stabbed."

"Makes sense," Layla said. "I think we're made that way. It's the way we're built. Humans and elves, I mean. We're basically the same, you know. We thrive when we're free."

"But is anyone ever really free?" I asked. "There are things that I can't just do. Things that are beyond my control. Things I can't change."

"Limitation isn't the opposite of freedom," Layla said. "If you think about it, gravity is a limitation. It holds you on the world. But it gives you the opportunity to live, to exercise your freedom. All liberty, I think, comes with limitations. Limits give us an orientation, a playing field where we can exercise our freedom."

I scratched my cheek. "I like that thought. You know, I've always thought something like that. As a believer, I've felt that I'm free, subject to no one except God. But at the same time, I'm bound to be a servant to all. Kind of a paradox."

"We're free to serve, free to love," Layla said. "Sometimes I think we discover more about ourselves and we find more joy when we stop fighting against limitations and embrace liberty within our sphere."

"I agree," I said, yawning. "Right now, I'm going to embrace my freedom to sleep. Hopefully, I'll dream about you naked because I want you right now, but I don't have the energy left to do a damn thing about it."

Layla giggled as she spooned herself behind me. I wasn't even remotely comfortable, but I was so tired it didn't matter. I closed my eyes and fell asleep.

CHAPTER THIRTY-THREE

"Rise and shine!" the glowing green ball in flight that I knew was Trixie said in too chipper a tone for what was probably no later than five in the morning.

I still didn't have my phone, so I was relying on my biological clock. As exhausted as I'd been the night before, it would probably feel like five in the morning for a while.

I wouldn't know if I had enough rest until I got up and the blood started flowing.

Lord, I missed coffee. I'd even settle for crappy AA coffee at this moment. If I was ever injured and needed blood, they'd have to run it through grounds and a filter before they added it to my body. I'd probably reject the transfusion otherwise.

"They're there! They're there!" Trixie squealed. "We have to go, Caspar! Get up! Get up! Get up!"

I mustered the energy to get up out of my makeshift bed. Even my often-popped air mattress back at the junkyard ranch was more accommodating than this dirt-and-blanket bed.

"They're at Elrand's place?" I asked.

"Not exactly," Trixie said. "When I got there, I could tell that the magic wasn't coming from the stones. Elrand was casting something subtle like we thought he might!"

"Like an SOS, a distress call?" Layla asked, rubbing her eyes.

"Exactly!" Trixie said.

"All right, Trixie. Where are they?"

"The drow are in a cave south of there. They're sealed in with magic, but nothing you can't get past!"

"I can dispel magic forcefields?" I asked.

"It's a cave!" Trixie trilled. "You have earth magic!"

"Oh, yeah," I said. "So long as I can avoid a cave-in."

"Flex those earthen muscles," Layla said. "Blast the earth around the cave open from above, and we can pull them out of there."

"Where are the legion and the loyalists?" I asked.

Trixie shook her head. "I couldn't find them."

"Of course not," I said. "Do the drow in the cave appear to be unguarded?"

"Yup!" Trixie said. "How great is that?"

I sighed. "It isn't."

"It's obviously a trap," Layla said. "My father knows we can find them. He can't be so foolish as to think that Elrand wouldn't use magic. He went to Elrand's stone circle. He knows he can do it, yet he didn't set up dampeners."

"That makes sense," I said. "Totally a setup."

"So, what do we do?" Trixie asked.

"Get the rest of the fairies ready," I said. "It might be a trap, but what choice do we have?"

"The drow probably aren't being fed. They may have cave water, but that's it. If Elrand had earth magic, he could break out of there himself."

"He doesn't," I said. "Not without the five stones to help him access it. But he has aether and air."

"We can't just leave them in the cave," Layla said. "Trap or not."

I nodded. "What Brightborn might not realize is that you'll be leading the revolutionaries, Layla. He might be leading us into a trap, but we have surprises up our collective sleeve as well."

"All right, we need to gather everyone together so we can discuss our strategy."

"I agree," I said, nodding. "I want to include everyone in this decision. If they're going to be risking their lives, they need to have a say in how we do this."

"I agree," Layla said. "Crown or not, I'm not going to demand anyone fight if they aren't willing or don't believe in the cause. If someone is going to put their life on the line for a cause, no matter what that cause might be or how others might assess the threat, it has to be their own choice."

"I agree." I sniffed myself. "Damn, I smell like a man."

"You do!" Layla said, chuckling. "But you can rain shower yourself at any time."

"Might be a good idea," I said. "Some people might refuse to fight just so they can get a little fresh air absent me."

Layla giggled, "It's not that bad. Come on."

"Take the message to Illarion," I said. "I'll freshen up and talk to Gronk, Targigoth, and Brag'mok. They can relay the situation to the rest of the giants. We don't want to waste time, but everyone needs to know what they're walking into. Especially since it's likely that Brightborn is setting us up for an ambush."

Layla and I exchanged quick kisses. Agnus was still curled up on the floor, snoring. I'd let him snooze as long as possible. He wasn't useless in a fight. The first time we encountered B'iff, after the stabbing when we thought the giant was still our enemy, Agnus clawed the fuck out of his face. Still, fighting wasn't his forte. As a self-proclaimed deity, he preferred to do his smiting with words.

Clarence, on the other hand, was a force. He was a bear, after all. You don't want to mess with bears, no more than you want to mess with Sasquatch. It won't turn out well for you, no matter how many jerky sticks you toss at them.

I went and found one of the stones at the Ring of Bragdor to hide behind and stripped down. I formed a little rain cloud over my head, scrubbed myself down the best I could. No towel, I channeled air to blow-dry my body. It was the best I could do. I got dressed again in the clothes Aelfrich had given me before I'd realized he was an asshole.

Layla was discussing the plans with Illarion when I approached. I nodded at them as I walked past. They were discussing whether we could use Aelfrich as a trade, a prisoner exchange. I heard Layla say she didn't think it would work. Brightborn didn't value one person's life more than he would a strategic advantage. Getting Aelfrich back offered the elves less advantage than they gained by keeping the drow warriors from us. From what I could tell, Illarion agreed. We'd have to break the drow out of that cave by force and hope we had the resilience to withstand the ambush.

Hardly a flawless plan. I hoped that the giants had a few ideas, too.

I gathered Gronk, Targigoth, and Brag'mok and explained the situation. They surprisingly agreed that it was worth the risk to save the drow. I wasn't sure they would have made the same assessment a few weeks or even a few days ago. I wasn't sure what had changed since we'd left the junkyard ranch.

Perhaps it was that we were finally doing something. We'd gained some ground on Brightborn. We'd lost some ground on Brightborn. All things considered, I wasn't sure if we were in a better position now than we were back at the junkyard ranch. But now we were making things happen, not just waiting for things to happen. The giants knew that despite gaining the revolutionaries, we were weaker without the drow than we'd be if we got them back.

Was it just strategy? Or were the giants beginning to see that we were all more alike than different? That it wasn't a matter of giants and elves, humans and drow, or any racial distinctions. What mattered is what we were fighting *for*, and to a certain degree, what we were fighting against.

"What about Aelfrich?" I asked Illarion.

"I'll leave three elves here to guard him. I'd rather not bring him into the battle. Too much liability. Especially since he can wield magic. If he were to get free, it would complicate matters immensely."

I nodded. "Good plan."

"You ready?" I shouted to Brag'mok. Brag'mok nodded, then turned and said something to Gronk.

"Everyone, armor up!" Gronk shouted.

The other giants roared a "Broo-Hah!" in response. I wasn't sure what that meant, but I imagined it was a war cry. "Yes, sir," with a little more vigor and enthusiasm than mere obedience.

Their armor would come in handy. The elves were proficient archers. I expected they'd strike fast. Firing arrows at us was the most likely attack method they'd employ. They'd try to take as many out as they could before I could react. A whirlwind around us might make aiming arrows and keeping them on course impossible. If I churned the air fast enough, most of the arrows might not even get through.

If I knew where the elves were, I could call fire down on them. I could shake the earth. But I had my limits. I could strike hard. I could strike fast. However, as I'd discovered many times so far, after a while, my body gave out. It wasn't that my abilities waned or my access to magic faded, but I lost the ability to focus. If I pushed hard and long enough, I'd pass out.

That meant, whatever I did, I had to be careful about how I threw my magic around. Once I was tapped out, I was tapped out. I had to make sure I made it count.

Trixie and the other fairies buzzed in a circle around us, waiting until we were ready. Most of the giants carried broadswords or axes. The elves had spears, and a few of them carried bows that resembled Layla's. Jag had his guns, his right and his left. The giants had armored him. I wasn't sure how great he'd be in a real battle. He wasn't a soldier anymore, but he was certainly intimidating. The giants had given him a one-handed ax. Small for the giants, but a fairly hefty weapon for Jag. He was big for a human.

Layla was wearing her crown. It was sure to piss off her dad, but it invigorated the elves. Illarion raised his spear and gathered them in single file behind her.

"Trixie!" I shouted. "We're ready!"

I didn't have to ask twice. Trixie formed a giant portal, large enough to take our whole army to Missouri, and dropped it over us.

CHAPTER THIRTY-FOUR

"Where are the drow from here?" I asked Trixie after we appeared in a valley. The hills all around us were covered in trees, limiting our view of the landscape. "This isn't a great spot to be in if you're trying to avoid an ambush."

"Sorry!" Trixie said. "But the drow are right beneath where you're standing!"

I snorted. Of course they were. Brightborn had chosen a cave that ran deep in the middle of the Ozark Mountains. Yes, they are technically considered mountains. They were nothing compared to the Rockies or the Appalachians. The Ozark Mountains are more like large hills. None of them are high enough to have snow caps.

But Missouri has more caves than any state in the United States. One of the state's nicknames is "The Cave State." Most of the caves are found in the Ozarks. One of them was directly beneath us.

"Can you guys watch my back?" I asked.

Illarion and Gronk both nodded.

"Establish a perimeter," Gronk shouted.

"Back them up!" Illarion commanded in turn.

Layla rested Agnus on Clarence's back. Agnus stood there, stiff as a board, his back arched as if he didn't know what to do.

Clarence chuffed, and Agnus gradually relaxed his body.

Layla drew an arrow from her quiver and readied her bow.

"Are they really just going to let me open this cave and save them?" I asked.

Layla shrugged. "I don't see them anywhere. Trixie and the other fairies are scouring the mountains looking for the elves. If they get any sight of them, they'll let us know."

I sighed. "I don't like this at all. Something doesn't feel right."

"We knew it wouldn't," Layla said. "We anticipated a trap. Maybe they're taken aback that the revolutionaries are with us? They might be reevaluating their strategy. If they saw us appear here at all."

"I find it hard to believe that they don't know we're here," I said. "They wouldn't go to these lengths to hide the drow in a cave beneath the perfect spot to conduct an ambush if they weren't going to keep someone on watch."

"I agree," Layla said.

"Can we get them out?" Jag asked.

I nodded. "I'll have your girlfriend back in your arms shortly. I just want to be sure we know what we're dealing with here."

I touched Aerin's' sword. "Any thoughts?"

Be careful. I'm as perplexed about what's going on here as you are. All I know is that you have to get my sisters out of there.

"I agree," I said.

Layla glanced at my hand, touching the sword. "Does Aerin have any ideas?"

I shook my head. "She's stumped, too. But she's right. We need to get the drow out of that cave. We'll worry about whatever your father is planning afterward."

"Do it," Layla said. "If my father is surprised at all that we have Illarion and the rest aligned with us, we have to take advantage. The longer we wait, the more time he'll have to adapt his plan."

I nodded. I drew on earthen magic. I'd stopped an earthquake before. Now, it was almost like I was trying to do the opposite. I had to focus. As I did, I could sense the cave beneath my feet.

"You guys need to get out of here," I said to Layla and Jag. "I have to blow this cave open. Otherwise, I'll risk caving it in."

Layla and Jag nodded and stepped away from the area. Clarence followed them up the side of one of the hills with Agnus on his back.

"This might be messy!" I shouted. "Take cover! Watch for flying rocks!"

Collapsing the cave would have been easy. I'd just need to unsettle the earth. But I had to harness the earth and stone all around them. Most of it was limestone. It was heavy. I had to throw it hard to make sure none of it fell back in on the drow, and I had to maintain enough focus to ensure that the flying debris didn't take out anyone else.

The last thing we needed was to lose some of our number by friendly magical fire. Or, earth, technically, since fire was a different kind of magic entirely. But "friendly earth" just doesn't have the same ring to it as "friendly fire." In this case, though, it could be just as deadly.

I drew on my earthen elemental magic and focused on taking the roof of the cave up and away. I gathered air and aether and rose to hover over the shaking ground beneath me. I used more air magic to control the flying pieces of rock and divert them away, preventing them from hitting anyone.

Between flying all over God's green Earth the day before and wielding all this magic now, I didn't know how much more I could handle. Sweat beaded on my brow. My hands started to shake as I hovered in mid-air. If I lost focus, I'd go crashing into the hole forming below me.

I had to keep my mind alert. There was so much going on at once. Opening the ground, making sure that none of the debris hurt anyone, staying afloat.

I saw the drow in the cavern below. Elrand extended his hand. What was he doing? My vision started to blur. I couldn't hold on any longer. Then a breeze picked me up.

Elrand was casting magic without a stone circle.

As he lowered me, I saw Elrand's magic was connected to a stone on one of the hills. If there was one, there were more. We were in the middle of a stone circle.

"Quick!" Rina shouted. "We have to get Layla out of here!"

"Layla…" I was so oblivious to what was happening I didn't even realize it. As Elrand set me down on the ground, he shot more air at Layla as if he was trying to lift her off the ground.

"We're not going to make it!" Elrand shouted.

"Make what?" I asked. He couldn't hear me. None of them could. I clenched my fists. I had nothing left. I was spent.

Then I saw the magic swirling around all five stones. This wasn't Elrand's doing. Figures in black were standing atop the mountains surrounding us.

"Layla!" I shouted.

She looked back at me, her eyes wide in horror as her purple, celestial magic spread from her hand, where she wore her rings, and enveloped her body.

Magic of every color, corresponding with each element, shot up into the sky in a giant, swirling cone and drew Layla's purple magic into it.

A weapon…

They were going to use her as a weapon!

But why? What were they trying to do?

I tried to get to my feet, but my knees buckled beneath me. I couldn't draw on any more magic. My body wouldn't respond. I crawled over to Layla and touched her, trying to stop the magic. What could I do? I didn't know.

I focused on aether, thinking maybe that would work. But it didn't. I was too weak, and there was no telling if I could do anything with her celestial magic even if I had full strength. I could have harnessed the elements above us, the magic swirling around the stones…

Dammit.

That was why Brightborn had kidnapped the drow and trapped them in that cave. So I'd have to use my magic to save them. So I'd be helpless to stop this from happening.

I looked around. On one of the mountains, the elven king stood next to one of the sorcerers, his golden robe glinting in the hot summer sun.

He held something in his hand. A phone? Was he recording this? What the hell was he doing?

Layla and I were the only ones left in the circle. Elrand couldn't pull her out. He couldn't overpower the other sorcerers using the stones. The other drow, along with the giants and elves, were charging up the hills after Brightborn's sorcerers. But other elven legionnaires appeared beside the sorcerers with bows, showering them with arrows.

They had to take cover.

Layla's celestial power was expanding, flowing out of her body like a river and into the sky.

Until it wasn't.

She collapsed next to me. The elves on the hills retreated as Brightborn lowered the hand holding his phone and left with his legion.

I had nothing left. Layla had nothing left. We lay there in the middle of what we'd just discovered was a stone circle, gasping for air.

I touched Aerin's blade.

He's framing you, Caspar. You and Layla.

I sighed. I couldn't even put two words together to respond.

He's destroyed something using Layla's power and he recorded it, just like you did when you recorded your miracle. Whatever her magic was used to destroy, it will appear as though you're guilty of it. Both of you.

I clenched my hand on the hilt of Aerin's blade and forced myself to roll over. I put my other hand on Layla's hand.

"What did I do?" Layla asked.

"It wasn't you," I said, "but he made it look like it was. Whatever he did, it wasn't good."

CHAPTER THIRTY-FIVE

I was still catching my breath. The drow had been saved, but what was the cost?

The giants, elves, and drow were making their way back to our position as Trixie and the fairies buzzed overhead. Jag had one arm around Rina and his phone in his free hand. Based on the look on his face, it wasn't good.

"What is it?" I said, with Layla in my arms. "Is everyone okay? Did anyone get hit by arrows?"

"All of the giants are fine and accounted for," Gronk said.

"The drow are well," Rina added.

"As are the elves," Illarion said.

I took a deep breath. I was afraid that the shower of arrows the elven legion had released to slow everyone down had hit someone. It was sheer luck that no one was injured. But Jag still looked disturbed.

It wasn't because anyone in our group was hurt. The way Brightborn had used Layla's power... Someone was hurt somewhere. I suspected that was what Jag was finding out about as he scrolled through his phone.

"Please tell me it isn't bad," I said, wincing. "Did he destroy St. Louis?"

Jag shook his head. "The block on my phone was lifted a few minutes ago. The stories are just coming in. The news feeds are reporting that the Pentagon was attacked."

I snorted. "A military target. Of course."

"Are they saying who was responsible?" Layla asked.

Jag shook his head. "Not yet. It's just coming in."

"Brightborn was taking a video," I said. "It's only a matter of time before Layla and I are blamed. They'll consider us terrorists."

"We need to get out of here," Elrand said. "We'll carry you two. We can't run the risk that they'll come back and use Layla again. We have to get her out of the stone circle."

"Trixie!" I shouted.

The fairy queen spiraled toward me.

"Hi, Caspar." Trixie wasn't quite as chipper as usual. Even she recognized that we were in deep shit at the moment.

Hell, deep shit was an understatement. Deep shit would be enough shit to fill a small pool. We were in a flood of shit. As if God had said to Noah, build a toilet because I'm about to crap on the world for forty days and forty nights. *That* level of shit, and there wasn't any way we could flush this problem away.

"I don't understand why he would do that," Layla said.

I snorted. "Nothing unifies people like a common enemy. What I can do is on the level of what he could do if he attacked the planet with the battle crystals. I could command the elements, I could unleash earthquakes, I could flood cities and release tornados. You can't fight something like that with guns and bombs. You need magic to fight magic."

"So he's going to offer his aid, the aid of the elven legion," Layla said.

"Probably," Elrand said. "But he'll make the offer with a cost. He'll demand power and authority. Since you can travel anywhere in the world by fairy gate, he'll demand universal jurisdiction."

"His one-world government," I said, shaking my head.

"First thing's first," Brag'mok said. "We have to get out of here."

"Where can we go?" I asked.

"Here's the thing," Layla said, wincing in pain. "Dad's plan gets thwarted if you get caught. He doesn't want us to be found. The longer we're on the run, the more we evade the humans' attempt to stop us, the more leverage he has."

"So, I turn myself in," I said.

"Don't even think about it," Layla said.

"Why not?" I asked. "If it prevents Brightborn from getting what he wants."

"It won't stop him," Illarion said. "I don't know how your governments work, but if you are taken prisoner, all it will do is delay Brightborn's plans. He already has significant influence over the government. He'll still get what he wants, sooner or later. If you're gone, our chances of stopping him are next to nothing."

I sighed. "I get it. So we have to fight."

"But first," Elrand said. "We need to get out of here. We need to recover and regroup."

"Can we go back to the junkyard?" Rina asked.

I shook my head. "That location is compromised."

"The stone circles in Scotland?" Layla asked.

"Those are popular tourist spots," I said.

"We need to go get Aelfrich," Illarion said. "But after that, we can go back to the North Pole."

"*Noooooooo!*" Agnus shouted as he approached us, riding on Clarence's back. "Too cold!"

I snorted. "I hate to say it, but it makes the most sense. We'll be off the grid."

Layla shook her head. "But without a new place to stay now that the spire from before was compromised."

"Not true," Illarion said. "We had our spires there, too. Those aren't booby-trapped. I can promise you that. Aelfrich didn't build ours. We did. We have enough room for everyone."

"It's the only choice we have right now," I said. "Sorry, Agnus. I don't like the cold, either. But we need a place to regroup."

"Fine," Agnus said. "Methinkst thou art a general offense and every man should beat thee."

I smirked. "Trixie, take us back to the pole!"

With all of us gathered on the edge of where the cavern used to be, Trixie formed a fairy gate over us and dropped it over our heads.

For a second, I was relieved. We were out of that stone circle. We were clear of Brightborn. Then I felt the cold. My relief was short-lived, and I still couldn't walk.

CHAPTER THIRTY-SIX

Illarion helped us get settled in the spires. They'd sort it all out. Layla and I needed to rest. At least the spire had beds. I'd slept on the ground and popped air mattresses for so long I'd almost forgotten how amazing a bed felt when you were tired. It wasn't the best bed that money could buy. It was firmer than my old bed at the apartment, but it was a thousand times better than the ground or the floor, and I wasn't complaining.

It was the worst time to sleep. I didn't have a choice. I needed to rest. I felt like I imagined Santa Claus must feel when he returns to the North Pole after busting his ass every Christmas. Only, I didn't have the satisfaction of having brought toys to all the good boys and girls throughout the world. I'd saved the drow, and I was happy about that. But if the whole world was against us, had I done much more than delay the inevitable?

Brightborn couldn't kill me because I was soul-bound to Layla. He wouldn't kill her unless he absolutely had to. But he'd wipe out everyone who supported me. He wouldn't hesitate to take down the giants, the drow, probably even the other elves.

Sure, he wanted to preserve anyone who could wield magic for his new world order. At least, that's what we'd been led to believe when he'd kidnapped the drow. Maybe he didn't care about that, and it was all a ruse to get us into the stone circle he'd erected in the Ozark Mountains.

Maybe his plan all along was to trap us between the mountains and weaken me so he could use the stone circle to extract celestial power from Layla so he could frame us as a "common enemy" that the world could unite against. All so he could march in as the world's knight in shining armor, the hero who would save the planet not just from climate change but from the greater scourge—the vile threat that was me.

It wasn't long ago that I'd feared I might be the Antichrist. That notion had been thoroughly disposed of. If anything, Brightborn fit the bill. However, the world would now see me as an existential threat.

I could wield magic. Layla could, too. They saw Layla with celestial power flowing through her, me lying there beside her. They'd already seen what I could do with the trees. At least, the government saw it. So did a few others. They knew I was powerful, and they were right.

But I wasn't the threat. I was trying to save the world. Brightborn was the one who would destroy our civilization with his desire to emerge as emperor supreme.

When Layla and I woke up, it was quiet. Too quiet. Why was it so damn quiet in the spire? Giants are never quiet. There was always a chorus of grunts and farts following them wherever they went. With all the drow and elves, not to mention Jag with all his bravado, I figured there'd be a constant stream of chatter throughout the spire, and it was too cold for everyone to be outside.

"What the hell?" I looked out of the room where Layla and I were and didn't see a soul.

"Where is everyone?" Layla asked.

"I wouldn't have said 'what the hell' if I knew."

"Maybe the rapture came, and we were left behind," Layla said.

I snorted. "You know I don't believe in that interpretation of Revelation."

Layla shrugged. "You're the one who is always saying you should be willing to admit that you could be wrong about doctrines."

I chuckled. "Fair enough, but if that was the case, I find it hard to believe that Agnus got raptured and we were left behind."

"Or Jag," Layla said, chuckling.

"Of course." I smirked. "The Bible says something to the effect of being alert, not being asleep when he returns. Maybe that passage was a lot more literal than I expected."

"Come on," Layla said. "They have to be somewhere nearby."

Layla and I found some warmer clothes. Not the coats we'd brought, but we found a couple of elf parkas. These spires had housed all the revolutionary elves. There weren't doors or locks. We headed out onto the ice surrounding the spires.

I would have used fire magic to warm myself up, but after what I'd just been through, I didn't want to get caught in a situation where I'd channeled too much magic before I needed it. Surely Brightborn hadn't attacked. We'd have heard it. There'd be bodies around.

"You want to fly up and take a look?" Layla asked.

"We can see far enough," I said. "I'd rather conserve my energy. Just in case."

Layla shrugged. "The stone circle, maybe? Ice Henge?"

I narrowed my eyes. "Seriously?"

"I'm not going inside it! I just mean that maybe they're there."

I chuckled. "I know that much. I just couldn't believe you'd named the thing Ice Henge."

"It fits, doesn't it?" Layla said.

"Sort of," I said. "I mean, Stonehenge works because the thing is made of stone."

"Whatever," Layla said. "Like any of the names for the other henges make any sense."

"I'm sure they do for people who know the reasons for their names."

Layla shrugged. "What else would you call it?"

"I don't know," I said. "Do we have to name it?"

Layla chuckled. "We're calling it Ice Henge. It's already decided."

"By whom?" I asked. "The council of henge-namers?"

"That's not a thing!" Layla said. "I decided. And so, it's done."

"I don't get a say?"

Layla raised an eyebrow. "Bitch, please."

I laughed as we made our way across the ice. We arrived at the stone circle. There wasn't any evidence of anyone nearby. There wasn't any residual magic in the stones. Nothing at all.

I poked my tongue into the inside of my cheek. "You might be right about that rapture shit, after all."

"I know, right?" Layla said, rubbing her brow.

"Even Agnus and Clarence seem to have abandoned us," I said.

Layla frowned. "The strangest thing."

"Well, we might as well go back inside," I said.

"I agree. It's cold!"

Layla and I made our way back to the spire. I glanced at the panel by the front door.

"Shit, we never got our hands programmed into this thing."

Layla bit her lip. "We got out just fine."

"Yeah, because normal spires, those not set up as traps, let anyone out with no problem. Like a door on any house. The deadbolt locks to prevent people from the outside coming in. Anyone on the inside can turn it and unlock it without a key."

"Shit. We're stuck here, out in the cold," Layla said.

I wrapped my arms around the front of my chest. "Yeah. I mean, I could fairy portal us somewhere else. But I don't want to leave until I know what the hell happened to everyone."

Layla nodded. "I agree. There aren't' any signs of a struggle. If they left on purpose, someone will be coming back to—"

Layla's words were interrupted by a familiar buzzing. I turned to see a green orb—a familiar fairy.

"Trixie!" I said. "What the heck is going on?"

Trixie giggled. "April fools?"

I cocked my head. "It's August. How do you know about April fools day anyway?"

Trixie shrugged. "I'm a fairy. Many of us are tricksters. It's a holy day! Always has been!"

"So, what's the joke?" I asked. "Where is everyone, really?"

"Back in St. Louis!" Trixie said.

I bit the inside of my cheek. "In St. Louis?"

Trixie giggled. "The big guy, the one with all the muscles..."

"Jag?" Layla asked.

Trixie nodded. "That's the one! By the way, is that his real name?"

"It's his last name. His first name is Will; Jag is short for his last name. Whatever. It's beside the point. What about him?"

"Oh, yeah, yeah, yeah." Trixie laughed. "When you two fell asleep, Jag realized, welp, no cell service at the North Pole! Crazy, right?"

"Totally. Verizon needs to get on the ball with that," I said.

"Wait," Layla said. "You're saying they left us here so Jag could go check his text messages?"

"No, silly!" Trixie said. "He had to check the news! He found out, Brightborn's video was put out. The government blamed you for the attack on the Pentagon."

"Of course they did," I said.

"But somehow, your other video got out, too," Trixie continued. "Someone leaked it! Then, people started noticing that you and Layla were in pain in Brightborn's video. They said, you know in those little comments under the videos, that it looked like you were scared. Like someone was manipulating you!"

"Well, they were!" Layla said.

"So, when that other video came out, the very first one with Brag'mok on it, people started rioting! It's out of control, Caspar! They're all carrying signs, like, Free Caspar, and pictures of a cartoon ghost for some reason, and Down with the Elf King."

"Wait," I said. "The people are rising up against the government?"

"Bingo!" Trixie said. "Come on! They're all rallied at the Arch!"

Layla and I exchanged glances. Then I started laughing. "I can't believe it."

"Me neither," Layla said, shrugging. "But if the people are rebelling, this might be our best chance!"

"I agree! Trixie, take us to the Arch!"

CHAPTER THIRTY-SEVEN

We appeared beneath the trees I'd grown. No one had cut them down, which came as a surprise. I'd expected they'd do whatever they could to get rid of all the evidence that suggested I might be anything other than a terrorist threat since the government had *attacked* us.

I mean, rapid tree growth is hardly a terrorist act. Well, except from the perspective of those who have dendrophobia. It's a real thing. Google it.

My whole army was assembled under the Arch: the giants, the drow, the elves, and yes, even Clarence and Agnus. You'd think people would be shitting themselves, seeing a bear on the loose in the city. But the crowd that had assembled there, filling the field around the Arch, wasn't fazed.

"What is going on here?" I asked.

Jag chuckled. "They're here for you. They're ready to march."

"To march on what?" I asked.

Jag shrugged. "I don't know. Isn't there a federal courthouse downtown? I don't know that they are going to march all the way from St. Louis to Washington, DC. But Trixie could take everyone there."

I chuckled. "I don't know about that."

I waved at the crowd. One man stood at the front, a black man who I recognized. I couldn't mistake his wide smile from a mile away.

"Cecil?" I asked, walking up to my old friend. I'd healed his daughter one day when he'd showed up at my church. Since then, time and again, he'd surprised me. He'd supported me several times when I needed support the most. It just dawned on me that I'd sent him the video.

"We're here for you, Reverend!" Cecil said.

"Holy smokes," I said. "You realize the government wants me arrested, right?"

"We know," Cecil said. "But we ain't gonna let that happen, Reverend. If they want to take you down, they gotta take all of us down."

I looked over the crowd. I had no idea how many thousands of people there were. The last time I'd seen this many people gathered in one place was back in Kansas City when the Royals won the World Series in 2015. They say more people flooded the city that day than the whole population of Kansas City. All for the celebration parade. They'd had parades like that in St. Louis, too. But the Royals had gone so long without one, and the city connected so well with that team that it brought people out from under the woodwork.

That's the closest thing I could think of that was like what I saw here. A sea of people, as far as the eye could see.

And I had my army—all armed, all ready to fight if need be. I had protection.

"This is unbelievable," I said.

"Believe it," Cecil said. "We know you weren't behind that attack."

"We were set up," I said.

"We know," Cecil said. "Everyone knows it. That elf king might be able to pull the wool over the eyes of the President and Congress, but he can't fool the good people of this country!"

I smiled. "So, what do we do from here?"

"We make our demands!" Cecil said. "They know what we want. We want the truth. No more lies, and we want that elf king exposed. We want the truth out! What your friend Brag'mok said in the video. We ain't gonna let that elf king do what he did to his planet here. If we're gonna save this planet, we're gonna do it ourselves. We don't need his lies and false promises."

"You know what," I said, turning to Jag. "I think you might have had a good idea from the start."

"You mean marching on Washington?" Jag asked.

I smiled. "Hey, Trixie! Do you think you can take all these people to Capitol Hill? I think it's time we stand up to the government and make our demands."

"Capitol Hill?" Trixie asked.

"Washington, DC," I said, nodding.

"All these people?" Trixie asked.

"Every one of them."

Trixie giggled. "I might not be able to do it alone! Thankfully, I'm not alone!"

A whole swarm of fairies appeared around us. At least a hundred of them, all with glowing green auras. The people gathered around, near, and behind Cecil gasped—not out of fear, but in awe and wonder. Most of them didn't even know fairies were real until now, much less had they seen one.

I grabbed Aerin's sword. It seemed like the right thing to do. Then I raised it into the sky. "Who wants to take this message to Washington?" I shouted.

The crowd cheered. I wasn't sure how many of them heard me, but the word would spread.

Golden portals started forming over all of us. Trixie had the largest one, of course. She took care of my regular crowd. The other fairies buzzed around the crowd, forming portals and lowering them over the people. Large swaths of people disappeared into the fairy gateways.

Trixie lowered her portal over us—the giants, elves, and drow—and we reappeared on the steps of the Capitol building in Washington DC.

I hadn't been there since a school trip in the seventh grade. It was a tradition in my school district. Seventh graders, if they had permission, took a spring trip to the nation's capital. I remembered the whole bus trip from Missouri clearly.

The capital city hadn't lost any of its luster since. If anything, I was more in awe of it since I understood better than ever before the significance of the place. It wasn't just a place where out-of-touch politicians gathered to throw shade at each other, although it had become that. This was a place where monuments to freedom stood tall. It was a place where thousands had marched before, even millions, for civil rights, to protest injustice, to stand up for equality. If Brightborn took charge, if he ruled the nations, would he allow something like this?

The crowds cheered, even as they laughed, and some cried when they appeared on Capitol Hill. I imagined some were frightened. They probably didn't realize what was coming. They may not have realized that I fully intended to send them home again via fairy portal.

Still, the shouts and the chants filled the air. These people believed in me. They didn't believe the lies. They were demanding that the government sever ties with Brightborn.

Layla and I walked up the steps of the Capitol building. I didn't know if Congress was in session. We weren't there to be unruly or disruptive, but we were going to be heard.

The skies were clear. It was every bit as hot in Washington DC as it was in St. Louis, but it was a beautiful day, made more beautiful by the voices of the people rising up. The city wasn't ready for this. We didn't have protest permits. They didn't see us coming.

But we were here. This was our chance.

There were so many of us that even as the police started to arrive along the perimeter, they didn't dare reproach us. Maybe I was a wanted man. They might have been trying to get to me. But they couldn't. Even if they could, it wasn't like they could hold me.

"Long live the revolution!" Illarion shouted, raising his bow into the sky.

The people cheered.

Jag stepped up. "They can take our lives, but they can never take our freedom!"

I snorted. "Okay, William Wallace."

"Shh," Jag said. "It's the only thing I could think of."

I laughed, filled with joy. "You realize, Jag. In the movie, it wasn't long after he said that they cut off his penis, right?"

Jag stared at me wide-eyed.

I laughed again. "It's just a movie."

The crowd might have recognized the source of Jag's line. Maybe they didn't. They didn't care. They roared their agreement with Jag's *Braveheart* quote in response.

"Plant a tree on the Capitol steps!" someone shouted.

I chuckled. I would have, but that would involve destroying property, and I wasn't about that.

"Maybe on the White House lawn!" I shouted back.

The man who'd shouted applauded, along with a few standing near him.

I wondered how these things went. Like, did we keep shouting until we were acknowledged? Or, did we just make sure that our voices were heard and then go back to our lives and hope that the politicians would grant us a few concessions, have press conferences and offer platitudes without action?

There was too much at stake for that. We weren't here just for us, just for our American freedoms. We were standing up for the world. We were standing up against a dictator who fashioned himself as the world's messiah.

Thunder suddenly roared above us, and then a loud crack as lightning split the sky.

"What the heck? The sky was clear!" I said.

Layla grabbed my arm. "It's my father and his sorcerers."

The ground started to shake as the storm continued brewing overhead. A funnel cloud started to form over our position.

"You can do this," Layla said. "You can stop this. You're stronger than they are."

I nodded. I didn't know where Brightborn was or where he and his sorcerers were operating from. "Trixie," I said. "Find them. I'm going to stop this. Let me know when you've zeroed in on their location."

"You got it, Caspar!" Trixie said.

It was an act of desperation. Brightborn saw his plan to frame me for his own terrorism had failed. He might be able to lure the government to his side, but I had the people. In a nation that is governed by the people, for the people, the government can only do so much if they want to get away with it without wholesale rebellion.

I drew on the elements of air and aether and shot into the sky. The people cheered as I flew overhead. A lot of firsts in one day for these folks. Fairies, fairy portals, and now a flying person.

I might not be able to fly at superspeed around the planet and turn back time. Not like that's what would happen, despite what happened in the *Superman* movie. I couldn't save the lives that were lost in the Pentagon attack. But I sure as hell wasn't about to let Brightborn literally rain on my parade.

I was using air and aether already. I thrust the hand holding Aerin's blade in front of me.

You've got this!

I did. I knew it.

I unwound the funnel cloud that was forming and blew the

storm off to the east. More dark clouds formed out of nowhere. I wasn't sure how they did it, but again, the clouds started to spin. The elven sorcerers were bound and determined to form a tornado. Again, I thrust air into it and overpowered their efforts.

Could I keep doing this? Not forever. Brightborn had a whole legion working to cast these storms. No single legionary or sorcerer was a match for me, but I couldn't last forever. Brightborn had figured this out already. This was another attempt to exhaust my magic, then he would unleash his hell.

This wasn't going to work. Not unless Trixie found out where they were operating from so I could go there and take them all out. Another tall order. They were trained soldiers. Even with Aerin's help, it would be me against who knew how many.

I turned back. Elrand ran up to me as I landed, and Layla grabbed my hand.

"We have an idea!" Layla said.

"What's that?" I asked.

"This whole place," Elrand said, "has stone monuments everywhere. It's like a stone circle."

I bit my lip. "Shit. Let's hope Brightborn doesn't figure that out. Not with Layla in here."

"He can't do it if we do it first," Elrand said. "He's focused on the storm. If we connect the monuments as stones and form the temple and seal it with our control, he won't be able to touch us."

I nodded. "Smart. I don't know how long I'll last trying to fight off these storms. He has too many legionaries!"

"But in the circle," Elrand said. "It'll only take a fraction of the power to do just as much."

I nodded. "Do it."

Elrand spun around, casting aether and connecting it to different monuments. The statues at the Peace and Garfield circles. The Capitol building. The Ulysses S. Grant monument. We drew on other stones, too, some farther away. It wasn't a perfect circle, but we had enough monuments that it formed a prism, a sanctuary that allowed me to focus my magic more precisely.

Elrand and I cast our magic into the air, now amplified by the temple we'd made, and dissipated the storm. The people, crowding all around us for the march, were in awe. There were a few screams from those who didn't know what was happening. I'm sure it was terrifying.

But there were also shouts of joy, gasps of wonder, and plenty of cheers.

Trixie buzzed in. "They're on the opposite side of the National Mall!"

I looked, and sure enough, they gathered around the Washington Monument, between the towering phallus I imagined was meant to symbolize the insemination of a new country and the Lincoln Memorial.

I'm sure my interpretation was off base. But that's how my mind works. I can't help it.

If they figured out what we were doing, they had enough stone structures—larger ones—that they could use them to do the same.

As I took off and flew toward them, I could see that was exactly what they were doing. No wonder I couldn't draw enough magic before to slow down their storms.

We had more numbers. But Brightborn was there, and he had a host of legionaries around him.

The giants and drow were making their way through the crowd. I just had to distract the legion long enough until they got there. Drawing Aerin's blade as I landed, I allowed her power to course through me. With Aerin's skill, I had a chance—if not a great one.

I wasn't going to get to Brightborn alone. I couldn't take out the whole legion. But if I could wield my sword and interrupt their attempt to cast tornados over my supporters, and they'd have to shift focus.

I grabbed the hilt of the sword with both hands and relaxed my body. "You've got this one, Aerin."

Gladly! the drow princess said, communicating in my mind through our connection to the blade as she took control.

Aerin didn't hold back as the legion rushed me. She pivoted on one foot, slicing through the spears of the first to reach me.

Aerin was careful and calculated about her strikes. Kneeling and spinning, she took the elves down by cutting at their ankles, severing their Achilles tendons, and dropping them by taking out their knees.

The drow didn't like killing. She'd sliced a few throats in the battle before, but if she could avoid it, she incapacitated our opponents.

Still, she cut through the legionaries like a harvest reaper. Every legionary who went down brought us closer to Brightborn. Every magic-capable legionary she incapacitated, the fewer who could cast.

There were still a dozen or more elves surrounding Brightborn. They drew their bows and fired arrows in our direction. Aerin cut them out of the air one after the next. Damn, I looked like a badass when she took the reins. I still had my abilities. I extended one hand and hurled a ball of fire at the elves who were firing on us.

One of their sorcerers shot a blast of water into the air. It met my fire, resulting in a cloud of steam. I cast again, this time using earth, throwing up stones from the ground and hurling them at the legionaries.

I winced when an arrow struck me in the shoulder. I drew on aether to heal the wound as I pulled it out.

Careful, Caspar, Aerin warned. *I can't do as much when you're channeling magic. I might mess up your spells.*

"Got it," I said. I was about to let Aerin take over again when I heard loud steps behind me. The giants were charging. The drow were not far behind, along with the revolutionaries. For once, we had Brightborn outnumbered.

I screamed as I rallied with my friends, and we went for the elven king.

The legionaries fought back as the giants crashed against them, but they didn't stand a chance.

We had him! Finally! Brightborn was going down!

With Aerin's blade in hand and Brag'mok in front of me clearing the way, I gripped the hilt and swiped at Brightborn.

My blade passed right through him. It didn't cut him. It passed through him as if he was a ghost.

"What the…"

An astral projection, Aerin said. *He's here in spirit, but his body is elsewhere.*

I sighed and my heart sank. "Of course."

Brightborn laughed. "Impressive, Cruciger. But do you really think you and your protestors can stand against us? Your government has nuclear weapons. People with sticks and signs aren't going to stop us."

I snorted. "The people know the truth now, Brightborn. People know what you're up to."

"Some believe you," Brightborn said. "But you're still a wanted man, Caspar. How long can you hide behind your crowds?"

Layla came up behind me. "Stop this, Father!"

Brightborn's apparition laughed. "You're wearing your mother's crown, I see."

"You murderous fuck!" Layla shouted. "You killed my mother!"

Brightborn sneered. "You've taken to her sedition, I see. I hoped it wouldn't come to this, Layla. I wanted you to join me, to emerge as the chosen one to lead us to our glory."

"There's nothing glorious about what you're doing," Layla retorted.

Brightborn smiled. "Stand with me, or be cut down like your mother."

"You're a bastard!" Layla shouted.

Magic started to swirl around us like it had in the stone circle after I saved the drow.

I grabbed Layla. "He's trying to draw out your power again!"

"Get me out of here!"

Where the hell was he? Why couldn't the fairies find him? He was trying to use these monuments to wield Layla as a weapon again. But this time, I wasn't exhausted. I took off through the air with Layla in my arms. I soared up over the Capitol building, past the Supreme Court. We were in the clear.

We floated there for a moment. I don't know how Superman made it look so easy when he flew over Metropolis with Lois Lane. I could fly, but I didn't have his super-strength. Holding onto Layla while she clung to me wasn't easy. I wanted to kiss her, but I was afraid I'd drop her, and that wouldn't be romantic.

I took us back down to the ground, then I kissed her deeply. She kissed me back.

"Intimacy break!" Layla said, pulling away. "We have to find him! He can't be far from here."

I nodded. "Trixie!"

The fairy appeared. "Yes, Caspar?"

"Can you find Brightborn?" I asked.

Trixie shook her head. "He's gone. He was here. I sensed him in the middle of all that. But he's used all these monuments as stone circles, as portals."

I sighed. "If he can use any stone or rock structure as a stone circle, he could travel almost anywhere."

Layla nodded. "We'd best get back to the crowd. They came here for a reason before my father attacked. They're going to need a little assistance getting home."

I smiled. "You're right."

"If you hang out without them around you, I'm not sure it's

safe," Layla said. "My father is right. You might have the people, but he has the government. They came after us with snipers before."

I nodded, picked Layla up, and flew back to the steps of the Capitol building.

The people were still gathered there. They were cheering and chanting my name.

I raised my hand to quiet them.

I didn't have a microphone. I didn't know how well they'd hear me, but I had a few things to say.

"Our government has been compromised. Our leaders have aligned themselves with a tyrant. But we are not beholden to our leaders! They only have power when we follow, when we decide to grant it to them!"

The people cheered. When their shouts quieted down, I continued, "They want to see me arrested for the elf king's crimes. But I will not yield. I am here, with you, to fight. This is our country, not theirs. This is our world, not theirs. Like our forefathers, whose names are enshrined all around us, we will not go quietly into the night. We will not stand by while they oppress us with lies. We will not stand by while they cede the authority we gave them to a power-hungry king.

"But we must do more than defeat evil. We have to do better, too. We need to rise up and meet the challenges of our day. We need to fight not only for our personal liberties, but for our world, for our planet, for our faith in our God or whomever we choose to worship, and have faith for a better tomorrow! Today, we stand together. Humans, elves, drow, giants, and fairies. Not as one race over another, not as different tribes, but as a single people, dedicated to making a better world.

"We thwarted the king today. But he'll be back, and we have more to fight than his legions. We stand against the authorities that stand alongside him. But we have more than they do. We have belief in each other. We have a unity that will not falter against their oppression. And we have faith in a better world, in a vision of tomorrow that's better than today. Will you stand, not just with me, but together? Will you all stand side-by-side and demand a better future, a future where justice, not lies, prevails. Will you stand as one against those who'd divide us?"

The people shouted their cheers. It was so loud that I almost had to cover my ears. I looked at Trixie and nodded. "It's time to go home."

CHAPTER THIRTY-EIGHT

I walked through the doors of St. Ensley's, the church formerly operated by the Elf Gate cult. I wasn't sure if we could stay there. I didn't know if we could go back to the junkyard ranch. The government was still trying to find a way to take me down. But if they did, they'd have to do it now in defiance of the will of the people.

We came to St. Ensley's because we didn't know where else to go. The revolutionary elves weren't as populous as the loyalist elves who were with Brightborn. Even so, with all of them on top of the drow and the giants, the church was the only place large enough to fit us all inside. However, we couldn't stay there.

"To the North Pole?" Illarion asked, stepping up beside me.

I shook my head. "Brightborn knows about that place. Oddly enough, I think we're safer now in the open, around people who support our resistance."

"Our revolution!" Illarion said.

I smiled. "Right. *Vive la révolution!*"

Illarion patted me on the back. "You impress us all, Your Highness."

I almost choked on my tongue. "Your *what?*"

"You are married to our queen," Illarion said. "She might have the regalia and authority, but you are royal now, too."

I scratched my cheek. "Well, you can just call me Caspar. I'm not here to rule over anyone. All I can do is lead people to be the best version of themselves."

"That's why we succeeded," Illarion said. "We all have our strengths. Our gifts. We all played a role."

"We haven't succeeded yet, Illarion," I said. "We marched on Washington, but so far, there's no sign that they've responded to our message. Brightborn is still out there. He's still planning to take over the world."

"But we did succeed," Illarion insisted. "We succeeded in standing up as one. You have united the peoples, Caspar."

"There are still powers that stand against us," I said.

Illarion shook his head. "The prophecy was never about the powers that be. It was about the peoples. You've fulfilled the prophecy in every way."

I snorted. "I hadn't thought about it that way. There's still a lot to do. We might have won a battle, but the war still rages."

"But now we can fight it," Illarion said. "We have you. We have the people. We have each other. We have a chance! Because of you, Caspar."

I nodded. "Thank you for saying that."

Jag was fiddling with some of the cameras and such that were still set up in the old church.

"What are you doing there?" I asked,

Jag shrugged. "They can't silence you now. You up for another speech?"

I laughed. "Is it needed?"

Jag grinned. "I don't know. Your speech in Washington has already gone viral."

I furrowed my brow. "Viral? I didn't realize I was being recorded. I didn't think it was anything special. I was just shooting from the hip."

Jag smiled. "It was great! I got the whole thing, and I wasn't the only one. There are dozens of other videos. Some of you flying around. Some of you cutting down the elven legion. Some of you confronting Brightborn and giving your speech. This stuff is all over the internet. The government couldn't silence us now if they wanted to."

"We still need to be careful," I said.

Jag nodded. "We will be."

Layla was sitting in a chair in the corner by herself.

I walked over to her, bowing my head. "My Liege…"

Layla flashed a closed-mouthed smile and nodded in return.

"What's wrong?" I asked, sitting next to her and taking her hand in mine.

Layla opened the codex, the manifesto her mother had written. "This is all I have from my mother, and this is the first time I've had a chance to sit down and think about what happened. My dad *killed* my mom, Caspar. I'm so furious I feel like I could explode."

I squeezed Layla's hand. "I know. I wish there was something I could say that would make that pill a little easier to swallow. But I can't. It's horrific. The whole thing. I can't imagine how it must feel to realize that the man who raised you had blamed giants all the while when he'd done it himself."

"I know that revenge doesn't make things better," Layla said. "But he needs to suffer. I'm not just talking about killing him. My father is a fucking sociopath. He doesn't have an ounce of emotion or compassion in his body, but he needs to feel *something*. He needs to feel the pain I've felt for years and everything that's rushing back into me now."

I sighed. "You know, at the moment when I was holding Aerin's sword in my hand and thought I was about to cut him down. I'd like to say it was Aerin in control. I'm not so sure she was. I think that might have been me."

"I'm not sure whether I wish you took him down or if a quick death would have been too good for him," Layla said.

"Well, taking him down with Aerin's blade, I can't say what would have happened," I said. "That sword has some strange powers. I'm still not sure what to make of it. The first time I grabbed it, I didn't even hit anyone, and it separated the Unseelie fairies from the elves. Then, since Aerin had it enchanted with fire before, it sometimes comes ablaze when I wield it. At other times when Aerin's in control, it's just a sword, but the way she uses it is not normal. I know she's well trained, but when it cuts through flesh, I can sense something in the hilt. I'm not sure what."

"Does Aerin know what it is?" Layla asked.

I shrugged. "I haven't talked to her about it. I mean, until we fought off the elves at the spire trap at the Pole and took down the legion at the National Mall, I didn't notice. It's magic. Magic stuff is weird. I've gotten used to that, but I can't help but wonder if there's more to what happened when I cut down those elves... Well, when Aerin did it through me."

"You should ask her," Layla said. "When you get a chance."

I nodded. "I'll worry about that later. Right now, I want to make sure you're going to be okay."

Layla pulled closer to me and interlaced our fingers, then rested her head on my shoulder. "I will be. Eventually. But I don't like this anger, this hate. All directed at my father."

"He doesn't deserve forgiveness," I said. "Don't take this the wrong way, but I've learned that sometimes we have to let go of the past, forgive others just to get them out of our heads. You know what I mean? Like, your father has hurt you enough. The more space you give him in your head, the more he hurts you, over and over again."

"I know," Layla said. "It's been so long, but this information is new. I can't forgive him, Caspar."

"Maybe forgiveness is the wrong word," I said, squeezing

Layla's hand. "But somehow, we have to find a way to let go. We can't let the people who hurt us in the past continue to hurt us in the present."

"I know killing him won't make me free," Layla said. "It won't get rid of the hate. But he has to die, Caspar."

I nodded. "I never thought I'd say this about anyone. But I think you might be right. I'm not sure there's any other way to end this war."

CHAPTER THIRTY-NINE

We went back to Canada. It was Clarence's idea. I was starting to hear him speak. He wasn't like Agnus. He didn't have that attitude. He was more calm, calculated, and reserved.

And, he was a bit of a bear.

Ha-ha. Yeah, I know. I'll be here all week.

By that, I mean he's a little grumpy. I couldn't blame him for that. I mean, we took him out of his native environment to the North freaking Pole. He went into hibernation at a time of the year he normally wouldn't. Then we woke him up and took him to Scotland, then to Missouri, now finally back to his home.

I think it was the displacement that allowed me to connect with him. I didn't have much of a home either. Not anymore. Hell, the closest thing I'd had to a home in recent memory was the small apartment sitting above an Irish pub.

Damn, I missed that place. Almost as much as I missed the Reuben sandwiches they served at O'Donnell's.

Before that, when I was married, my wife and I had a small brick house in St. Louis' Bevo neighborhood. Then the divorce happened, and I just couldn't stand to look at those same walls anymore. When she moved out, I drank away a few of my mortgage payments.

The apartment was nice, but then came the junkyard ranch—a literal garbage heap. A farmhouse that was falling apart. If it was within the city limits, it would have been condemned. But we'd made it into a home. I suppose I never expected we'd be able to stay there forever.

The North Pole spire trap had been even more short-lived.

But now we were moving to Canada. Why in the world were we moving to Canada?

Clarence had his own reasons. For him, it was home. But we didn't go to Canada just to drop him off. It was the one place we'd been that Brightborn didn't know about.

"Until you arrived," Clarence told me, "I hadn't seen a human in years. Not that deep in the forest."

That was all the convincing it took. No humans. Not that I dislike humans. I am one, after all. The citizens of St. Louis supported us. However, we needed a place where we could rest, a place we could call home, even if we were going to portal in and out of there to other parts of the world so we could carry on the fight. When you have hundreds of soldiers to house, it's hard to find a place in a city or even near a city while remaining discreet.

Aelfrich was still our captive—bound to his cage. But we didn't tell him where we were. He couldn't know. If he got out, well, we'd have to move again. So, we kept him inside one of our new wooden spires.

Yes, *wooden* spires.

Illarion had a set of crystals of his own. An older style of home, he said, that had fallen out of fashion in New Albion. But they used to be standard housing on New Albion a few centuries back.

They looked like trees—albeit much larger than usual trees. These had serious girth. I'm talking a hundred feet in diameter, at least. They twisted up, like the North Pole spires, but didn't go much higher than the tree line. They were just tall enough that when I went to the upper rooms, I could see for miles over the top of the canopy of leaves.

I built most of them. Elrand helped, too. So did a few of the other elves. I just had more "juice" to channel into Illarion's crystals than the rest did. I enjoyed the process. Growing these wooden spires was more like sprouting trees than it was like building the spire I'd made at the North Pole.

We didn't use a stone circle to focus my magic. We could have, but we weren't sure how Brightborn was using them. If we used one, would he be able to track us and portal to it? Not worth the risk.

So I made one spire at a time. Took a nap, then made another one. It involved a lot of earth magic, a good deal of water, and some aether. No fire, this time. Fire and wood aren't compatible. A little air helped speed up the process. Channeling earth through a crystal is a little tedious. Air tends to lighten the magical load a bit.

Sure, it wasn't the most efficient way to construct a village for my army, given what I could have done with a stone circle to focus my energies. It took a lot out of me. But compared to traditional construction, it was crazy fast and a lot less work. An amazing process. It was insane that for the elves, it was commonplace.

I suppose a lot of what we think of as natural—like the sun rising, a child being born, a tree growing from a seed—is miraculous in its own way. The only real difference between what we deem "magical" and the things we deem commonplace is our experience. What's mundane for one man is another man's miracle.

Still, only making one spire at a time, some folks had to spend a few nights under the moonlight. If anyone had any complaints, they were free to go live at the North Pole if they'd prefer. After all, there were empty spires there waiting for them.

No one took up that alternative. I think everyone had enough ice and snow—not to mention the brutal summer heat in Missouri—to last a lifetime. Here, in the Canadian forest, it was perfect. Sure, it would get chilly come wintertime if our war lasted that long. We could probably find a new place somewhere in a rainforest if needed. It would only take a week or so to rebuild. But for now, I was comfortable.

One problem? We were still too remote for phone service.

Jag went with Trixie on a daily basis to keep tabs on what was going on.

Word of our movement was spreading. Citizens all around the country were protesting the government's alignment with Brightborn, and the message was starting to be heard around the world. So far, most of the governments were downplaying the issue. They insisted that their relationships with Brightborn were cooperative, that the elven king respected their autonomy, and they continued to hail his efforts to bring some of the world's leaders together.

He had them buffaloed for now. They'd see the light eventually, but by then it would be too late.

Even as our popular resistance movement spread around the world, growing and gaining influence, Brightborn sank his tendrils deeper into the world's governments. It was becoming a powder keg of tension that could explode at any time.

For the most part, the protests around the world remained peaceful. How long would that last? The movement was bigger than me now. We continued leaking videos—testimonials from the giants and the revolutionary elves that told the truth of the atrocities Brightborn had committed on New Albion. Even Layla released a video detailing how he'd killed her mom.

I always encouraged everyone to remain peaceful and discouraged resorting to violence. Nonviolence is the critical answer to the moral and political challenges that we were facing. However, I knew by my own experience that there would come a time when we had to fight. I'd already killed—most recently, while Aerin wielded her blade through me. I knew more was coming. Things were only bound to escalate.

Mainstream media discounted our videos and testimonials as "fake news." Social media platforms were mixed. Some of them censored our videos. Others allowed them to stand. Another battle, this one between independent companies and the governments. As far as I was concerned, it was up to the people to decide who to believe. There will always be those who believe lies. The President believed Brightborn's. But I always believed in truth.

I'm not saying I'm always right. But I believe that truth, as a principle, is invariably stronger than falsehood, and since I loved truth, I wasn't afraid of being wrong.

Because I loved truth more than I loved being right.

When I was a minister, I felt the same way. Why should we be afraid of false dogmas? Did I believe in a God so feeble that a few misguided teachers could compromise His kingdom and His plan for my life and the world? No. I think the same thing applies when it comes to the truth—whether it's in politics, religion, or whatever.

Falsehoods are always vulnerable to themselves. Deceit is its own greatest threat. No lie can endure forever. Eventually, the truth manifests itself. So long as it's the truth that we care about the most, rather than whatever position we've married ourselves to, I believe that we'll all eventually find ourselves on the same side.

However, we can't have autocrats telling us what we can or can't listen to, what counts as true or false. No elected official, no corporate mogul, is an arbiter of truth. The people are, and they'll discover it, eventually, when the censors and the powers that be get out of the way and let the truth resonate.

It might take some time. It might be messy and contentious at times. But I believe that truth is its own best defense.

The whole prophecy was now revealed. And the final word from the prophet? In short, you aren't beholden to destiny. Make your own future. Stand up for what's right even if the whole world is against you.

That was what I was going to do. It might change me. It might force me outside of my comfort zone. I might have to do things that make me uncomfortable. Hell, discomfort had been my modus operandi as of late.

CHAPTER FORTY

I took a long walk in the forest. It was just me and Aerin's blade. I still didn't understand how the thing worked. When I'd first used it, Aerin had warned me to be careful. What was that about? What did I feel when the blade sliced through flesh?

It wasn't painful or even unpleasant. It was energy. With so many elemental powers running through my body, I didn't give it much thought.

I gripped the blade and held it out in front of me.

"You there, Aerin?"

Always.

"You can read my mind. You know what I'm thinking."

You want to know what this blade is doing.

I nodded. "So, what can you tell me?"

I didn't want to say anything. I didn't want you to worry about it.

"Worry about what, Aerin?"

I'm not alone in here.

"What do you mean you're not alone?"

I'm saying that every time we cut someone, a little bit of them gets absorbed into the blade. And the ones we've killed...

"They're trapped in there with you?"

Yes. But like I said, I have it handled.

I had to bite my tongue. I was holding the hilt. Technically, *I* had it handled, but this wasn't a moment for dad jokes. I was genuinely concerned.

"Do they have the same control you do?"

No. I was here first. I was the one who created this blade. It's my blade. The enchantment of fire that is bound to it is my enchantment. I have all the power here.

"So you're using the fire to keep them in their place?"

More or less. It's not as brutal as it sounds.

"You said anyone who was cut by the blade, part of them is in there? How does that work?"

It's just a bother. It's a shade, a shadow, of the person cut. Like a copy, but without a conscious mind. They aren't a real threat. Just an annoyance.

"But the ones who were killed…"

They are in here completely. But they aren't any match for me. At least, not now.

"Not now? How many more people can get absorbed into this thing before you're outnumbered?"

I don't know.

"If that happens, what will they do when I allow you to take over? When you wield the blade?"

I'm not going to allow that to happen.

"Just humor me, Aerin. What would happen *if* they overpowered you?"

They'd control you, too.

"Dammit, Aerin! Why didn't you tell me about this before?"

Like I said, Caspar. I didn't want you to worry!

"You didn't want me to get rid of the blade. What if I buried it somewhere!"

Then I'd be…

I sighed. "You'd be stuck. Lost there. Trapped without any outlet."

Yeah.

"Look," I said, "I'm not burying this blade. But when we go to battle, you *can't* kill people with it. Do you understand? When you're in charge, when I'm letting you wield the blade through me, can you access my magic?"

I don't do that.

"But you could!"

Aerin sighed within my mind. *Technically, yes. I could.*

"If someone else took over, if they overpowered you, they could use my abilities too."

I told you, Caspar. I won't let that happen!

I scratched my head. "Can I take back over on my own? Like, before, when you were done kicking ass and taking names, it felt like you just let go. You were finished, and you backed out of my body. You let me take over again."

I don't know if you could take over if I didn't do that. I mean, you'd have influence, like how you cast magic while I was still wielding the blade.

"You realize how dangerous this could be, right?"

I do.

"The war is coming, Aerin. I will need your help. But it sounds like the smaller wounds, like when we cut that elf's Achilles brings something like a shade into the blade. But it's just an inconvenience, right?"

Yes. They don't do much. Eventually, I think they'll fade.

I nodded. "From now on, no mortal blows. I can't handle close combat on my own. I need you. We can't kill. Not with this blade, anyway."

That's it!

"What is?" I asked.

A second blade! I might not be able to handle it as well. I haven't had a lot of practice with dual-wielding. But if we have a second blade, a common blade, we can use that if we have to kill.

I bit my lip. "All right. But again, let's try to avoid killing. I'm not the best person for close combat anyway. We can let the other elves, the drow, even the giants handle that. I'll see if I can get something."

Talk to Rina. She can get us a second blade—something I'll know how to handle.

I nodded and sheathed Aerin's blade again.

I could have flown back to our village, but I was enjoying the walk. Sort of. I was flustered. The whole notion of potentially being possessed by the people we killed... Well, that would unsettle anyone. I trusted Aerin. I had to. She'd never given me a good reason not to trust that she'd handle this.

But the way things were changing, the way tensions were bubbling up around the world, this temporary solace in the forest was bound to be short-lived. Soon, we'd have to fight, probably sooner than I'd like. All it would take is one news report, one trip back into phone range and back again for Jag to tell us that a bomb had been dropped, that people were under assault by their government.

With Trixie and the other Seelie fairies, we could go anywhere in the world in an instant. We could stand up for our supporters; we could fight back. I wasn't going to allow the people who supported our revolution to be slaughtered. If it came to that, we'd defend them.

Eventually, even if it killed me, I'd see Brightborn fall. I wouldn't let Layla kill him. She was angry. She had reason to do it. However, it would leave a bigger wound in her to kill her own father than she realized. I'd have to do it. It was my burden to bear.

I just couldn't use Aerin's blade to do it.

I literally wrote this book in the middle of the dog days of summer. According to Google the phrase "dog days of summer" either has something to do with astrology—when the sun occupies the same part of the sky as the constellation Sirius—or something to do with how actual dogs behave when it gets this ridiculously hot.

I have a small writing studio. I built it myself. I didn't have a ton of experience building anything. There's a line in this book about how Caspar hadn't built much of anything other than a birdhouse before he constructed that elven spire on the North Pole. He was channeling me, there. My studio is nice. I love it. I'm proud of it. I added a picture window for a full view of my property and French doors. The problem? The sun heats the place up like a greenhouse. I have an air conditioner that's supposed to handle a room twice this size. It isn't keeping up in our hundred-degree weather. So, as I'm sitting in my writing sauna, I have curtains on backorder. Hopefully that will eliminate the greenhouse effect and make my writing experience more tolerable.

I say all that to say this—when Caspar is bitching about the heat in that book, those parts really came from the heart. When he's traveling to the cold—that stuff was pure fantasy. Of course, in a few months, it will be cold again. Right now, I'm looking forward to it. When that time comes, I'll somehow remember these "dog days" more fondly than I experienced them. These writer notes are here to remind the future-me to appreciate what I have.

There's one more thing about my studio. My youngest son, Elliot, had a cat allergy. We had a cat when he was born. The cat moved into my office. He's no longer with us, sadly. But my studio used to be both hot and full of litter which the cat tracked everywhere. My cat, Indie—he was the inspiration behind Agnus. RIP, buddy.

Okay, now I wrote about the miserable heat and how my cat died. I didn't intend for these notes to get so *negative*. Dang. Well, whatever. It is what it is. So, to change that, I'll invite you to sit back, close your eyes, and imagine unicorns, rainbows, and what it must be like to be at Anderle's beach dreamhouse in Cabo San Lucas. I hear he's actually planning on stabling unicorns there. I wouldn't recommend it, though. They can be a real pain. You know what they say about unicorns. They're *always* horny. Like, constantly. And apparently, they love dad jokes.

-Theo

Thank you for not only reading this book but this entire series so far and these author notes as well.

I remember having summers at my grandparents in Moulton, Texas (near Shiner...the place they brew the beer if you know anything about it.)

During July and August, it was "the dog days of summer" because it was HOT.

Hot like *make you wish to crawl into a pool to dry off the sweat*-type hot.

Note I didn't say "wash." It was too hot for that.

My grandparents' lawn was all carpet grass. Now, for those who don't know, carpet grass isn't the best type of grass. However, it works in the South because it's hardy and willing to survive in the shade and the heat, unlike a lot of other finicky green grasses that you could select.

Further, it itches like a sonofabitch if you roll around in it. As children, I'm not really sure what else we were supposed to do but play outside, and that would usually mean we ended up rolling around in the grass. Usually, my grandfather would set up a hose and a sprinkler and we would play in the water, thinking Grandpa was the coolest man in the world.

It's interesting how I look back on those days and realize he would move the sprinkler, and we would play on different areas of the lawn during the week.

Sometimes I hate myself for realizing it wasn't all about my pleasure. I prefer to be ignorant and not realize Grandpa was watering different sections of the lawn as we played.

Either way, in the dog days of summer, one of the few enjoyments we had was playing out on the lawn, sprinkler blasting away and cooling us down.

Oh, and we helped Grandpa water the lawn. In these dog days of summer (it will be 108 degrees next Tuesday in Las Vegas), I hope you, your children or your grandchildren get a chance to find a way to stay cool.

If you need an idea, try setting up a sprinkler and making a jug of cherry Kool-aid. They go together very nicely during the hot months.

May you have a great week or weekend, wherever you are!

Regards,

Michael Anderle

BOOKS BY MICHAEL ANDERLE

Sign up for the LMBPN email list to be notified of new releases and
special deals!

https://lmbpn.com/email/

For a complete list of books by Michael Anderle, please visit:

www.lmbpn.com/ma-books/